One Dark Night

One Dark Night

JAID BLACK

HEAT
NEW YORK, NEW YORK

THE BERKLEY PUBLISHING GROUP
Published by the Penguin Group
Penguin Group (USA) Inc.
375 Hudson Street, New York, New York 10014, USA
Penguin Group (Canada), 90 Eglinton Avenue East, Suite 700, Toronto, Ontario M4P 2Y3, Canada
(a division of Pearson Penguin Canada Inc.)
Penguin Books Ltd., 80 Strand, London WC2R 0RL, England
Penguin Group Ireland, 25 St. Stephen's Green, Dublin 2, Ireland (a division of Penguin Books Ltd.)
Penguin Group (Australia), 250 Camberwell Road, Camberwell, Victoria 3124, Australia
(a division of Pearson Australia Group Pty. Ltd.)
Penguin Books India Pvt. Ltd., 11 Community Centre, Panchsheel Park, New Delhi—110 017, India
Penguin Group (NZ), Cnr. Airborne and Rosedale Roads, Albany, Auckland 1310, New Zealand
(a division of Pearson New Zealand Ltd.)
Penguin Books (South Africa) (Pty.) Ltd., 24 Sturdee Avenue, Rosebank, Johannesburg 2196,
South Africa

Penguin Books Ltd., Registered Offices: 80 Strand, London WC2R 0RL, England

Cover photo by Pete Leonard / Zefa / Corbis.
Cover design by Rita Frangie.
Text design by Stacy Irwin.

PRINTING HISTORY
Berkley Sensation mass-market paperback edition / April 2004
Heat trade paperback edition / June 2006

Library of Congress Cataloging-in-Publication Data

Black, Jaid.
One dark night / by Jaid Black.—Heat hardcover ed.
p. cm.
ISBN 0-425-21237-8
1. Women surgeons—Fiction. 2. Online dating—Fiction. 3. Serial murderers—Fiction. I. Title.
PS3602.L285054 2006
813'.6—dc22

2006041154

PRINTED IN THE UNITED STATES OF AMERICA

10 9 8 7 6 5 4 3 2 1

To my editor, Cindy, for making this book the best it can be. To my agent, Ethan, for his valued input and criticism. To my daughters for making me dinner when I was too focused on Thomas and Nikki to eat. To my dad for all the pride I see in his eyes. And, finally, to my mom . . . for never doubting this day would come.

Prologue

Sunday, June 8
3:10 A.M.

Even after fifteen years of working as a police officer, ten of which he'd spent as a homicide detective, the scent of death never got any easier to stomach. It was a hideous smell, especially if the flesh of the victim had been decomposing for a period of time, as was the case tonight.

Detective Thomas Cavanah stepped over the yellow crime-scene tape that had been woven across twelve feet of muddy ground and chain-link fence and walked toward the body of the decomposing victim. He ignored the whirring of lights from nearby police cars, the buzzing sound of vultures—also known as reporters—as they clamored around for a story, and concentrated on the crime scene.

She looked just like the others before her. Late twenties to mid-thirties. Light brown—maybe dark blonde?—hair. Average height. Well-endowed. Very dead.

"Cavanah!"

Thomas glanced up at the familiar sound of his partner's voice.

He absently watched Detective James Merdino flash his badge at a rookie cop securing the scene before stepping over the police tape. Thomas cast his gaze back down to the muddy ground, his thoughts on the victim.

The Unidentified Subject—UNSUB—who had done this woman in was the type who likes to play, he thought, his acute brown eyes immediately noting the several superficial lacerations zigzagging across her torso. Cuts like that weren't meant to kill—only to injure, to torture. To give hope of living where none exists. To play . . . .

His gaze flicked up to the woman's bared breasts. Or what was left of them, rather. A large hole had been dug out of her chest, a gaping wound where her heart should have been, revealing that, just like the others, that particular organ had been removed from her body—probably when she'd still been alive.

Thomas pinched the bridge of his nose. He took a deep breath and blew it out. When the perpetrator had finally allowed the victim to die, she had been grateful for it, he was certain.

"On my way over, the police dispatcher informed me that the heart was missing," James said, squatting down on the ground next to the victim. "I see they got that right."

"This dude is one sick bastard," Thomas muttered, his gravelly voice kept low.

"They all are."

Thomas's eyebrows rose slightly. "Not like this, bro."

James nodded down to the victim. "He tied her up like the others."

"Yes."

"Any signs of a struggle?"

Thomas snorted at that. "Hell yeah, she struggled," he growled.

"You know what I mean—"

"But whether or not she struggled *before* he tied her up I just don't know." Thomas frowned. "Let's hope the coroner can answer that one. We need something more to go on, because right now we have as much as we did when the last victim surfaced—nothing." He ran a hand through his dark brown hair, the muscle in his biceps bulging. "Why do I have a feeling Dr. Goldstein is going to say she's too badly decomposed to tell?"

"Because she is. They usually are." James sighed, standing up before his partner did.

"He's gotten good," Thomas murmured. "Too good. He knows how to cut them, how to hide them, never fucks up. Never leaves DNA traces behind."

"He will eventually. And when he does, my friend, we'll get his ass."

Thomas was silent for a protracted moment as he considered that. "Right now we've only got one thing going for us. His ego. It's getting bigger and bigger."

He glanced back down at the victim, his eyes narrowed in concentration. The laceration marks across her torso were almost artsy this time. "He's not just cutting them up and killing them anymore. He's taking his time, confident in his ability to keep from getting caught."

"And the more time he spends with them . . ."

"The more chance there is that he'll leave behind a fiber—anything."

James nodded. "We'll get him, buddy. I know we'll get him."

Thomas forced his intense gaze away from the victim's body. His brown eyes clashed with his partner's. "I just hope we get him before he gets anybody else."

Silence.

That scenario was as unlikely as the perp turning himself in, a fact both detectives implicitly understood.

Somebody else would die.

And given Lucifer's penchant for playing, it would happen soon.

Chapter 1

Sunday, June 8
11:10 A.M.

"How much blood has he lost?"

Dr. Nicole "Nikki" Adenike put the question to the O.R. nurse as she quickly scrubbed down, preparing for an emergency surgery. The victim had taken a bullet through the chest, just two inches shy of his heart.

"A hell of a lot. We can't even tell."

"Drug related?"

"Yep."

Not that it mattered. Not that she cared. It was Nikki's job to save the man's life, not to play judge and jury. When he was healed, he would be handed over to the Cleveland Police Department. Until then, she had a job to do.

"Has he been prepped?" she asked as they ran together from surgery toward the awaiting victim in the operating room.

"Prepped down in E.R."

The scene inside the operating room would have looked like

chaos to the casual, untrained observer. In actuality, the team of nurses and doctors attending to the victim moved with expert precision, the singular goal of saving the drug dealer's life paramount to all else.

"We have to move fast, so don't make me repeat myself," Nikki calmly intoned as she took her place next to the victim. "Nurse, gauze please."

For the next eight hours Nikki worked like Mozart before the piano, doing what she did best. Her hands were steady, her fingers skilled. She detached herself from the pandemonium around her, concentrating instead on picking out the bullet, restoring the victim's vital signs, and sewing up the obscenely gaping hole in his chest.

Easier said than done. There was a lot of blood loss. His vitals were touch and go. Twice she almost lost him.

But in the end, eight hours, a perspired brow, and a fatigued body later, the victim's chest had been sewn back up sans the bullet, his vitals improving if not fully restored.

He would live. He would be staring at the inside of a jail cell soon enough, but he'd live.

Her job was done. Today.

"You did good," Juanita Brown remarked as she swiped at the sweat on her forehead with the back of her hand.

Nikki smiled, then tiredly patted the young nurse on the back. Juanita was a terrific lady to work with, her favorite on the trauma surgery team. They'd been saving lives together since Nikki had been a resident surgeon. "You weren't too bad yourself, kiddo."

Juanita half smiled and half sighed. "Damn, I'm beat. I'd say let's go grab a bite to eat, but I'd rather go catch some Zs."

"Me, too. I'll grab a burger from a fast-food place on my way home."

"Watch out. That stuff will kill ya." They shared an insiders' smile at the allusion to the man they'd saved together barely a week earlier after he'd almost choked himself to death by swallowing hamburger bites too fast. "You on call tomorrow?"

"Nope." Nikki grinned. "I have a day off, if you can believe it."

"Well, enjoy it. I got stuck pulling a double shift."

"Hey, I've had my fair share of those. See you Tuesday, Nita."

"I'll be here."

Fifteen minutes later, Nikki had changed into her street clothes, settled into her Mercedes Benz, and was driving toward the apartment she rented out in a high-rise complex that catered to doctors and other affluent professionals who worked at or around Cleveland General. Only ten minutes away, it was a logical place to live when people were depending on you to show up at the hospital on a moment's notice in order to perform emergency surgeries.

The minute the hospital was out of sight, so too was it out of Nikki's mind. She had learned long ago the importance of leaving her work at work, to avoid burn-out.

She doubted that most people could appreciate the stress that is inherent in playing God in people's lives, to know that they lived or died depending upon how well you performed on any given day. There was no room for error; only for precision. An impossibility, given the fact that she was human.

Due to the nature of her occupation, it was vital to not only be a skilled healer, but also a skilled commander of people, whom her trauma team could respect. They looked to her for direction, for the ability to provide authority and leadership.

Not that she was complaining. Nikki loved her job; always had. She took a lot of pride in what she did and the fact that she did it so well. Nobody, however, can be precise, commanding, and authoritative all the time, so she looked forward to her days off as a time to recuperate, a time when she could be plain old Nikki instead of the respected surgeon, Dr. Nicole Adenike.

Exhausted, Nikki smiled as the looming high-rise complex in which she lived crept into view. She patted the grease-stained paper bag sitting on the passenger's seat beside her.

First a burger, and then a hot bubble bath. Damn, she loved her days off.

"Another body was discovered in the early hours of the morning outside downtown Cleveland's financial district. The victim, identified through dental records as thirty-three-year-old Linda Hughes, was a well-respected international tax accountant at the prestigious Waterson, Helman, and Pandley firm.

"Reported missing several months ago, news of her death nevertheless came as a shock to family, friends, and coworkers, all of whom described Linda to reporters as an affable, highly intelligent businesswoman and friend."

Nikki watched from the bathtub in which she was soaking as the news report played on the flat-panel TV display that had been mounted onto a nearby wall. She absently worked soap bubbles over her breasts, then up and down her arms, as the victim's shaken mother spoke tearfully before the cameras.

"If this can happen to my Linda, it can happen to any woman," Mrs. Hughes said, her voice quivering. *"My daughter was a smart woman. She never would have gotten herself into a preventable situation."*

Which meant, as the police no doubt already suspected, that Linda had trusted the man who had murdered her. It was kind of unnerving to think that this particular serial killer had ingratiated himself into the lives of so many women—so many smart women, at that. Doctors, lawyers, CEOs . . . the man whom the Cleveland press had dubbed "Lucifer" was nobody's fool, she thought.

The phone rang, breaking Nikki out of her reverie. She reached for the TV's remote and hit the power button, flicking the box off at the same time she answered the cordless. "Hello?"

"Hey Nik. It's Kim."

Nikki smiled into the phone. Kimberly Cox was her nearest and dearest friend. "After sixteen years, one would think you would quit identifying yourself every time you call. I do recognize your voice, my dear," she said teasingly. "I've only known you since, oh, college."

"Hey, you never know. We're both thirty-four now. Starting to lose brain cells and all."

"Uh huh." Nikki tucked a light brown lock of hair behind her ear. "What's up?"

They chatted for a few minutes, catching up on the past seven days, neither of them having had time to phone the other at all for the past week.

"As nice as that sounds, I'm too beat to go out tonight," Nikki said regretfully. "I feel like bumming around in my sweats and that piña colada–stained T-shirt I got when we vacationed in St. Maarten." She smiled when Kim chuckled nostalgically. "Want to do brunch tomorrow instead?"

"Sounds good. I really need . . . I need to talk, to see you."

Nikki's eyebrows slowly drew together. "Is something wrong, kiddo? If there is, I'll be right over—"

"Nothing that can't wait until tomorrow," Kim cut in.

"Promise?"

"I promise."

Nikki wasn't precisely certain she believed her, but decided to let it go. The last thing she wanted to be was a nag. "That little French bistro in the Flats. At, let's say, eleven?"

"It's a deal."

She hung up the phone a minute later, the next day's plans cemented. Whatever was worrying Kim, they would deal with it together tomorrow over crêpes, their usual method of enlightenment.

Tonight, she told herself, was for Nikki. And for her, um . . . research.

Chapter 2

Sunday, June 8
10:23 P.M.

Okay, so it wasn't research in the clinical sense. In fact, most people would probably chalk it up to reading porn, but in Nikki's eyes it was still legitimate research. That it, rather than work, involved the sex life she aspired to one day have was beside the point.

Her gaze skimmed over the books sitting in her lap. The titles said it all. She nibbled on her lower lip, wondering if she was depraved or if other professional women in high-stress careers fantasized about the types of situations she fantasized about.

Submitting to the Master.

The Definitive Guide to Bottoming.

Sexual Servitude 101.

Ugh. Her mother would roll over in her grave if she had any inkling that the greatest sexual aspiration her surgeon of a daughter possessed was to dramatically submit her body as a sensual offering to a dominant man behind a closed bedroom door.

Then again, her mother would probably roll over in her grave if she knew Nikki had any sexual aspirations at all.

She sighed, deciding that, if nothing else, her fantasy life would make for an excellent edition of the Jerry Springer show.

These deviant physicians say there is nothing wrong with getting handcuffed to a bed and made to perform fellatio on the alpha males in their lives. Stay tuned as we talk to doctors who like to get down and dirty. Coming up next on Jerry Springer . . . .

Nikki shook her head. Down and dirty indeed. She hadn't performed fellatio on a male—or done anything else with or to one, for that matter—in over three years. She was as celibate as a saint, she thought a bit grimly. Single and celibate. She didn't mind the former, liked it in fact, but the latter really sucked.

Moving the Domination/submission books from her lap to the coffee table, she stood up and made her way over to the computer. She absently switched on the power button, her attention temporarily snagged by the mirror suspended to her left on the wall.

She pressed her face in closer, wondering what it was that men saw when they looked at her. Did they think she was at all attractive? At least average, maybe? Or did they think she was ugly? Too serious? Too brainy? Too . . . something?

Whatever it was, she thought, it was definitely keeping her from scoring.

She chuckled at her own thoughts. "Scoring," she murmured. "You sound like a middle-aged pervert, Nikki. And a male one at that."

She sighed, deciding that that's what happens to a woman when her sex life is as barren as the Sahara. She straightened her shoulders, giving her features a serious, critical evaluation.

She wasn't ugly, she decided. Not gorgeous, but definitely not ugly. Nor was she plain. Her face was pretty in its own way, her eyes wide and green, her lips full and soft. Her nose was a bit longer than what was considered fashionable, and her smile was slightly crooked, but all in all she wasn't too bad. Unusual-looking, perhaps, but not too bad.

Her light brown hair was long and curly and typically rolled into a neat bun at the nape of her neck for work. Her coloring was good for someone who rarely had time to see the sun, a light beige given to tanning on the rare occasion she made it outdoors.

At five foot, six inches she was neither tall nor short. At one hundred forty-five pounds she was neither skinny nor overweight. She was just average—boringly average.

The only thing that stood out about her body, she admitted, was her chest. Even she, her own worst critic, thought she had nice breasts. They were large and round, and still on the perky side for thirty-four. Perhaps not the sexiest chest in the world, but it would do.

"So why are you dateless, Nikki?" she murmured to her reflection. She absently wondered if a makeover would heighten her appearance at all. "What the heck is wrong with you?"

Nothing was wrong with her and she knew it. The average man was intimidated by her professional accomplishments, a fact she had long ago come to accept. A cliché, perhaps, where career women are concerned, but a true one nevertheless. So it was either go dateless or couple off with fellow physicians who, like her, had little time on their hands to devote to a relationship.

Truthfully, she loved her career too much to care, for the most part. It was just on nights like this, when she was overtired from a long workday and allowing herself to indulge in the occasional therapeutic bout of self-pity, that she gave her lack of a dating life any thought at all.

Otherwise she was happy. Content in who she was, happy with her life. Besides, she silently conceded to the mirror before glancing away from it and sitting down in front of the computer, the dates she had gone out on in the past year had been far from earth-shatteringly profound.

A few months ago there had been Ted. A fellow physician and a nice guy, but oh so dull. She'd dated him for a few months, deciding to try and stick it out. Then *he'd* dumped *her,* wanting to be "friends." She hadn't been saddened in the least.

Before Ted there had been Mike. Another physician, another nice guy, another man who put the *d* in *dull.* Him she'd gone out with three times before they'd parted their separate ways, again of mutual accord.

And, finally, before Mike there had been Elliott. A physician. A nice guy. Dull. Yada, yada, yada. Same story, different doctor.

Nikki sighed, wondering for the first time if all three of those men had really been as dull as she remembered or if the fact that her fantasy life was a bit more dramatic than what was probably considered normal could account for it. Simply put, she couldn't imagine any of her former dates handcuffing her to a bed and then treating her body like a sexual offering to a dominant god. She blushed, mortified by the thought that she might be abnormal.

"You're a weirdo," she dismally muttered to herself as she brought up her email. "A definite weirdo."

She didn't know why she fantasized about sexual submission, only knew that she did. Perhaps it was because she was so in control in her professional and personal lives that she wanted to be helplessly out of control in the bedroom.

Perhaps it was because she knew she'd never be considered a great beauty, yet to have a man desire her in such an all-consuming way would make her feel like one. In all of the D/s books, the Dominant party spent hour upon hour lavishing attention on the body of his or her submissive counterpart, bringing them to climax over and over again. Due to the complexities required of the relationship, such as the complete trust the submissive must put into the Dominant, a D/s partnership is supposedly more bonding and emotionally rewarding than many other kinds of relationships.

Maybe her fantasies were all very Freudian in nature and somehow or another they stemmed back to her childhood, to a time when her mother's needs had always been paramount and Nikki's had mattered very little. Growing up, she had been a shy, chubby girl, an awkward kid with pimples and thick glasses who was more comfortable surrounded by books than by people.

Books never disappointed . . . people always did.

That was the lesson she'd learned early in life, and one that hadn't been easy to surmount. She couldn't count how many times she had tried to reach out to her emotionally vacant mother, how many times she had thrown her arms around her middle for a hug, only to feel her mother tense up. Eventually she had stopped trying.

A child takes experiences like that personally because they aren't mature enough to realize that the vacancy and neglect has nothing to do with them and everything to do with the one neglecting them. All a child understands is that they want the one they love to show love back. When that love is not expressed physically, through hugs and kisses and smiles, they take it to heart. Nikki had been no exception to that rule.

Maybe it was because she was plump and unattractive, the young Nikki had thought. Maybe her mother was disappointed by the fact that she wasn't a part of the "in" crowd. She didn't know. All she'd known at the time was that she ached for affection from a woman who was unable, for whatever reason, to bestow it upon her.

Nikki had loved her mother to her dying day—passionately, at that. Still did. And although she wasn't the type to sit around and bemoan her upbringing—for as an adult she was able to realize that her mother loved her in her own way and had been dealing with problems of her own—the emotional neglect Nikki had experienced at her hands had left her feeling very lonely and isolated as a child. She couldn't help but to wonder if that accounted, at least in part, for the types of all-consuming fantasies she now entertained.

Fantasies of being the sole recipient of one man's undivided sensual attention. Fantasies of being longed for, desired . . . *wanted*.

D/s requires, by its very nature, for the Dominant to be in tune with the emotional and sexual needs of his or her submissive. It would be impossible, after all, to place enough trust in a person to permit them to handcuff you to a bed if you suspected they didn't pay the proper amount of attention to the emotional and physical reactions elicited by their touch. It is crucial for the Dominant to be focused on the submissive's needs at all stages of the game.

Or at least that's how it was supposed to be, according to all the Domination/submission texts and fictional stories. Whether or not it actually played out like that in reality she hadn't a clue.

But damn did she want to find out.

Nikki took a deep breath, realizing as she did that she was unlikely to ever get her answers firsthand. She wasn't willing to chance something like *that* getting out about her, for if it did, her career would be irreparably damaged. She also didn't want to live a D/s lifestyle twenty-four hours a day and seven days a week. She only wanted to experience it behind the closed bedroom door. So, in the end, what were her fantasies worth to her?

She frowned. Unfortunately, a lot.

Perhaps if she could meet a like-minded professional . . .

She snorted at her thoughts. Yeah. As if a like-minded professional would advertise for a sexual submissive anywhere. He'd be just as afraid as she was of his own career being ruined by gossip!

Nikki sighed as she pulled up her web browser. If she couldn't experience D/s firsthand, she could at least live vicariously by reading stories about fictional women who had.

"Oh God!" I screamed.

I wanted him to take me, to ravish me, to plunge his stiff cock deep inside of my wet, awaiting pussy.

The metal of the handcuffs lay cold against my heated skin. The power that emanated from him was a tangible thing.

"Master! Please fuck me—Master!"

Nikki squirmed in her chair, the e-book having a decidedly pronounced effect on her libido. "I'm pathetic," she mused even as she drew her face closer to the screen. "Completely and utterly pathetic."

She decided not to think too much on that admission lest she grow depressed.

An hour later the e-book had ended, the Master and the sex slave had fallen in love, gotten married, and the heroine was pregnant. A typical romance, if a bit more brazen than most. She loved it.

Curious about the author, she typed her name into the browser's address space, added .com onto the end of it, and waited to see if she had her own site. Sure enough, she did. Nikki spent over an hour researching every title the author had written, for future reference, then clicked on the "Links" page, just to see what was there.

The author's favorite authors. The author's favorite vacation spots. The author's favorite—

Whoa! What was this?

Her eyes wide, Nikki backtracked up the web page.

"Favorite alternative sites," she murmured, reading the text aloud. Her wide green gaze zeroed in on one site in particular. "Dom4me.com," she whispered.

She gulped, her heartbeat inexplicably racing as she clicked on the hyperlink. *You are pathetic,* she thought excitedly as the website loaded and displayed on her screen. *You find a place that specializes in D/s personal ads and your body reacts like a kid on Christmas Eve!*

Nikki spent the next two hours giddily sifting through dozens upon dozens of ads. There were older men, younger men, short men, tall men, pudgy men, and muscular men—all of them Dominants, all of them looking for bedroom submissives.

She narrowed down her search to the five ads that appealed to her the most. None of the five had photographs attached to them, but all of the five were intelligent, well written, and posted by men who claimed to be professionals who, just like her, needed the utmost discretion concerning this part of their lives.

"I can't believe I'm doing this," she grinned as she opened up a word-processing program and began to type out a brief description and bio of herself. She kept the biography very general, not wanting anything to be traced back to her.

I'm a thirty-four-year-old professional woman, seeking to be sexually submissive in the bedroom but otherwise my partner's equal . . . .

After creating a special account for D/s email, she put a few polishing touches on the bio, then copied and pasted it into five separate emails and whizzed it off to the recipients she'd carefully chosen. That accomplished, she sat back in her chair and took a deep breath.

She had done it. She had actually replied to five D/s ads.

She sighed, convinced nothing would come of it.

"They're probably a bunch of phonies," she muttered, standing up.

She switched off the computer screen, doubting she'd hear a word back from any of them.

And if she did, she mused, all five of them would be fat, bald, ugly men who still lived at home with their mommies.

Chapter 3

Monday, June 9
11:17 A.M.

"Mmm mmm. These are excellent, Nik."

"Agreed," Nikki cheerfully concurred around a mouthful of strawberry jam and butter crème crêpe. She chewed the bite and swallowed. "The best I've ever had. Bar none."

Kim smiled absently.

Nikki stilled, her eyebrows drawing together quizzically. "What's wrong, hon?" She set down her fork. "You sounded weird on the phone last night, too. What is it?"

Kim closed her eyes briefly, rubbing her temples as she sighed. There were visible bags under her eyes, Nikki noticed for the first time. As though she hadn't slept in days. "Kim?" she quietly prodded, worried.

"It's happening again," Kim murmured. She opened her eyes and found her best friend's gaze. "Just like last time. Only worse."

Nikki's eyes widened. "You mean . . ."

"Yeah. That." Kim snorted, glancing away. "God, I'm a freak," she mumbled.

"That's not true," Nikki said softly, her gaze gentling. "You are . . . gifted."

Kim half smiled and half groaned. "I'm just lucky I have you to talk to. Can you imagine me confiding this . . . this . . . mess to anyone other than you?"

No, Nikki couldn't. But she didn't say as much.

She couldn't blame Kim for keeping that aspect of herself a secret. Admitting that one had visions, premonitions, ESP—whatever you wanted to label it—might go over well in some New Age artsy circles, but you might as well wear a tattoo on your head that said "Looney Tune" if admitting to it in theirs. They lived in the heart of Ohio, for goodness sake.

Nikki hated conceding to a prejudice, but if anyone *except* Kim had confided their psychic abilities to her, she wouldn't have believed them. She didn't know why she felt that way—such occurrences were very possible from a physiological standpoint. Possible, just not probable, as humans tend to utilize a very small portion of the brain.

But Kim . . . how could she not believe studious, upright Kim? A teacher of physics at the prestigious Eastern Academy, an elite boarding school in Hudson, her best friend was as sensible and logical as people come.

"You said the occurrences have gotten worse." Nikki thought back on the last time, the time when Kim had been able to locate a missing bracelet in an area she'd never before been to or even heard of. Not a big deal, really. Just kind of neat. She cleared her throat, then lowered her voice, not wanting anyone to overhear their conversation. "How so?"

"They've become clearer, crisper. It's hard to explain. . . ." She sighed as she ran a punishing hand through her blonde hair. "And darker."

"Darker?" Nikki murmured. "What do you mean?"

Kim's eyes were intense, her expression pained. "I'm envisioning awful things, Nik. Stuff worse than you can even begin to imagine." She shook her head slightly. "I don't know what to do, don't know how to turn it off. It's awful. Awful!"

Nikki blew out a breath, uncertain as to what she could possibly say to put her friend's mind at ease. Then again, she conceded, sometimes there wasn't anything that could be said. Sometimes the best therapy was simply to listen, to allow your friend to vent. "Go on," she said encouragingly.

"In my dreams," Kim whispered. "It's awful. The images of blood and screams . . ." She let her sentence trail off as she took a deep breath. Nikki's eyes widened.

Kim smiled softly. "You're a terrific friend, Nik. I feel better having told you even that much. But I came here to forget. Let's just eat our crêpes, okay?"

"Oh sure," Nikki said dryly, trying to lighten the mood a bit. "Drop a bomb like that and then leave me hanging." She smiled as though teasing, but she was serious. Kim had never dreamt morbid things before. That she did now was a bit unsettling.

Nikki had known Kim since their undergrad days at Youngstown, the mental click between them instant and strong. If one were to judge solely by outward appearances, they would have seemed ill-suited as best friends back in those days. Kim heralded from an extremely affluent family, while Nikki's upbringing had been lower middle class at best. Kim was tall, blonde, and fashionable, while Nikki had been a shy, plain Jane of a bookworm with almost no fashion sense.

And yet, surprising as it was to the superficially minded, they had hit it off from the moment they'd met in English Lit and had been all but inseparable ever since. What the superficially minded hadn't realized, of course, was how much Nikki and Kim had in common on the inside—everything from emotionally vacant parents to a love of French bistros to a disdain of shopping.

Their personalities went together like red beans and rice, like peanut butter and jelly, or as the running joke had been a few years later thanks to MTV, like Beavis and Butthead. Nikki had been shy and socially awkward, never feeling as though she fit in anywhere. Kim had felt much the same way; she'd just done a better job at hiding it. "Always smile," had been Kim's motto. "Never let the assholes get you down."

At any rate, they had both been enrolled in the same pre-med accelerated program and had finished their bachelors' in two years' time. Whereas Nikki had continued on, enrolling in medical school at nineteen, Kim had decided against it, physics by then her raison d'etre.

After leaving the accelerated Northeastern Ohio University College of Medicine (NEOUCOM) program behind, both women had headed for Harvard, allowing their friendship to further grow and strengthen. Nikki had been in medical school, Kim in the physics department, but they had spent time together every night after classes let out, having decided prior to arriving in Cambridge to share an apartment.

They had struck up a deal from the beginning. Because Nikki had come from such humble beginnings and possessed little money, rather than getting further in debt and taking out loans to pay for her share of an apartment in Cambridge, Kim covered all the bills. In exchange, Nikki had done all the cooking, which she loved to do anyway while Kim had never taken to it.

Those years had been a blast. They had grown up together, become women together, taught each other, and learned from one another. Kim had given Nikki fashion sense, and Nikki had given Kim the security of knowing she was loved not for how much money she'd inherited but simply because she was Kim.

They had watched each other fall in love for the first time, and then held each other when their hearts had been broken for the first time. They had shared each other's victories and felt each other's disappointments. That Kim was purposely withholding information from her now, after their long and meaningful history, was disturbing.

"I'm sorry," Kim said. "I'll confide more in you when I feel up to recounting it, okay?"

Silence.

"Kim . . ." Nikki sighed. "I don't want to press you—really, I don't." She ran her hands through her hair as she expelled a breath of air. "But you didn't ask me to meet you today just to eat crêpes, and we both know it."

"I don't want to be a burden, Nik. I know things at work are crazy for you right now. Dr. Sorenson has it out for you and—"

Nikki waved that away. "I can handle Dr. Sorenson. He's such a whiner that the chief of staff doesn't put any stock into what he groans about anyway. Honestly." She gave her friend a level look. "Besides, Kimmie, you are my best friend. If you can't unload on me, then what kind of a friend am I?"

Kim considered that for a moment. "Okay, fair enough. But I have to warn you . . ." She sighed. "Nikki, these images are not pleasant."

"I'm a surgeon. There is little I haven't seen."

"Touché."

Nikki offered her an encouraging smile. She lowered her voice. "Go on, sweetheart. Tell me. You need to get this off your chest."

Kim was quiet for a prolonged moment. Eventually, however,

she made eye contact and lowered her voice to the same hush as her friend's. "There is this woman . . ." She shook her head. "I don't know who she is, or even what she looks like. The image of her face in my dreams is so muted as to be nonexistent."

"Go on," Nikki murmured.

Kim quietly cleared her throat. "She is enraptured with this man. This man who, just like her, I cannot see. Except for his eyes." She shivered. "His eyes are the most chilling, icy blue. Anyway, that's neither here nor there."

Nikki nodded, but said nothing.

Kim leaned in closer. "She goes to meet him. Funnily enough, considering that she cares for this man, I get the impression this is the first time she'll have ever met him face to face."

Nikki's forehead wrinkled, but she said nothing.

"I know. That makes no sense. Anyway, after that, the images flash forward to this black space. A dark room? An abandoned house? I don't know. It's so dark I can see nothing but silhouettes. I'm able to see what is happening to the man and the woman by a single ray of moonlight that penetrates wherever it is the couple is standing. Other than that, I get no impressions of where they are." She frowned. "The scent of water is strong—very strong."

Kim sighed, looking away. "That's when it becomes awful, Nik. The things he does to her . . ."

She glanced back, making eye contact. "This woman is tortured for hours. And when I say tortured, I do mean tortured. I'm not talking a little bit of pain here. I'm talking being raped so brutally that blood flows down her legs. And while he's raping her, he's also stabbing her. He stabs her just right, so that the cuts don't kill her until he's ready to deliver the death blow. So he can keep pumping away inside of her while she's still alive."

Nikki's eyes widened. She shifted in her chair, slightly uncomfortable but engrossed in the tale. "Jesus." She blinked, then blew out a breath of air. "No wonder you've got bags under your eyes. You must not be getting a wink of restful sleep. How long have you been having this dream? Is it the same one every time?"

Kim shrugged. "More or less. It varies in detail now and again, but yeah, it's basically the same dream."

"How many nights now?" she asked again.

Kim sighed. "Fourteen."

"Fourteen!" Nikki frowned. She didn't know what to make of this. She also didn't know what to suggest to make Kim feel better. She'd have bags under her eyes the size of Texas if she had been haunted every night of the past two weeks with images like that.

"And, almost the worst thing about it is that the entire time he's doing this to her . . ." Kim briefly closed her eyes while she took a deep breath.

"Go on," Nikki whispered. "Tell me."

"The entire time he's doing this to her he's humming—humming the theme song from the movie *Somewhere in Time*."

"Have you thought about talking to someone, hon?" Nikki reached across the table and gently placed her hand over Kim's. "You know, a professional?"

Kim scoffed. "I'm not crazy!"

"I know that!" Nikki said with just as much force. "I didn't mean it that way, so don't go getting your feathers ruffled." She squeezed Kim's hand. "I'm a surgeon, not a psychiatrist, but surely there has to be something on the market that can stop dreams. Then again, maybe not. But you should at least find out!"

"No way." Kim pulled her hand out from beneath Nikki's and made one definitive slash with it through the air. "No way am I going to a shrink. Uh uh. No."

Nikki sighed. Her friend was as stubborn as a goat. Yet another trait they had in common.

"Kimmie," she said quietly, "a recurring nightmare does not a premonition make. All of your verifiable premonitions have been small, almost insignificant in scope. And they have *always* occurred while awake, never in slumber. This sounds more like disturbed sleep patterns than anything else! Lots of people experience recurring dreams. You should see a doctor."

"Maybe you're right, but . . ." She blew out a breath of air. "I can't."

"May I ask why? It's hardly a mark on your character."

"Work," she admitted. "If they ever found out . . ."

"They won't. Besides, we don't know that this is a premonition. As I said before, it could be something as simple as a recurring dream."

Kim looked at her skeptically. "I really don't think so, Nik," she whispered. "But let's use the best possible scenario and say that you're right. Even so, what do you think would happen to my job if it was found out that I keep having disturbing recurring dreams about rape and torture?"

Her career would be over. Nikki frowned. She couldn't deny the truth of that argument. An elite boarding school would never have a potential nutcase on staff. Not that Kim was crazy, but they'd treat her as though she were.

"Fair enough," Nikki murmured, feeling as defeated as Kim looked. She was silent for a moment, and then, "What are you going to do?"

"I don't know." Kim forced a grin. "Sell my memoirs and become fabulously wealthy?"

Nikki snorted. "You're already fabulously wealthy," she muttered.

"Okay. So I'll give the proceeds to charity, then."

"Kim . . ."

"Don't chastise me, okay?" She sighed. "Look, Nik, I'll figure something out. I promise. But you have to understand that I can't let something like this get out."

Nikki smiled supportively, but on the inside she was still worried. "Sure," she whispered. "I understand."

Kim smiled back. "I wish you did understand." She glanced away, her look thoughtful. "But you can't possibly know what it feels like to be a freak," she murmured.

Not true, Nikki thought, biting down onto her lip. It might not be exactly the same thing, but her intense D/s longings made her different, unusual. She didn't really want to know just how unusual. And, like Kim, she didn't want to chance her career being ruined if word got out.

Those were the reasons why she hadn't confided her yearnings to anyone. Embarrassment was why she hadn't even confided them to her best friend.

"You're not a freak," Nikki softly reiterated. "You're just gifted."

"Boy oh boy, is this hombre gifted or what?"

Detective Thomas Cavanah snorted at Dr. Felix Goldstein's sarcastic assessment of Lucifer's work. He'd known the fifty-year-old coroner for over five years and highly respected him. "Or what," Thomas murmured.

"His cuts are clean, precise. His hands are steady."

"How pro do they look? Are we talking Boy Scout level, a surgeon, what?"

"Maybe a surgeon, but not one that graduated at the top of his class. Somewhere in between is my best guestimate," Felix said thoughtfully. He threw a white sheet over the remains of Linda Hughes, then motioned for Thomas to follow him into an adjoining conference room.

"Well, that only leaves a million or so occupations to plug into the databases," Thomas said dryly. "Thanks for clearing that up, Doc."

Felix smiled. "I wish it were that easy." He sighed as he took a seat behind the desk. "Because of how my field is portrayed in the media, people think my job is simple." He held up a hand. "The coroner examines the dead, runs a few tests, and the perp is nabbed. If only it really were that straightforward."

One corner of Thomas's mouth hitched up in a gesture of camaraderie. He knew exactly how Dr. Goldstein felt. In the movies, a cop's job was more science than art. In reality, the opposite was true. There was a lot of science involved, these days more so than ever before, but it still came down to intuition, gut instinct, problem-solving skills, and tenacity. In a word, art.

"So," Thomas said as he took the seat across from the coroner. He tugged at his suit, feeling big and uncomfortable in it. At six-foot-three and carrying around two-hundred-forty pounds of solid muscle, he had never warmed up to the professional-suit attire of a detective. He belonged in a football jersey and sweats. "You got anything new?" he inquired, his gravelly voice sounding sharp for a man who hadn't slept in two days.

"Actually, yes," Felix said, surprising him.

Thomas's eyes slightly widened. He ran a callused hand across his five o'clock shadow. "Well hell, Doc, why didn't you say so?"

"Very rarely do I get to make such a dramatic announcement. Allow me to savor it, eh?"

Thomas smiled. "What do you got for me?"

Felix sighed. "Not as much as I'd like, but at least it's something."

The detective sat up straighter in his chair. "Go on," he prodded.

"We've got a fiber."

Yes. "It doesn't belong to Ms. Hughes? You're certain?"

"Positive."

Thomas's eyes narrowed. "What kind of fiber?"

Felix frowned. "Now there's the shit part."

"The shit part?" He grunted. "What are you saying, Doc?"

"I'm saying that the fiber was too threadbare to positively ID." The coroner sighed. "When I burned it down to analyze, there just wasn't enough there, buddy."

Thomas closed his eyes, momentary defeat gnawing at him.

"But . . ."

"But?" His eyes flew open. "There's a 'but'?"

Felix smiled. "A small one, but yes, there is a 'but.' "

Thomas threw a hand toward the coroner. "What is it?"

"Just my hunch." Felix steepled his fingertips together. "My hunch will never hold up in court—you know that, Detective. The defense would shred it to bits."

Thomas waved that away. All he needed was a lead. He'd find evidence that would hold up in court once he had something to go on. "Tell me."

Felix nodded. "Leather. I think the fiber was black leather."

Thomas chewed on that for a protracted moment. "Any particular reason you think that?"

"None. Just experience, Detective. Nothing more, nothing less."

But experience made up for plenty. He inclined his head and then rose to his feet. "Thanks, Doc," he murmured, holding out his hand for a shake. "Let me know if you find anything else."

* * *

*Kimberly Cox arrived back home a little past two in the after-*noon. She felt drained by the time she opened up the doors to the colonial-style brick mansion nestled within the elite suburb of Hudson, where she lived, worked, and had been raised.

To outsiders, she led a charmed life. Having been born the sole heiress of a multi-millionaire father, she had wanted for nothing her entire life. Indeed, she had never felt the social pressure to outperform others in the way that many of her school peers had. She had grown up knowing it wasn't necessary, counting herself blessed that she could choose to work at a profession she loved rather than feeling obligated to choose one merely because it was high-paying.

She didn't have to keep up with the Joneses; the Joneses were too busy trying to keep up with her. Not that she bothered competing.

Much to her social snob of a father's dismay, his only child had never cared much about coming off to others as pretentious and worldly. She was just plain old Kim, a spinster schoolteacher who loved working with kids and was passionate about physics—a subject most people fell asleep just thinking about.

Kim valued logic and reason, higher thoughts and self-contemplation. She did not value this . . . this *thing* . . . that she had become.

She sighed a bit wearily as she padded into the bedroom, exhausted from a lack of sleep these past two weeks. She could only pray that the fates would grant her mind a bit of surcease and permit her to get some much-needed rest this afternoon.

Sleep without dreams. Sleep without nightmares.

She was beginning to forget what it felt like.

"Please," she whispered to the walls as she stretched out onto the four-poster bed and closed her eyes. "No blood. No death. No screams."

Her dreams of late had been a bit more complicated than what she'd expounded upon to Nikki. Not much, but a little. She hadn't seen the point in going on and on about all the little details, though. She'd given her best friend the gist of it all, and Nikki had been correct in that talking about them aloud had helped her to feel less burdened. Perhaps Nikki was right. Perhaps she truly was suffering from nothing more than a recurring nightmare.

It wasn't as if Nikki needed to be forewarned or anything, Kim reminded herself as she took a deep breath and blew it out. Her best friend was a sensible, logical, intelligent female. Not the type to get herself into weird scrapes like the woman in her dreams.

Kim smiled, bemused. Besides, she told herself as she drifted off into blessed slumber, Nik would never be into things like *that*.

Chapter 4

Monday, June 9
4:37 P.M.

"You've got mail."

Nikki clicked the mailbox icon on her screen, her hands shaking slightly ever since the computerized voice had announced that there was something in her electronic inbox. She blew out a breath, mentally chastising herself for reacting like a teenager to email from men she'd never so much as met before.

So what that they happened to be into things she possessed the courage to imagine only in her wildest, most wicked dreams.

She smiled as she pulled up *submissivegrrrl*'s inbox, the account she had created before responding to the personal ads. She was pleased that all five potential candidates had written her back. She took her time reading through the correspondence, mentally noting which ones she had the most in common with.

In the end it came down to two men, both of them living and working in the Cleveland area. Bachelor #1 was Paul, a thirty-eight-year-old accountant living on the east side. A divorcé, he was a single father of two kids and, understandably, didn't want his young sons to know about this part of his life.

Discretion was Paul's middle name. Perfect.

But it was Bachelor #2 who really snagged her attention. Perhaps because she liked his photo more, perhaps because his writing had a poetic flavor. It was fluid and graceful, masterful and certain. It felt like the writing of a Dominant, if such a style of writing existed.

Dear submissivegrrrl,

To answer the question foremost in your mind, I have been involved in the D/s lifestyle for over nine years. I am a professional by day, a Master by night . . . .

Nikki savored the entire email, her mind already wondering what he would be like in the flesh. If he looked anything at all like his photo, then he was as handsome and well-built as he was dominant. She smiled.

An added bonus. She was more interested in the dominance.

Bachelor #2 was a thirty-six-year-old schoolteacher named Richard. A divorcé like Bachelor #1, he had a daughter who lived with him full time.

Nikki smiled as she clicked the "Reply" button in her email program. She typed up a five-paragraph response, indicating her interest and expounding upon their commonalities. Before clicking "Send," she attached a photograph of her body in profile, her face turned away from the camera. She wasn't comfortable enough yet to show him more.

But this was a start, she thought, feeling equal parts excitement and nervousness. If he liked what he saw and wrote back, maybe she'd work up the courage to send him a photograph of her face.

She bit her lip, her heart racing. Maybe, one day, she'd even meet him.

"Black leather." Thomas grumbled those words to himself as he plunked down into his office chair and ran agitated hands through his hair. "Shit."

By itself, a black leather fiber wasn't much to go on. All kinds of people wore black leather jackets. Damn—he didn't even know if the fiber had come from a jacket. It could have come from gloves, a pair of pants, or even a pair of underwear from a novelty store.

The hell of it was, black leather could be found on anyone. From Hells Angels sporting black leather jackets to sixty-year-old grandmas carrying black leather purses, it was a common material. Apparently too common, he thought on a frown.

Thomas yawned as he stretched his muscles. His body was tired from a lack of sleep, but his mind kept refusing to rest. There was a correlation here somewhere, he knew. A correlation he was missing.

He stood up and trudged to the back of his office, and then into an adjoining planning room where he had photographs of Lucifer's victims pinned up in a straight line across two walls. He took his time studying the death-scene photographs, looking once again for that small lead he knew was there if only he could find it.

All of them had been tied up.

He frowned. That didn't necessarily mean anything. Lots of killers tied up victims before they whacked them. It made torturing and killing them easier because they were defenseless to fight back.

There was also the bondage aspect inherent in tying a victim up. Most serial killers who also fit the profile for sexual sadists, which Lucifer definitely did, were aficionados when it came to collecting bondage porn. That this killer in particular had reenacted bondage death scenes with the victims wasn't exactly noteworthy as far as an investigation goes. Still, it was something. Information to file away in the corner of his brain, to be retrieved at a later date.

Thomas's eyes flicked from the photograph of Linda Hughes to the photograph of Carrie Stoddard. From Carrie to Marsha Graham. From Marsha to Lisa Pinoza. From Lisa to Genevieve—

His gaze flew back to Lisa Pinoza. Lisa was the only victim they'd found who had still been alive when police had arrived on the scene. She'd been badly injured, left for dead. She'd died of her injuries less than ten minutes later, unable to tell them anything about her attacker before she'd taken her last breath.

She had also been the only victim not missing her heart.

That was important. Why?

Thomas tried, for the hundredth time since police had found Lisa four years ago, to analyze that question from a psychotic thinker's point of view. Why would Lucifer take the heart of every victim except for this one? What set Lisa apart from the others?

His gaze flicked down to the stats below her death-scene photograph.

Name: Lisa Marie Pinoza. Race: white. Age: 31. Marital status: married. Children: a five-year-old son and a three-year-old daughter. Occupation: waitress at The Sacrament, a bar in downtown Cleveland.

Thomas stilled, thinking about the other discrepancy between Lisa and the rest of Lucifer's victims. She was also, the stats reminded him, one of only two victims who wasn't a white-collar professional. A victim who did not, for lack of a better description, wield a lot of power in life.

Black leather. Tied up.

Power.

He scratched his jaw. His partner, James Merdino, had spoken with Lisa's husband after the murder. He'd said it was a dead end, that there was no new information to be gleaned from the spouse.

Thomas narrowed his eyes as he considered that. Moments later, he turned off the light in the planning room and made his way out the door and toward his vehicle.

It wouldn't hurt for Cavanah to speak with Lisa's husband himself. Nothing might come of it, but then again, there was always the small chance that something would.

Waiting for the computer to boot up, Nikki threw the towel she'd been wearing since her bath into a nearby hamper, then pulled on a T-shirt and sweats. Today had been a grueling day at work. She had lost a five-year-old boy who'd been playing with his father's gun. The gun had gone off, and the bullet had lodged in the child's chest.

She was more glad than she could say that she wasn't on call tonight or tomorrow. She needed the time to recuperate, to forget.

She always aimed to leave work at work. But every once in a while a particular patient would get through the carefully constructed emotional walls she had placed around her heart. Today had been such a day. She'd never forget the sweet innocence of that five-year-old's face. Or the look of unadulterated guilt and anguish on the father's.

Nikki sighed as she plopped down in front of the computer and pulled up her Internet account. She checked her primary account first, the one at which friends and professional acquaintances emailed her. After answering those emails, she switched over to her

D/s account, grinning when *submissivegrrrl*'s inbox revealed another message from Richard.

My sweet submissive Nikki,

For almost two weeks now we've been emailing back and forth. With every day that goes by, I find it harder and harder to concentrate on work when all I want to do is rush home and check to see if you've written me.

She smiled. She felt the same way. Nikki was too well trained and controlled to let her mind wander during an operation, but as soon as the procedure was finished, her thoughts would invariably turn to Richard. She was growing to like this D/s fantasy lover of hers. A lot. She wasn't quite ready to meet him, but she knew the day would be upon them soon.

I understand your hesitancy in regards to meeting me—truly, I do. So I will endeavor to be patient, beautiful one, knowing that when I earn your trust, I will also earn the honor of meeting you in person.

*You're a special lady, Nikki. Everything about you is exciting and intriguing. From your submission fantasies to your profession, there is nothing about you that escapes my awe. I sometimes find it difficult to believe that you are interested in the likes of me, a lowly underpaid schoolteacher, but I will never look that particular gift horse in the mouth. *smiles**

Nikki smiled back to the screen. There was nothing lowly about being an underpaid schoolteacher. To her way of thinking, it was one of the noblest professions in existence.

She continued reading.

With the same passion and intensity with which I respect you, so too do I desire you, sweet Nikki. I will treasure your last email to me forever. . . . I mean that.

She blushed, recalling that email. Divulging her most secret yearnings hadn't been easy, but telling them to Richard had felt right.

At Richard's gentle prodding, she had revealed her most intimate fantasy to him—the very one she daydreamed about at least twice a week.

The fantasy involved being handcuffed to her Dominant's bed while being "made" to perform for his pleasure. She would suck his penis first, opening her mouth like a good little girl (she loved to be called that in her fantasies!) at the Master's request. When his cock was stiff with need for her, he would settle himself between her thighs and thrust inside, then ride her body into wave after wave of delicious, submissive orgasm.

In her fantasies, her Dominant was in love with her and would tell her how much that was true over and over again as he thrust in and out of her welcoming body. She had neglected to mention that part to Richard, not wanting to appear pathetic, as though she expected him to love her before they truly knew each other.

Still, they were her fantasies. She could dream about whatever she wished, love included.

I am a Dominant by nature, Nikki. It's not something I need to pretend at. To me, there is nothing more sacred or sexy than the trust a submissive places in her Dominant.

I can make all of your dreams a reality. I can fulfill fantasies you didn't even know you had . . . .

I want all of you, Nikki. Your body, your soul, and your heart.

I hope I'm not scaring you off . . . please tell me if I am! I just feel so connected to you, as if everything between us fits. I know it sounds crazy when we've never met, but why else would we email back and forth several times a day—long, detailed emails that reveal our truest selves to the other—unless both of us are coming to the same conclusion?

*Please tell me I am not making a fool of myself here. *smiles**

Yours,

Richard

Nikki took a deep breath and blew it out. Richard was right. As insane as it sounded, she too felt the connection growing between them. It became more and more pronounced with every email they sent off to each other.

And it wasn't just sexual compatibility, either. They seemed well-suited as friends, too—and as lovers in a general sense. They shared the same political and religious beliefs, the same . . . everything! He was almost too good to be true.

A little unnerved by how fast her feelings were developing, but smiling contentedly nonetheless, she hit the "Reply" button.

The Cleveland PD wasn't even sure Lisa Pinoza had been one of Lucifer's victims. The fact that her heart had been intact when she'd been found had set her apart from the other women enough to warrant suspicion that she'd been done in by someone other than Lucifer—an altogether new perpetrator. Perhaps even her husband, Vincent. But Vincent's alibi had been squeaky clean—it was kind of hard to fake being in jail.

The CPD had then tried to ferret out possible lovers Lisa had taken up with, even though James Merdino had reported back that Lisa's husband had believed her to be faithful. They'd never come up with anything solid, so perhaps Vincent Pinoza had been right.

Thomas, however, doubted it. All signs pointed to Lisa having willingly met the man who'd murdered her that fateful night, for reasons other than friendship. Unlike his partner James, Thomas held no doubts but that Lisa had planned to dally with this man on the night of her death. He was also certain he knew precisely who that man was:

The devil himself.

The manner in which Lisa had been tied up was eerily similar to Lucifer's other victims. Same knots, same type of hemp rope. Even some of the stab wounds she had sustained had been, although not as well thought out, proficiently clean.

Not everyone at the CPD considered Lisa Pinoza one of Lucifer's victims. Thomas did. What he needed to understand now was why Lisa's murderer hadn't put the same amount of effort into killing her as he had into the others, which would include why he hadn't taken the heart.

The stabs Lisa sustained had been brutal, angry. Not the clean, precise, orderly cuts found on the other victims' bodies.

Thomas ascended the cement steps leading to Vincent Pinoza's modest home. The tiny postage-stamp-shaped house was small but well manicured on the outside, he absently noted.

He lifted his hand to the doorbell and rang it, tugging on his tie as he did so. Goddamn, he hated suits.

A minute later, and wearing nothing but a towel around his middle, Lisa's widower showed him into the living room.

"We were young when we got hitched. Young and stupid." Vincent sighed and lit a cigarette. He ran his hands through his wet, shoulder-length brown hair, the bottom strands falling to rest on the Harley-Davidson T-shirt he'd thrown on after escorting Thomas inside the house. "But I loved Lisa a lot, always had. We'd been going out since high school, didn't you know?"

Thomas shook his head.

"I did drugs back then," Vincent admitted. "Heavy shit. Coke. Heroin. You name it and I did it." He took a long drag from the cigarette. "Been clean since the day she died," he murmured in a faraway voice.

"Did Lisa start looking for a way to escape?" Thomas asked softly.

Vincent's eyebrows rose. "You mean did she fuck someone else? Yeah, she did."

The detective's body stilled.

"Hell," Vincent said. "Looking back I can hardly blame her. Here she was stuck with a deadbeat husband and two kids, supporting all four of us *and* my drug habit on a waitress's salary. Shit, I'd have looked for an escape, too."

Thomas said nothing. He didn't want to interrupt Vincent's train of thought.

"Lisa was good people," Vincent said reflectively. "Had a lot of aspirations in life—aspirations I never had. She wanted to go to college, didn't you know?"

Thomas shook his head.

"Yeah, well, she did." Vincent took another long drag from the cigarette. "When we got married the deal was I'd work to put her through school. She wanted more out of life than this neighborhood. Can't say I blame her."

"But you started using drugs and she never got that chance. Did she?"

Vincent blew out a long puff of smoke. "That's about the size of it." He frowned. "I can't tell you how many times I tried to quit. I knew Lisa'd leave me if I didn't. But I couldn't stop. Not until I had to. Not until Lisa was dead and the only thing the kids had left in life was me."

Thomas nodded. He absently yanked at his tie, wanting to pull the damn thing off. "For the kids' sake I'm glad you did," he muttered. His eyes narrowed a fraction. "Do you know who she was having an affair with, by chance?"

"Not a clue."

"Are you certain she was having an affair?"

"Positive."

"How?"

Vincent sighed as he ran a hand through his damp hair again. "Lisa was depressed the last three years of our marriage. Ever since the second baby came along. But then, a month or so before she got killed, all of a sudden she was real happy. Know what I mean?"

Thomas thought that over. He inclined his head.

"It was like she had a reason to smile again." He frowned. "I hated her for it back then because I knew the reason wasn't me."

Thomas waited for Vincent to make eye contact. "Did you have anything to do with her death?" he bluntly inquired.

"No." Vincent's nostrils flared.

"You knew I was going to ask," Thomas said unapologetically, believing him. Vincent wasn't smart enough to figure out how to have his wife murdered while he was in the slammer, his alibi airtight. That took a cunning that the detective's experience told him this man lacked.

Vincent frowned. "You know something? I thought about it a time or two when I was flying high. Killing her, I mean. She was my wife and she was fucking someone else. But could I kill Lisa? No way, man. I loved that woman. I'd have probably killed the guy she was screwing if I'd got my hands on him, but not Lisa."

"How do you know the reason was another man? It could have been any number of things that made her feel less depressed."

"It was definitely another man." Vincent shook his head. "She flat-out admitted she was in love with someone else."

One of Thomas's eyebrows rose almost imperceptibly. "Did you tell the police that?" he asked softly.

Vincent waved that away. "Yeah. Of course. This is all old news, man." He took a final drag from the cigarette before snuffing it out into an ashtray. "Damn, I still miss her. I know she fucked around toward the end, but if I'd gotten my act together, we'd be married thirteen years next month." He straightened in his chair. "Anyway, as I told you when you first got here, I don't have any new information. I wish I did. I'd like to tear the bastard who raped her and killed her apart with my bare hands."

Thomas inclined his head as he rose to his feet. That he could understand. More than Lisa's husband would ever guess. "Thank you for your time, Mr. Pinoza." He held out his hand to shake it. "I appreciate it."

Vincent returned his firm handshake. "Any time," he said as he led him to the front door. "Let me know if you find anything."

"Will do."

Thomas traipsed back to his car, the wheels in his head racing. Why would James have neglected to mention in the reports he'd filed on Vincent Pinoza the possibility that Lisa had had a lover? He scratched his five-o'clock shadow, wondering if a mistake had been made somewhere down the line in the paperwork.

Thomas had been down in Savannah visiting his mother when Lisa's body had turned up. James had hurriedly faxed the paperwork to him to look over, to bring him up to speed. He hadn't thought to question his partner about Vincent upon his return because the paperwork had made it seem like a dead end.

He frowned as he revved up the Cadillac's engine. There must have been a careless mistake in the paperwork.

A distinct possibility. And one he'd have to look into.

Chapter 5

Monday, June 30
7:52 P.M.

My sweet, submissive Nikki,

*Today is our 3-week anniversary. *smiles* I can hardly believe it's only been 3 weeks when I feel as if I've been waiting for you my entire life. I have to admit I'm finding it increasingly difficult to remain patient in my wait to see you face-to-face. I just want to know that you're real, that we are real.*

I want to thank you for your last email, for sharing another part of your soul with me. I can't begin to appreciate the amount of stress you must be under each day at work. . . . I find dealing with 8th grade history students trying enough.;-) My respect, and passion, increases for you a hundredfold with every new glimpse into your being you grant me . . . .

Nikki paused from her reading as she glanced up from the computer screen. She turned around in the swivel chair at her desk in the den, her gaze seeking out the report she hadn't yet read.

She sighed as she stood up to retrieve it, feeling bad that she'd gone so far as to hire a firm to check Richard out. But a woman can't be too careful these days, she reminded herself. It never hurts to make certain you've checked—and double checked—your facts.

Opening up the large manila envelope, she tugged at the sheaf of papers inside until they were firmly in hand. There was a photograph of Richard—the same photograph he'd emailed to her three weeks ago—along with a bunch of reports. She read the cover letter first.

Dr. Adenike,

Everything about Mr. Remington checked out just fine. He is, indeed, a thirty-six-year-old single father and a teacher of history at Shaker Heights Middle School . . . .

She smiled as she read the rest of the cover letter, elated that her suppositions about Richard had turned out to be true. He hadn't lied about who he was. Richard was the real deal.

Nikki took a deep breath as she clutched the report to her chest. Now that she knew he was legit, all she had to do was work up the nerve to meet him.

*Over the course of the month they spent in devoted email ex*change, Nikki grew ever fonder of Richard. She felt as though she knew him, as if their email exchanges were bonding them together before they'd even met face-to-face.

Perhaps it was because she was allowing herself to open up her soul to him, to bare parts of her psyche to Richard that she had never before permitted a man to glimpse. The Internet offered a sort of safe haven to express oneself in, a way to get to know another person without masks or façades.

She was baring her true self to Richard, telling him of her hopes and dreams, of her vulnerabilities as well as the things in which she had self-confidence. She took comfort in the knowledge that he was just as open with her.

She would sense it if he were lying, she told herself. No man was *that* good an actor. The two of them were definitely bonding.

She had shown him photographs of her face and he had liked them. She had even sent him a photo of her bared breasts late one evening when she'd had a bit too much wine to drink. He had liked that photo, too, telling her he'd always treasure the spontaneous webcam photo she had snapped solely for him to view.

Surprisingly enough, Nikki hadn't felt dirty or bad about sending Richard that photograph. She told herself she should have, but everything just felt so . . . right. She had been nervous and giggly, surprised by her own audacity, but she had enjoyed sending him the risqué picture.

Perhaps because the photograph symbolized a letting go of the old Nikki, an ability to be a sexual being where before she had been too shy and lacking the self-esteem to do so. She had gotten rid of the thick glasses and uncoordinated outfits ages ago, but until she'd "met" Richard she had still felt like that insecure plain Jane of a bookworm she'd been at eighteen. Now she was beginning to feel like a caterpillar who, at long last, was ready to emerge from her cocoon and become a beautiful butterfly.

And yet, despite their growing closeness, a part of Nikki still shied away from meeting the man she had come to idealize as the perfect D/s lover. She chalked it up to nerves, to cowardliness. To a fear of failure. And perhaps, if she was honest, to a fear of success.

By the time their month-long anniversary arrived, she realized that Richard was growing more and more desperate for a physical meeting. She had known from the beginning that his patience would endure but so long, and she sensed that his limits were about to be reached.

Could she blame him? she asked herself as she sat down in front of the computer and hit the power button. If their roles were reversed, she knew she would have begun to doubt that he was serious about ever meeting her.

Just coffee, he'd said in his last email. *Coffee and conversation. *smiles**

Nikki smiled at the memory. It didn't seem like a lot to ask of her, she mentally conceded as she logged on to her *submissivegrrrl* account. Coffee and conversation. A well-lit, public meeting place. A café in the Flats, perhaps?

Her smile faded when she signed on to find no new email. This was the first day that Richard had neglected to write to her.

She sighed, realizing that she couldn't blame him. A cyber relationship could last but so long. Apparently one month was near enough to that limit.

Slightly down in spirits, yet still uncertain as to whether or not she was ready to take the next step and meet him, Nikki pulled up Richard's last email and reread it.

My sweet, submissive Nikki,

Please, darling, give me one chance. A chance to see you, to hold your hand, to look into those soulful green eyes and experience the pleasure of having you reveal yourself to me in the flesh.

You won't regret it, darling. I'll see to that . . . .

Her body became involuntarily aroused as she continued reading.

I know how to satiate all of your deepest hungers. How to make you gasp, make you scream, make your eyes roll back into your head in an ecstasy hitherto unknown . . . .

She believed him, she thought, blowing out a breath. Her nipples hardened against the T-shirt she wore.

I know your every longing. I know you, my Nikki. This is about more than sex, and I think you realize that. This is about the kinship of souls, the kinship of minds.

I want much more than your body, sweet, submissive Nikki. I want your soul, your heart . . . .

She swallowed against the lump in her throat. Did he realize how profoundly his words affected her? She had confided in him before about how emotionally neglected she'd always felt growing up. To have someone use such strong emotion against her now just to get her into the sack would be beyond cruel.

She bit her lip. Richard wouldn't do that—no, not Richard. He had no reason to. A man who looked like that, and who was intelligent and witty to boot, could get any number of willing women into his bed. He didn't need to prey on her.

"Always the cynic," Nikki murmured.

She took a deep breath and blew it out. She had already hired a detective agency to check him out, and the report had come back clean. No arrests. No history of mental illness. Nothing that could give her pause. "What would a cup of coffee and some intelligent conversation hurt?" she asked the walls of her apartment.

And maybe, just maybe, things would be as wonderful in real life as they had been online. If that was the case, they could move into the next phase.

And Dr. Nicole Adenike would finally know what it meant to submit her body to an alpha male.

Nikki sighed as she stood up. She turned away from the computer, leaving it on while she went into the kitchen to make herself some dinner.

She wasn't going to make a potentially life-altering decision on an empty stomach. She'd ponder her choices while she peeled the potatoes.

Huddled up in the bathtub, Kim wrapped her arms around her knees, staring at nothing. The nightmare she'd been enveloped in an hour ago, the one that had awoken her from a dead sleep, had been her clearest yet.

It had also been the most horrific.

This time she had seen what the attacker was wearing, though the woman's figure was still too hazy to discern anything from. She had also gotten a clearer picture about where they were—next to some sort of a building. In an alleyway, perhaps?

Kim bit down hard into her bottom lip as she came to the definitive conclusion that, like it or not, she truly was dreaming about things yet to come. Things that hadn't happened yet . . . but would.

"Shit," she muttered to the walls. "What do I do?"

She couldn't do *nothing,* which was, unfortunately, precisely what she wanted to do. But she wasn't a cop, either. She could hardly go tracking the killer down, guns blazing, like some rebel with a cause. The killer would laugh his ass off before he did her in, too.

But that woman . . .

She shivered. That woman in her dreams was going to die. How could she live with herself if she sat back and waited for it to happen, knowing she hadn't done one thing to at least try to stop it?

"What do I do?" she whispered to herself as she drew her legs in tighter against her chest. "What do I do?"

"You've got mail."

Nikki's head shot up from where she was grating cheese for the salad. Almost thirty minutes had gone by—she'd forgotten that she'd left the computer on.

Wiping her hands on the apron she wore, she sipped from her glass of wine before setting it on the marble countertop, then turned around and walked into the den.

She clicked the mailbox icon as she sat down in the chair, grinning when she recognized the familiar screen name.

FallenAngel.

Richard.

Nikki opened up the email, her heart thumping pleasurably in her chest as she read it.

Have you given any more thought to meeting me, my sweet? I deplore pressuring you in any way. My only excuse is that I know we were destined by fate to be together. We have so much in common . . . and we have bared our souls, our hearts, to each other.

What do you say, beautiful Nikki? Will you give me the distinct honor of meeting you in the flesh?

She took a deep, fortifying breath and blew it out as she clicked the "Reply" button.

YES!! Nikki typed, her mind made up. *YES!!*

Chapter 6

Monday, July 7
8:20 P.M.

"He's really neat." Nikki grinned as she handed Kim a glass of wine from over her kitchen counter. Kim was seated at a bar stool on the other side of it. "We're going to meet for coffee a week from tomorrow."

"How were you two introduced?"

Nikki blushed. She cleared her throat as she poured herself a glass of the merlot she'd opened. "We met online," she muttered.

Kim snorted. "Oh yeah. I'll just bet he's a real doll," she said dryly. "He's probably eight hundred pounds, bald, and still lives at home with his mother."

Nikki had figured the same thing when she'd answered his ad, so she couldn't blame Kim for her skepticism. "Nope. I've seen his photo. And," she quickly added when her friend threw her a *he-could-have-sent-you-anyone's-photo* look, "I had him checked out by a detective agency." She smiled. "He's definitely legit."

"Smart thinking," Kim conceded. "In this day and age you can't be too sure."

"Tell me about it."

"Just look at those poor women who died at that Satan worshipper's hands. If they had practiced more caution, I bet they'd still be alive."

Nikki's face scrunched up. "Satan worshipper? This is news to me."

"Hmm . . . maybe the killer is not a Satan worshipper, then. I don't know." She shrugged. "You hear so much gossip in the media these days, it's hard to make a coherent story out of any of it. Anyway, the one the press calls 'Lucifer' is who I meant."

"Oh—oh! I know who you mean." Nikki frowned. "Now that you mention it, I do recall a reporter speculating that the murders could be occult-related. I doubt it, though, because I've followed the case a bit—not much, but a little." She shook her head slightly. "It makes for sensational headlines anytime the word 'occult' is thrown into the mix, but that doesn't make it accurate. As someone once said, believe nothing you read and only half of what you see."

Kim's look was thoughtful. "To be honest, I don't watch the news much, so what I pick up on is just bits and pieces here and there." She grinned. "So the one report I did actually see was a sham, huh?"

"Oh yeah," Nikki informed her. "The police flat-out said the killings were definitely not occult-related the day after the story you are thinking of aired. The CPD's rebuttal, however, was given about two seconds of airtime . . . after the weather was reported!"

Kim snorted. "The real Lucifer is probably some middle-aged disgruntled accountant type."

"I wouldn't doubt it." Nikki sighed. "An accountant type. That singular possibility makes you wonder about *all* men."

"Exactly. Psychos are supposed to look like psychos. Not like some guy named Howie who does your taxes."

Nikki grinned. "True enough." She took a sip of merlot. "Speaking of psychos and being extra careful," she said as she set down the wineglass, "I wanted you to know where we are meeting. Just to have all my bases covered. Richard is a great guy, but you know me." She winked. "I'll die a cynic."

"No, no, that's not cynical," Kim said, her gaze drifting away. "It's smart. You should never meet a man you don't know for a date without telling someone where you'll be."

"True. You probably shouldn't even meet one you *do* know without telling someone where you'll be! Anyway, the rendezvous is scheduled for 7:00 P.M. at Jake's, that rustic little café/bar down in the Flats. I've never been there before, but I hear it's really cute."

Kim nodded, but said nothing.

One of Nikki's eyebrows rose. "You okay, hon?"

"Hm? Yes." She shook her head to clear it. "I was just thinking about . . ." Kim sighed. "I've been having the dream again. It stopped for a while and then all of a sudden it came back full force."

Nikki's eyes showed her concern. "You feel like talking about it?" she quietly asked.

Kim was silent for a moment, then inclined her head. "Yeah. Yeah, I think I would." She picked up her merlot, drained it, and then set the wineglass down on the countertop. "Come on," she said as she stood up, "let's go talk in the living room."

"And then what happened?" Nikki whispered.

Kim simultaneously shrugged and sighed. "The same as before. It's not that there was anything different in the dream, per se, it's just that the images and impressions of what's going to happen were a lot more vivid than usual. At this stage I'm sure this is more than a recurring nightmare, Nik. I don't know how I know, I just *do*."

She ran a hand through her long, blonde hair. "When the dream begins, I am seeing things from an aerial perspective, like if I was a ghost hovering over the scene or something. That's how I got a better look at the crime scene this time, and what separated it from previous dreams. There was this bridge and then a dock. . . ."

Kim scrunched up her face, pieces of it still fuzzy. "From there the image zooms in on this dark space. I get the feeling this crime is going to take place next to a building. A building near a dock of some sort. Or something. Arrg! I just don't know. It's so frustrating!"

Unfortunately, that location could be just about anywhere. Cleveland alone boasted numerous similar establishments.

"You should go to the police." Nikki folded her arms under her breasts, her expression as serious as it was troubled. "It can do no harm and perhaps a lot of good if you tell them everything you know."

"The police?" Kim frowned as she snuggled into the leather sofa in Nikki's living room. She picked up a pillow beside her that had been placed there for decorative purposes and absently toyed with it in her lap. "They'll think I'm crazy. Nik, you know that."

"Maybe. Maybe not. They probably deal with psychics all the time. . . ." She cleared her throat when Kim gave her a *yeah-right* look. "Well, even if they do think you're crazy, you'll at least have done your part." Nikki inclined her head. "Then the burden of guilt is theirs rather than yours."

"I don't know. . . ."

"I'll go with you," Nikki said, her tone permitting no argument. "You have to do this, Kim." Her gaze gentled a bit when she realized how nervous her friend was. This would be the first time Kim had been obliged to reveal her dreams to someone other than

Nikki. "I know you better than anyone. You won't be able to look yourself in the mirror again if you don't do this."

Kim sighed, her eyes briefly closing. "I know." She opened them back up, her gaze locking with Nikki's. "I just hope they don't laugh me out of the building."

Nikki's nostrils flared at the mere thought of it. Nobody but nobody had better dare make light of Kim in Nikki's presence. If they wanted to snicker behind their backs after they left, fine. But Kim was embarrassed enough about her visions as it was.

"That won't happen." Nikki frowned, then qualified her statement a bit. "That *better not* happen."

"I know this sounds crazy—believe me, I know that. But . . ." She sighed, her voice trailing off as she glanced away.

Thomas wasn't certain what to say. In all the years he'd been on the force, he'd never once had a psychic approach him. That was stuff for the movies, not for the CPD. And this particular psychic—Kimberly Cox—was telling him she was having dreams about the devil himself.

He had been tracking this killer for *nine years*. He was obsessed with him—perhaps a bit too obsessed. Because of that singular fact, Thomas had failed to meet certain expectations in his personal life, more frequently than he felt comfortable admitting. After awhile, the grueling hours he put in hunting his nemesis—his obsession—eventually got under the skin of every woman he'd ever dated.

And yet all these years and failed relationships later, Lucifer was still alive and well, still raping and torturing victims before killing them off in a belated act of mercy . . . or was it a final display of power? There were periods when he got scared and stayed underground until he couldn't take it anymore and needed the release a kill provided—sometimes those periods lasted over a year—but inevitably he always reemerged, even more sick and sadistic than before.

It had been years—*years*—and now Kimberly Cox, a shy teacher of physics from the snooty Eastern Academy, claimed that she could help narrow down where and possibly when his next kill would occur. A bit too easy for Thomas's way of thinking. Life didn't work like that.

"Listen, Dr. Cox . . ."

"You don't believe me," she whispered, her eyes unblinking as she looked away from him once more. "I knew you wouldn't believe me."

Something about her seemed so sincere. Thomas didn't doubt for a second that the Ph.D. schoolteacher believed herself to be a psychic—he himself merely doubted that she actually was one.

"Look, lady," Detective Ben O'Rourke said on a frown as he surged to his feet. Ben wasn't assigned to this case, but he'd been the officer who had found Linda Hughes's body, so had been collaborating with Thomas on parts of it. They'd been going over notes together when the ladies had come in.

Linda's remains had been discovered by accident when Ben had been off duty, heading home after a night out with buddies at a bar in the financial district. He'd immediately secured the crime scene before reporting it to headquarters.

"It's not that we don't believe you," Ben began in a patronizing tone of voice that clearly said just the opposite.

"Bullshit," Dr. Cox gritted out, rising to her feet. Her nostrils flared as she locked gazes with Ben. "This was a waste of my time. *You* are a waste of my time. I knew I should have kept it all to myself."

Ben's eyebrows rose but he said nothing.

Thomas ran a hand through his short, dark hair, sighing. "Please," he murmured to Kimberly Cox, "have a seat." He motioned for her to sit down again, then threw Ben an exasperated look.

People complained that Thomas was too surly and abrasive. Clearly those people had never met Ben, he thought with a frown.

"No, thank you." The schoolteacher's nostrils flared. "All I'm trying to do is save some poor woman's life. Do you think this is easy for me, coming here when I knew I'd be ridiculed? Because it's not. Far from it, in fact!"

That Thomas could believe. If word got out about this little visit, her schoolteacher days in Snootyville would be over.

"Please," Dr. Cox's friend murmured to her. "Have a seat, Kimmie. We'll leave soon."

Thomas's gaze darted over to the friend. Dr. Nicole Adenike was her name. She was a respected trauma surgeon at Cleveland General, a fact he'd quickly found out as soon as he'd been informed that the ladies were waiting in his office. The first thing he always did was check out an informant's history. In this case he hadn't had to look far—a couple of beat officers had recognized her face from having escorted perps into the hospital to have their injuries cared for.

Ben too had been familiar with Dr. Adenike. Thomas imagined that she and Ben wouldn't be getting along very well during future hospital visits. Anger was radiating off of her in waves. She didn't seem to hold Thomas in much higher regard.

This particular informant, or informant's friend, rather, had been glaring daggers at Thomas from the minute she'd whisked her schoolteacher friend into his office and witnessed as Ben had all but laughed at Kimberly Cox's "information." Add to the fact that Thomas, while not as abrasive about it as the extremely unsubtle Ben had been, was still just as skeptical, and it showed. Apparently the pretty surgeon's estimation of Thomas had plummeted even further when he'd failed to believe everything that came out of Dr. Cox's mouth as though it was the gospel truth.

Too bad, too. Dr. Adenike was damn cute.

Thomas had to admit, histories didn't come cleaner or more solid than the surgeon's. Or, for that matter, her friend the alleged psychic's, either. A circumstance that had his instincts on guard. Nevertheless . . .

"Listen," Thomas said, his gravelly voice kept low. He raised his eyebrows at Dr. Adenike when the daggers she was glaring at him impossibly turned more lethal. "Whether or not I believe Dr. Cox isn't the issue here. Even if I believed all this, it isn't much to go on. A bridge, a dock, a building . . . that could be anywhere. Hell, it could even be another city."

"It'll be Cleveland," Dr. Adenike stated through semi-gritted teeth. "She's certain of that. She's already told you as much. Kim doesn't make things up."

Nicole Adenike was a stubborn, loyal woman, Thomas thought as he leaned back in his chair and scratched the stubble on his cheek. He liked that trait in a female. Required it, in fact. If there was one thing a big, surly cop with a jealous streak a mile long couldn't hack, it was dating a woman whose word he couldn't be certain of. Too bad she hated his guts, he mused—otherwise, against procedure or not, he would have been forced to ask her out.

"I know," Thomas murmured, "that Dr. Cox believes it will happen in Cleveland." He locked eyes with Dr. Adenike, one eyebrow raising in a gesture she probably took as arrogance. Maybe it was. "But from my perspective, can you see how far-fetched all of this sounds?"

Dr. Adenike's nostrils flared and she glanced away, color rising in her cheeks.

Very telling, Thomas thought. Perhaps she did know how ludicrous it sounded. But because of her loyalty to Dr. Cox, she believed it all anyway.

"I'm leaving," Kimberly Cox said quietly, picking up her purse. She managed to look graceful despite the way Ben had treated her—Thomas would have a talk with him about that later. "I did what I came here to do. I've told you everything I know. What happens from here is up to you, Detective Cavanah. Come on, Nik. Let's go."

Dr. Adenike nodded and surged to her feet. Thomas watched the surgeon turn around and head toward the door, her posture rigid with anger. When you're a cop, you learn how to read body language well. Not that any five-year-old couldn't have picked up on the trauma surgeon's body language just now. Her tense jaw, flared nostrils, and rigid back were saying something in between "fuck you" and "I spit on your grave."

Thomas sighed. He mumbled something incoherent as he absently ran a hand through his hair. "Do you know what the killer will be wearing?" he heard himself ask, if a bit skeptically. He expected, of course, that the "psychic" would have no answer for that.

Dr. Cox's cheeks burned red. She must have known he was trying to make her feel unashamed, which she might have appreciated on some level, but she also realized that he didn't exactly believe her.

"Ye*sss*," she hissed. "He'll be wearing a black leather jacket and a black ski mask. I'm not sure how she will be dressed, but her hair is long and flowing."

Thomas stilled, his muscles clenching. The two angry women were already marching out of the office door, so they hadn't noticed his reaction. He glanced up at Ben, his mind racing.

"Oh, come on," Ben snorted, his hands folding across his chest. "Don't tell me you believe any of that bullshit for a second!"

But then, Ben didn't yet know about the black leather fiber that had been found on Linda Hughes's body.

Thomas frowned as he stared at the empty seats the women had vacated. Had Dr. Kimberly Cox had an actual "out there" experience?

Or had she made a lucky guess?

"What a waste of time!" Nikki half yelled and half growled.

Kim frowned, throwing her an *I-told-you-so* look. Not that Nikki could see it: her concentration was fixed on the road, visible through the windshield of the Mercedes.

"What an arrogant jerk!" Nikki continued on. "I wanted to smack that attitude right off of his face!"

"Yeah, I know. That Ben O'Rourke guy was a real asshole."

"Ben O'Rourke?" Nikki glanced over to Kim then back to the road. "I was talking about Detective Cavanah." She grimaced. "Men like him are so irritating! They think they know it all."

Kim conceded to that point. "Yep. He's another jerk. Not nearly as big of a jerk as that Neanderthal in his office, though." Her forehead wrinkled. "Was there something familiar about that guy to you?"

"Who? Ben O'Rourke?"

"Yeah." Kim frowned. "I feel like I've seen him someplace before, only I can't place where."

"I can. The jerk is always hanging around the hospital. If he's not getting patched up from some brawl or another he himself was in, then he's escorting detainees in for treatment."

"Oh." Kim thought that over for a second. "I guess that must be it, then. Maybe I saw him one of the times I went down to Cleveland General to pick you up for dinner."

"Maybe."

Kim sighed. "I just hope I never run into him again." She shook her head. "And I pray those two detectives are, if nothing else, discreet. I don't want what we did today getting around."

"I feel sorry for the women that end up with those two arrogant asses," Nikki seethed. "Did you notice neither of them wore wedding rings?" She harrumphed. "Well surprise, surprise! Who would have them?"

Kim chuckled at that. "Hey. You and I are still single, too. Please don't equate a lack of nuptials to a lack of character."

Nikki grinned, her good humor restored a tad. "Point taken." She shook her head, her expression turning serious. "I'm sorry I pressed you into that, Kimmie. Those cops were real jerks to you, and you didn't deserve that."

"Nik," Kim said softly. "It's not your fault. Besides, I was expecting it." Her eyebrows rose. She glanced over at Nikki, more than eager to put the morning's events behind them. "You feel like crêpes?"

Nikki smiled, ready to forget their less-than-pleasant experience at the CPD. Regardless of what Kim said, Nikki still wished she hadn't pushed her friend into the situation. But, she conceded, what was done was done. "Sounds good."

Chapter 7

Tuesday, July 15
3:15 P.M.

Peanuts, walnuts, almonds, Nikki mentally grumbled. Everything but pistachios. She grunted as she pushed the shopping cart another three feet, stopping before a second display of nuts at the local grocery store. "Ah," she muttered, "here we go."

There was only one carton of pistachios left, she noted with a frown. She didn't want to have to return to the store for another shopping expedition anytime soon, but one carton wasn't liable to get her through one week, let alone two!

Pistachio ice cream, pistachio pudding, pistachio anything—her favorite indulgence. Rarely did she whip up a dessert that didn't somehow feature pistachios in it. Kim had teased her about that fact back when they'd shared an apartment in Cambridge. Many a night her best friend had good-naturedly complained that if she was fed any more pistachios she'd probably grow a shell.

"Where the hell are the pistachios?" a deep male voice growled, forcing Nikki's attention two nut displays over. Her eyebrows rose as she watched the man verbally castigate an unsuspecting stock boy, and then narrowed when she realized just who the horrid male customer was.

Her lips pinched together disapprovingly. Too bad Detective Grouch was such an ass, she thought grimly. It was a shame when a fellow pistachio connoisseur was also a first-rate jerk.

Detective Cavanah apparently shopped at the same grocery store Nikki did. The football jersey and sweats he wore declared him off duty, as did the lack of a gun holster. But somehow the officer looked even more dangerous in his street clothes, she decided. Perhaps because it was easier to see just how heavily muscled he was all over, from his vein-roped arms to his solid chest to his powerful thighs.

"The pistachios," the stock boy replied undaunted, "were moved over to make room for the walnut-and-almond display."

"Walnuts and almonds, walnuts and almonds." The grouch rolled his eyes. "I don't want that girly food. What does a man have to go through these days to find a basic pistachio?"

The stock boy frowned, finally somewhat exasperated. "He has to walk two displays over. Somehow, I think you'll survive the grueling trip."

The grouch muttered something under his breath about smart-ass teenagers as he stomped off, prowling in Nikki's direction. The detective glanced up just then, his body momentarily stilling when his gaze clashed with hers and comprehension of who she was dawned.

His dark eyes narrowed a bit, leisurely raking over her face, and then down lower to her breasts. His gaze paused there a lingering moment before slowly returning to her face.

A tremor of awareness coursed through Nikki, causing her heart to beat in a strange way. It was an awareness she recognized, but one she couldn't explain. Nor was it one she wished to analyze or dwell upon.

She frowned. Vein-roped arms or not, Thomas Cavanah was and, as far as she was concerned, always would be, a first-rate jerk. She picked up the last carton of pistachios and held onto it for dear life.

The grouch studied her quizzically for a moment or two, wondering at her actions. Finally he glanced down and, noticing that she'd managed to snatch the very last carton of pistachios, scowled. "What the hell?" he muttered.

Her spine straightened, her posture defensive. "I believe this just isn't your day," she sniffed. "I guess you'll have to go to Howard's down the street and try to find some pistachios there."

His dark eyes narrowed. "I just came from Howard's," he bit out, his tone even surlier than it had been. "They're out of pistachios, too." He grunted. "You're just doing this to get back at me. Put down my nuts and back away slowly, lady."

Nikki's face slightly colored when two strangers glanced up and gave them a bemused look. Her nostrils flared as she cocked her head and glared at her nemesis. "These are *my* nuts," she hissed challengingly. "Finders keepers. Losers weepers."

His eyebrows shot up. "I see we passed the third grade," he growled.

She smiled sweetly—too sweetly. "And I see that you're leaving here nutless." She ignored the amused expressions of the passersby as she turned to saunter off.

"Please," Thomas said, his voice a bit desperate. "Don't do this."

A momentary pang of guilt lanced through her. She could, after all, empathize all too well with a fellow pistachio aficionado who was out of his stash. She quickly quelled the emotion, forcing herself to remember that the aficionado in question was also the jerk who had humiliated her friend.

"I wonder what I'll make with them," she said tauntingly, turning her head to look at him from over her shoulder. "Ice cream? Pudding?" She tapped a finger against her cheek, pretending to give the question consideration. "Or perhaps I'll just eat them plain." A light brown eyebrow shot up. "There's nothing quite like the sound of popping one from its shell, is there?"

She could have sworn she heard him whimper.

Good.

Nikki smiled in satisfaction. "Have a nice day, Detective." She sauntered off, her hips sashaying, leaving Thomas to stare after her. "It's a shame," she said, turning her head to glance at him one last time, "that you are nutless."

Thomas stared after Doctor Evil, a bemused expression on his face. It really was too bad she hated his guts, he thought, watching those hips of hers defiantly swish back and forth. She had a nice . . .

He ran a hand over his five o'clock shadow. Come to think of it, she had a nice lots of things.

Thomas stood there in the middle of the fruit-and-nut aisle, unsubtly appreciating the view of Dr. Adenike's well-rounded backside until she turned the corner and was out of sight. Blinking, he glanced down, frowning when it again dawned on him that the woman had taken his nuts.

He grunted. For her sake, she better eat those pistachios plain, he silently grumbled. If word got out that she'd made a pudding of his nuts, there'd be hell to pay.

Chapter 8

Tuesday, July 15
7:15 P.M.

What a jerk! she mentally wailed for what had to have been the tenth time since she'd returned from the grocery store. She frowned, the realization that she'd been thinking about the detective ever since their earlier run-in not settling well. She had other things to think about, other men—one man in particular, she reminded herself. She didn't need to waste any more of her precious free time considering what a colossal ass Thomas Cavanah was.

Nikki took a deep breath and blew it out as she studied herself in the full-length mirror adjacent to her bedroom's walk-in closet. She couldn't remember having ever been this nervous about going on a date before. She felt like she was sixteen again.

But then, she'd never gone out on a date with a man like Richard before, either. A man who knew everything there was to know about her before they'd even met. Her dreams, her hopes, her aspirations . . .

Her fantasies. The ones she'd kept to herself for years before having met her *FallenAngel.*

The only things he didn't know about her, in fact, were her last name and where she worked. Deciding that some things were better left a secret until they met and she could verify her suppositions about him in real-time, she had carefully omitted from her emails any references to her last name or to Cleveland General.

Nikki closed her eyes and breathed deeply, trying to calm her raging nerves. When next she opened them, she gave her looks one last critical assessment.

The spaghetti-strap black dress she wore was thigh-high and semi-low-cut, showing off what were, in her estimation, her two greatest assets in a purely physical sense—her long legs and her full breasts. The dress was classy and chic-looking. Perfect for coffee and conversation at a trendy eatery.

Perfect for Richard, whose favorite color on a woman was black.

Nikki had never dressed to please a man before. This was the first time, and she wasn't altogether certain how she felt about it. The independent part of herself said to grow up and quit acting like a little girl—a woman should dress for herself! But the other part of her, the part that became aroused by images of sexually submitting her body to a man, rather liked it.

Still, she didn't want to place too much mental importance on this meeting. If things worked out—great. But if they didn't, she wouldn't be crushed. Disappointed, but hardly crushed.

Over the passage of the last month she had grown to care for Richard, or, rather, for the man he presented himself as being. If he turned out to be that man in real life . . .

She blushed. She could easily envision herself falling fast and hard for such a lover as Richard.

But if he didn't turn out to be that man in real life . . .

She would survive. She'd be a bit down for a day or two, but she would rebound.

Nikki smiled at herself in the mirror as she raised a manicured hand to the back of her neck and let her hair loose of its confining bun. She was Nikki tonight, she reminded herself, as she shook out her light brown hair and left the curls to flow to the middle of her back. Nikki—not Dr. Nicole Adenike.

"Well," she murmured to her image in the mirror. "It's time to go meet your fallen angel."

She frowned, something about that name causing some bizarre sense of déjà vu, triggering some . . . *something*. Her forehead wrinkling, she tried to figure out what that something might be.

Almost all of the handles and their corresponding email addresses used in ads at Dom4me.com were dark and a bit devilish. She supposed it helped create a certain aura of forbidden mystery. There had been other similar names, such as DarkKnight, DarkMaster, FallenMaster, DevilishDom, etcetera.

Nikki inelegantly snorted at her reflection. "Always the cynic," she muttered. She shook her head once, then turned on her heel and headed for the door.

Tonight, she told herself with a grin, could very well be a major turning point. It had taken a month for her to work up the nerve to meet Richard, but the night was finally here.

This meeting held the possibility of changing her life forever.

Thomas felt like a damn fool.

He'd gotten together a team of ten police officers he trusted with his life, ten overworked and underpaid men, to work a week-long stakeout based on the premonition of some weird rich chick from Snootyville who believed herself to be a psychic. Worse yet, he couldn't get the image of the kooky lady's best friend (and her well-rounded rump) out of his mind.

Goddamn, he was losing it.

His men had been in place every night the past seven nights from 6:00 P.M. until closing time. They were stationed in various points around the Cleveland Flats—that, after he'd given it some thought, being the most logical place in Cleveland to look, mostly because of the bridge and the dock in Dr. Cox's dreams.

All of the officers were in undercover clothes, their well-trained gazes on the lookout for a woman with long, flowing hair who may or may not be accompanied by a man wearing a black leather jacket.

Thomas frowned as he glanced at his watch. 9:57 P.M. It was a Tuesday night. Most places in the Flats would be closing within the next few minutes.

"Hey, buddy, I hate to be the negative one here, but it doesn't look like our boy is gonna show."

Thomas sighed as he ran a palm over his stubbly face. "Shit. I don't know what I was thinking."

James Merdino clapped him on the back. "You've got nothing to feel ashamed about, man. Don't do that to yourself."

He closed his eyes and breathed deeply. "I just want that son of a bitch so bad," he murmured. Thomas opened his eyes, staring at nothing. "I'm letting my personal obsession cloud my judgment."

"Hey," James said. "Given your history with the bastard, any one of us would have felt the same."

"It's no excuse—"

"It's plenty of an excuse." James nudged him in the shoulder with his elbow. "Hell, even Ben O'Rourke gave up his night off to come out here and help. You know you are a respected cop when a bad-ass bastard like that lets you come between him and getting laid."

Thomas snorted at that. "Getting laid. Now there's what I should be doing."

"You still seeing Lucy?"

"Nope." He slid his gun into the holster, and then turned to James. "Get on the radio and call it off," he growled, changing the subject. Thomas had never been real big on discussing his dating life. Not even with the man he called partner and best friend. "This is useless."

James stared at him for a suspended moment before inclining his head. "Will do." He turned to walk away.

"Hey, James," Thomas said, recalling something he'd forgotten to ask him about. "Remember Vincent Pinoza?"

James stilled. He cocked his head, glancing back at Thomas. "Yeah. Lisa Pinoza's husband, right?"

"Yeah. Something strange . . ."

James lifted an eyebrow.

"I can't find your original paperwork on the interview. Did you file it somewhere?"

James narrowed his eyes in thought. "It's hard to say. That's four years ago now. It should be there, though."

Thomas slowly nodded. "I must have missed something. Thanks, buddy. Sleep good tonight."

He watched James walk away, the wheels in his mind racing. His partner was right: The paperwork had to be at the station somewhere.

There was no point in asking him about Lisa Pinoza's affair until he found it.

* * *

Black stiletto heels clicked on the pavement as she walked into the alleyway to retrieve her car. She was a bit sad, a lot disappointed, yet somehow not surprised that her dream lover had failed to materialize.

It was so black out tonight, so dark and eerie. She should have left the café earlier rather than waiting for him to show up clear until closing time . . . .

She stilled. Something didn't feel quite right out here tonight, she thought, her heart inexplicably pounding. Something was making the tiny hairs on her arms stand on end.

She felt watched. Trapped.

Hunted.

She picked up her pace, the stiletto heels sounding loud to her ears in an otherwise deserted alleyway. She walked faster and faster—*faster!*—she was almost to the car. Just a few more steps and—

"Nikki."

She spun around, frightened. Her eyes were wide, her heartbeat thumping. She saw no one.

This felt like something out of a nightmare.

"Nikki. My love . . ."

She backed up slowly, terrified. She couldn't see him, could only hear him. She'd never heard that voice before, so she knew he was a stranger, and yet his love for her was real, a tangible emotion transmitted in the way he spoke to her that was so thick with need and longing you could cut through it with a knife.

Oh God! Oh please someone help me! she mentally wailed. She tried to scream, tried so damn hard to scream, but she felt like a deer caught in headlights. Her voice was frozen. *Someone help me!*

The attack came swiftly, without notice. She had been expecting him to be in front of her, yet two strong hands seized her from behind, pulling her roughly up against a solid chest.

She screamed long and loud, a piercing sound that carried into the night. Finally—*finally!*—she could scream.

A heavy hand roughly slapped over her mouth, her scream cut off as she struggled with her attacker.

Him? Her dream lover? Oh please no—*no!*

One moment she had been struggling with him in a darkened alley and—she blinked—where was she now? Frightened, she looked around. She felt groggy and disoriented. She was in pain . . . *oh God oh God it hurts so much!*

He was going to rape her. Oh no—*noooo!*

She was naked, tied up, her body obscenely splayed out. Hemp rope held her outstretched hands bound to two slabs of wood shaped like a cross. He stood before her broken body, his penis stiff, the knife in his hand gleaming.

"I love you so much, Nikki. Your heart will belong to me. Forever."

He rasped out those words as he plunged his erection into her, the knife in his hand promising that something even more horrific than this brutal rape was still to come.

She wanted to scream—*oh please someone save me!*—but she was gagged. In that moment she knew she was going to die. She was only thirty-four and she was going to die.

Oh God—noooo!

Kim gasped as she bolted upright in bed, sweat pouring off her soaked forehead in rivulets as she abruptly awoke from the worst, most intense vision she'd had yet. Her breasts heaved from under the drenched cotton of her nightgown, her nipples hard against the saturated material as the chilled AC hit them.

It took her a long moment to orient herself, to realize where she was and to come to terms with the fact that she was nowhere close to where she needed to be. "Nikki," she breathed out, her blue eyes wide. "Oh God . . .!"

Kim threw the blankets off of her body and raced toward her closet to throw on a pair of jeans and a T-shirt. The police didn't believe her, she knew. There was no sense in going to them now, no time to grow angry over their lack of intervention.

Saving her best friend would be up to her, she realized, horror stabbing her in the gut. She raced down the back stairs of the colonial brick mansion, stopping only long enough to grab a butcher knife from the kitchen.

Nikki. *Oh God . . .*

"Last call. We're closing in fifteen minutes."

Nikki sighed as she glanced around the eatery a final time, the bartender's words reminding her of the hour. It was 10:15 P.M. and Richard still hadn't showed. By now she knew that he wouldn't.

The café was supposed to have closed fifteen minutes ago, but due to some cocktail party in honor of one of the people running in an upcoming election, it was staying open a half hour past its scheduled time. She took a deep breath, attempting to quell the pang of disappointment lancing through her.

Either Richard wasn't real or he had shown up earlier, saw her, and decided he wasn't interested. Either way, nothing was going to come of the month she had spent getting to know her fantasy D/s lover.

Nikki smiled a bit sadly. Then she motioned for the waiter, ready to pay her tab.

* * *

Thomas paced back and forth in the kitchen of his apartment, his muscles taut, his instincts screaming. Something was not right. Something was not as it should be.

He glanced at his watch. 10:29 P.M.

He had made it home in just under ten minutes. He could make it back to the Flats in just under five if he raced.

But it wasn't like the Flats was a small area. There was a ton of ground to cover. Several bridges, the docks . . .

A building by the docks. A building with an alleyway on one side of it.

He kept trying to assure himself that he was being obsessive, that nothing out of the ordinary was going down in Cleveland tonight, but it wasn't working. That schoolteacher kept creeping back into his mind. She had seemed so sincere, so troubled by the fact that she had these "visions" rather than embracing them as proof of some unseen ability.

Thomas based most of his better decisions on instinct—was it too much to believe that maybe the schoolteacher had that same ability, only on a different, possibly even advanced level? And so what if she was wrong. Would it hurt to go back one last time and do a security check over the Flats?

"Shit!"

Thomas swore under his breath as he grabbed his keys and stomped out the front door. His mind wouldn't rest until he'd done a final check. Might as well get it over and done with.

Chapter 9

Tuesday, July 15
10:31 P.M.

Nikki rubbed her hands up and down her arms to ward off the chill bumps as she slowly walked toward the alley. "Quit freaking yourself out," she muttered to herself.

Okay, so she hadn't remembered where she'd parked the Mercedes. Worse things have happened to better people, she decided.

Still, it was weird. She could have sworn she'd parked her car behind the bistro, but when she'd come outside it hadn't been there. At first she'd been angry, assuming it had been stolen, but then she'd spotted it in the little alleyway separating the eatery from another establishment.

The tiny parking lot had been jammed full when she'd arrived, cars spilling over into the adjacent alley. She'd been nervous when she'd arrived, her mind preoccupied with thoughts of Richard.

It was possible she'd parked her car in the alleyway and simply hadn't been paying much attention. Lord knows she'd done that at the mall a time or two—thinking she'd parked in one spot, only to find it five aisles over.

Conceding that she was freaking herself out over nothing, she walked faster toward the Mercedes, her stiletto heels clicking against the pavement. The car was there. The keys were in her hand. What thief would steal her car, then chance being caught by bringing it back? Get real Dr. Moron!

Still, Nikki had always valued gut instinct, and hers was telling her to stay alert. Her heartbeat racing, she kept her eyes wide open and her ears in tune with her surroundings as she clutched her keys so tightly her knuckles turned white.

She walked quickly toward the car, faster and faster, her breasts bobbing up and down as she moved. Almost there . . . almost—

"Nikki."

She stopped abruptly, whirling around to face the direction her name had been spoken from. She swallowed against the invisible lump in her throat, her heart beating so hard it felt like a rock in her chest.

No one. She saw no one.

"Nikki. My love . . ."

Her eyes widened. Panic, ice-cold fear, engulfed her.

In that moment of dawning, chilling awareness, she understood what she had done. She backed up slowly, perspiration dotting her forehead, as the realization that she had spent the last month exchanging emails with a madman caused her to feel as though she might vomit.

"Richard?" she asked in a small voice. "Richard, is that you?"

She knew it was. That was probably not his name, but it was the same man.

Scream, Nikki, damn you! Scream!

She wanted to scream—dear lord in heaven how she wanted to.

But when she opened her mouth this time, nothing came out. Her lips parted, closed, parted, but her vocal chords were frozen.

The attack came swiftly, without notice, from behind. She had expected him from the front—how had he gotten behind her?

His hands were on her—*oh God!*

The scream finally came, bubbling up from her throat and wailing out like a platitude to the heavens. *"Help meeee!"*

He brutally slapped a palm over her mouth, struggling with her as she tried to fight him off. He was big, so damn strong.

The keys—yes, her apartment key . . . !

She struck out at him blindly, trying to jab the key in her hand into his thigh. She was so hysterical and frightened that she had no idea whether or not the key had made contact. All she knew was that Richard was bellowing, that he had released her—

Oh God—run! Run Nikki! Run!

She fell to the ground instead, the jarring action of his abrupt release causing her to plummet. She cried out as she fell, pain ripping through her as her knees banged against concrete.

"Bastard! Fucking sick bastard!"

Nikki blinked. She had thought those words . . . but she hadn't said them.

"Kim," she whispered, her heartbeat racing like mad. "Oh my God."

Nikki wrenched herself up off of the ground, crying out from pain as she did so. She maneuvered her body around with some difficulty, only to find the most horrific sight imaginable.

A man in a black leather jacket and ski mask—*Richard!*—pulling a butcher knife out of his wounded arm . . . and stalking toward Kim with it. Kim, whose leg lay battered beneath her, the ankle either sprained or broken.

"No!" Nikki wailed. "Nooooo!"

Richard stilled, his head twisting to the left to regard her. Intense, chillingly blue eyes clashed with her wide green ones.

"It's me you want, fucker!" Nikki screamed, anger, fear, revulsion, and a million other emotions ripping through her. She clutched the key in her hand tightly, holding it like a talisman. "You spent an entire month planning this moment! Come and get me, coward!"

A police siren pierced the night, the loud wail sounding to Nikki's ears like a trumpet sent from the gods. She cried out, tears of relief stinging the backs of her eyes, as she watched Richard take one last thorough look at her before disappearing into the shadows.

Nikki limped toward Kim, her breathing labored, her arms outstretched, her entire body shaking. She needed to hug her, needed to know she was all right.

"I'm so sorry," Nikki said shakily.

One police car turned into two. Two into three. Then four and five. She ignored them all as officers scurried from their patrol cars and surrounded them on all sides. Her only thought was to get to Kim.

"Oh, Kimmie," she cried out, her voice sounding guttural, as if tamping down on barely controlled hysteria. "I'm so damn sorry."

Kim tentatively smiled, a black eye quickly forming from where she'd apparently been struck. "Hey," she said, her voice aquiver, "all in a day's work. We schoolteachers are used to stuff like this. Happens all the time."

Nikki half laughed and half cried. She hobbled the rest of the way to Kim, then fell down to her knees, no longer able to stand. The pain was jarring, numbing. She ignored it. "How did you know?" she asked weakly, dizziness assaulting her. "The dreams? Oh God—"

"Are you two all right?"

Nikki's head shot up, the sudden movement making her so

dizzy she felt nauseous. She turned a wild green gaze up to the owner of the masculine, gravelly voice. She could hardly see him, headlights from police cars all but blinding her. On all fours, her hair hanging in limp clumps every which way, her eyes crazed, she looked more injured-animal than human in that moment.

"It's okay, Dr. Adenike," the gravelly voice gently assured her. "You and your friend are safe. Officers are tracking your attacker as we speak." His voice was very deep, very rusty, and very soothing. Not to mention very familiar. Why couldn't she place it? "I won't let anything happen to you."

"B-But—the man . . . R—Richard . . ."

"You're okay," he repeated. The gravelly voice drew closer. She squinted, trying to see him in spite of the headlights. She was certain she knew that voice, but couldn't place it with a face. "Lucifer is long gone."

"Lucifer?" she heard Kim call out. "L-Lucifer?"

Nikki blinked. Now why was that name familiar? She knew she was in shock, realized her thinking process was slowed and surreal from the adrenaline rush and crash. But she should know that name. . . .

Memories assailed her. TV news reports. Dead women. Raped. Tortured. Missing organs. A man they trusted.

Lucifer.

Oh. My . . .

Lucifer—*FallenAngel*—Lucifer.

Oh. My. *God.*

Nikki clutched her heart, her breathing becoming dangerously rapid. She felt two strong hands grab onto her, holding her in a way that permitted her to feel secure enough to do something she'd never done in her life.

She fainted.

Chapter 10

Wednesday, July 16
4:07 A.M.

It was shaping up to be one hell of an enlightening evening. Lucifer had escaped once again, but the CPD had collected more information on the serial killer and his predilections in three hours' time than they had in the past several years.

1. The predator was now wooing women through the Internet—a fact the CPD had suspected with at least three of his previous victims, but weren't sure about until tonight. The last email Linda Hughes had ever sent, for instance, contained a reference to meeting an online acquaintance named Allan for a drink. The CPD, however, had found no residual traces from any emails sent by Allan, or any other potential suspect, on the victim's computer. They were forced to conclude that if Linda had been wooed via the Internet, she had set up a web-based email account through which to correspond with him, so that

no traces of him could be located on her computer's hard drive. Linda had most likely done that to protect herself professionally. She died never having realized that she had played right into her murderer's hands, that her secretiveness was a predator's twisted dream come true.

2. Like a fisherman who had discovered a new, successful lure, it was probable that Lucifer's next strike would occur on a woman he seduced via the Internet. It made a lot of sense, though. He liked professional women, powerful women. Liked bringing them down, removing their power. But professional women don't have a lot of time on their hands, tend to be too beat from a long working day to go out at night. The Internet makes for a convenient pickup scene and provides an endless pool of potential victims.

3. Lucifer considers himself an expert on D/s and bondage, and uses that knowledge to lure women looking for such an expert—again, the CPD had suspected this, but hadn't been able to confirm it until tonight. This explained the whip marks on Linda Hughes's corpse, as well as the bizarre markings on another victim. It also explained his proficiency with ropes and tying women up.

4. He had used the alias Richard Remington—a fact that probably wouldn't do them much good because he likely changed his name every time. Still, the alias would be looked into.

5. He was a big man, strong and tall.

6. Blue eyes.

7. Black leather jacket.

8. Probably fancies himself in love with his victims, most likely believes the romantic delusions he spins to lure them in. This, if true, probably explained the removal of the victims' hearts. Or at least explained it as much as it could possibly be explained.

9. Crazy as a two-dollar bill. That, however, the CPD had already known.

Thomas poured himself a cup of coffee from Dr. Nicole Adenike's expensive brewer before shuffling into the den to watch Leon Walker work. Leon had been on the force for over twenty years and was the CPD's resident computer whiz.

"Talk to me, buddy. You got anything new?"

Leon shook his head. "Not yet. Still working on it." He sighed, his ebony face showing fatigue. "On top of everything else, the asshole knows computers, too."

Thomas's eyebrows drew together. "What do you mean?"

Leon glanced up. "*FallenAngel* looks like a legit email account. . . ."

"But it's not," Thomas ventured, frowning.

"Nope."

Which probably meant the real *FallenAngel* was some fourteen-year-old kid into heavy metal who had no idea his account was being faked by a serial killer. Shit. "What is it, then?"

"Don't know. Looks to me like the emails are rerouted to another server."

"Can you find that server?"

"Gimme time, Cavanah."

Thomas sighed. After all these years he should have guessed that

Lucifer had covered himself from all angles. "I'm going to go speak with the victim again. See if she can remember anything new."

Leon nodded, his attention once more riveted on the computer screen. "I'll let you know if I find anything."

Nikki was in a daze, recovering from the greatest shock of her life. Lucifer. She could still scarcely credit it.

For a month she had been emailing back and forth with a serial killer, had even started to feel the beginnings of love for him. Like a fool she had believed the things he'd said to her, had believed *in* him.

Good Lord in heaven, she was a moron. A moron who had escaped being raped, tortured, and murdered by the skin of her teeth. She shivered, the realization as numbing as it was terrifying.

"Feeling any better?"

Nikki glanced up, the familiar gravelly voice breaking her from her reverie. Detective Thomas Cavanah. Her nemesis. On a typical night, anyway. She decided that a truce was in order, at least for this particular night.

She studied the homicide officer for a prolonged moment, getting her first good glimpse of him since this entire ordeal had begun. He was a big man, she noted just as she had back in the grocery store, muscular and solid. As tall as he was broad. His hair was dark and cut short, his eyes brown.

Thank God his eyes were brown, she thought. It made conversing with him easier. That last officer, Ben O'Rourke, had possessed blue eyes—she doubted she'd ever again look at blue eyes quite the same way.

"Yes. Thank you." Nikki cleared her throat. She offered him a half-hearted smile as he handed her a cup of coffee. She blew at the steam rising up from it, then took a long, measured sip.

"It'll get better, you know," he murmured, taking the seat on the sofa beside her. "I know it doesn't feel like it right now, but eventually it'll get easier."

She could see how muscular his legs were even through the material of his denim jeans. The muscles seemed to ripple as he bent his legs and sat. She glanced up at his face. "I hope so," she whispered. "Because right now I'm about a step away from needing to be institutionalized."

He didn't smile, but his dark eyes gentled. She sensed he wasn't the type who smiled much.

"Well, if you do need to be institutionalized, at least you'll get some good drugs for your trouble." He winked, winning a small smile from her. "See there," he drawled, his gravelly voice a purr. "You're doing better already."

Her gaze clashed with his. His brown eyes flicked down to her lips, then back up. She glanced away, blushing for reasons she couldn't fathom.

He was just being nice, she reminded herself. He was trying to provide calm and hope where little existed.

Thomas cleared his throat. "I know it's been a difficult night . . ."

"But?"

He sighed. "This is the part of my job I hate. I know you're just wanting to retreat to your shell to lick your wounds. . . ." He waited for her to make eye contact. "But I need to find this bastard, Dr. Adenike."

"Please, call me Nikki."

"All right, Nikki. And you call me Thomas."

She nodded. "Okay," she whispered.

"Have you been able to recall anything else about your attacker?" he asked, his tone patient. "His shoes? Any tattoos? Any . . . anything?"

She sighed, her eyes briefly closing. "I wish I could say yes, but . . ."

"But you can't."

She frowned, her head slightly shaking in the negative. "No. I'm sorry."

Thomas was silent for a moment as he studied her face. Finally, he inclined his head. "If there is anything else you remember, anything else at all . . ." He held out his business card to her. "I jotted my home phone on the back. My work phone and cell phone are on the front."

Nikki breathed deeply before responding. "I'll let you know if I come up with anything, but you have copies of all the emails we sent back and forth. That was the extent of our relationship. Oh, and I did have him—or Richard Remington, rather—checked out by a detective agency."

Thomas's eyebrows drew together, though truthfully the information didn't exactly surprise him. It was just further proof of what a careful woman Dr. Adenike was. She had done everything she could do and then some to play it smart. "And?"

She shrugged. "The report is laying on the counter in my kitchen. Feel free to take it. Anyway, Richard Remington is definitely a real man. As a matter of fact, he's a teacher at a middle school. But I'm willing to bet my last dollar he isn't the man you are looking for."

Thomas's frown was thoughtful. The doctor was right about that. He'd check into it, but it probably was a dead end. If there was one thing Lucifer was not it was stupid.

Nikki's nostrils flared as she looked away. "I, an allegedly intelligent woman, was taken in by the fantastical musings of a serial killer." She groaned, mortified by her own stupidity. "I actually believed that he was falling in love with me. My God, I'm pathetic."

Thomas was silent for a suspended moment. She glanced back at him, the quiet making her curious as to his thoughts.

"I think he did fall in love with you," he murmured, his gravelly voice kept to a minimum. "In his own sick, twisted, delusional way, of course." He inclined his head. "But I hold no doubts that he believed what he wrote to you."

Nikki shivered. "If he thinks raping, torturing, and killing are signs of love, well, that's pretty damn sick."

"Hence the term 'psychopath.' "

She found her first genuine smile, even if it was a small one. "Touché."

Thomas rose from the sofa. He held out his hand, waiting for her to make the first move and reach out to him. She could tell that he didn't want to frighten her, was probably assuming she found the touch of all men repulsive at this point.

She didn't. Richard—or whatever his name was—was not a man. He was the demon the press had dubbed him.

Nikki accepted his hand and shook it. "I'll let you know if anything else occurs to me, Detective."

He winked. "Go get some sleep."

"Thanks. I think I will."

Thomas nodded, then turned to walk away.

"Detective—I mean Thomas!" She stood up, waiting for him to turn around. When he did, she blushed. "Those emails . . ." She cleared her throat, the crimson in her cheeks growing more pronounced. "If they get out to the press, my career is over."

His forehead wrinkled. In that moment she was aware of the fact that he hadn't had time to read them yet. No, of course he hadn't. He'd spent the majority of his time on the phone with various officers and forensic specialists, first at the hospital where she and Kim had been checked out—the hospital where Kim was still under observation—and then again when she'd been driven back home.

"When you read them," she muttered, glancing away, "you'll understand." She sighed, looking back to him. "Anyway, if you can keep those emails out of the press until I figure out a way to save face at work . . ."

"Not a problem." Thomas inclined his head, curiosity as to what the emails contained evident in his dark eyes. "I'll see to it that those emails never see the light of day."

"Thank you," she whispered, her head slightly bowed.

"You're welcome."

Her head shot up. "Oh—one last thing."

One of his eyebrows rose.

She sighed. "The pistachios," she muttered. "They're in the kitchen. Go ahead and take the damn things."

He stared at her for a protracted moment, an enigmatic twinkle in his eye. "You think because you're a woman I won't take you up on the offer," he drawled.

Nikki frowned, a telling gesture.

Thomas held back a smile. His intense gaze swept over her. "I'd let a pretty lady come in between me and many, many things, Doc. . . ." He shook his head slightly. "But not between me and my nuts." He winked down at her, then turned and strode away.

Open-jawed, Nikki could only stare at him as he disappeared into the kitchen.

Chapter 11

Wednesday, July 16
8:10 p.m.

Feeling rejuvenated after sleeping for eight solid hours, Thomas booted up his home computer, slid the CD containing the email exchanges between "Richard" and Nikki into the e: drive, and settled in for a long working night.

He'd been itching to read them ever since he found out about their existence, this being the first writings the police department had on file of Lucifer. And then, after his little pistachio thief had blushed so prettily when referring to them . . . well, call him nosy, but his curiosity had increased tenfold.

She was an intriguing woman, Dr. Adenike. He could understand the predator's obsession with intelligent, strong, driven women—and with Nikki in particular. She wasn't classically beautiful in the fashion-magazine sense, but she was a beauty in her own way, a woman who held a certain exotic allure. She was sexy, sensual-looking . . . he could understand Lucifer's attraction. What he could not understand was the desire to murder her over it.

A feeling of inadequacy on "Richard's" part, no doubt. The need to prove his power by robbing his victim of hers.

Dr. Sydney Horace, the CPD's forensic psychologist, had skimmed through the emails already. Later, probably within the next few days after consulting with an FBI profiling specialist, she'd render a more complex summary on this particular killer.

The newly discovered knowledge on Lucifer would help immensely as the psychologist would then be able to make guesses on everything from the killer's profession to what style shoes he favored. Or at least that was the hope.

Dr. Horace's brief perusal of the emails was how Thomas already knew about the predator's penchant for Domination/submission games and a few other details. What he didn't understand was how Nikki came into play in all this. And why a successful, accomplished woman such as herself would agree to meet a man who admitted to the types of fantasies the forensic psychologist had briefed him on.

Thomas opened up the first email. It was time to have some questions answered.

Talking to you has been so freeing, Richard. I feel as though I can tell you anything. You have no idea what a relief that is to me. I've had D/s fantasies for years, I just never labeled them as such. Until, one day, I came across this website and started reading.

It changed my life forever, made me feel a bit less abnormal, if that makes sense. Anyway, it was comforting to come to the realization that lots of women like me—professional, "together" women, fantasize about sexually submitting to a man. About playing slave to his Master, prisoner to his jailor . . . .

About giving up all power to a man behind the closed bedroom door and trusting him to do what he will with her body.

Thomas blew out a breath. He felt like a real asshole because of it, but his cock was hard enough to cut a diamond. Shit.

The yearnings I have are more needs than cravings, more goals than simple curiosity.

Images of submission, of handcuffs and blindfolds, fill my mind whether awake or asleep. Thoughts of crying out my Master's name in orgasm—

Whoa! Thomas shifted in his chair, his erection damn near painful.

This certainly explained a lot, he thought, suddenly in the mood for a cool drink. Namely, it explained why Dr. Adenike didn't want these emails circulating in the press.

It also accounted for why all of Lucifer's victims, countless numbers of professional, intelligent women, were duped into meeting dominant, yet allegedly gentle, "Richard." They thought they were meeting a likeminded, sane professional male who was into the same kind of D/s games they enjoyed playing. Nothing more, nothing less, as Dr. Felix Goldstein was fond of saying.

Who would have guessed a female trauma surgeon was into those games?

Thomas sipped from his lukewarm coffee and continued working. For the hour or so he'd been reading, it had been hard not to envision Nikki in the types of situations she was so graphically describing, difficult not to see her tied to his own bed, screaming out his name as he pumped her long and hard. But calling him "Master" while he rode her—

That he'd never thought of before. Suddenly he was thinking about it.

Envisioning scenarios like that, especially given the damn near deadly meeting these emails had led to, made him feel like a big jerk. Unfortunately, feeling like a jerk didn't matter in the least to his raging erection.

Nikki was the victim here, he reminded himself. Thomas's job was to protect her, to find Lucifer, not to get distracted with images of mounting her.

He sighed. If the pistachio thief's writing got any sexier, he'd get up and make a glass of iced tea. For now, lukewarm coffee would have to do.

Until now, all of my D/s fantasies have been just that—fantasies. You are the first person I've ever opened up to about my longings.

I really think I want to meet you, Richard. I'm just a bit scared. Forgive me, k?

I know in time I'll be ready. But this is a big move for me, mentally and emotionally, and I need some time to settle into that.

*But . . . *smiles* . . . remember how you told me that you wanted my heart? Call me insane, but I think you just might already have it . . . .*

Jesus. If only she'd known he meant that he wanted it in the literal sense.

Thomas felt his anger growing. These women had all trusted the bastard. They had revealed their innermost selves to him, only to have that knowledge used against them for vile, sick purposes.

Okay, I'm blushing! I can't believe I just admitted that—I've never even met you!

But I feel as though I've known you my entire life, Richard. Am I imagining all of this, or do you feel it too?

I'll look for your email when I return from work, just as I always do. Take care of yourself.

smiles

Your "sweet, submissive" Nikki

Thomas frowned, jealousy knotting in his gut. He felt like a moron for experiencing an emotion like that over emails she'd written to a serial killer, but there it was. He didn't have any claims over Dr. Adenike, but the jealous feelings were still there.

He closed out the email. He opened up the reply from Richard and began reading.

My sweet, submissive Nikki,

I know precisely how you feel, my darling. It's crazy to me, too—I've never felt this way before! But yes, I too feel as though I've known you my entire life.

You already own my heart, sweet Nikki. I look forward to the day when I have yours irrevocably within my grasp . . . .

The sick part was, Thomas thought, the wacko hadn't lied to her. Just as he'd told Dr. Adenike last night, Lucifer probably had believed his maniacal musings. Probably still did.

And, for sure, he had wanted Nikki's heart. Just not in the way the surgeon had imagined while reading the emails.

Thomas thought back to a line from the movie *The Exorcist*. The experienced priest, when preparing to perform the exorcism on a possessed Linda Blair, had first explained to the younger priest working with him how the devil operates.

He mixes lies with the truth, the older priest had said.

Just as Lucifer did, with his victims. The Cleveland press had no idea how close to the truth they had come when, a few years past, they'd dubbed him the king of all demons.

Thomas ran a hand over his freshly shaved jaw, his mind working out another detail. For the first time in nine years he truly understood how all of the victims could have been that "stupid."

The thing of it was, none of them had been stupid, a theory a couple of the detectives in the CPD had previously held firm to. The assumption many of them had harbored all of these years was that these smart women had all made one stupid mistake—a mistake that, unfortunately, had cost them their lives.

But that wasn't true, Thomas now understood. All of them, from the first victim to the last, had been expertly lured like prey, their desires and emotions used against them by a vicious, meticulous hunter.

The predator knew how to get to them. He knew how to feed on emotions and needs that had been neglected by other men in the victims' pasts in order to seduce them into meeting him.

Now what Thomas had to figure out was how to turn the proverbial tables around. He would use the very things that made Lucifer tick in order to lure the hunter to another hunter.

Himself.

Chapter 12

Thursday, July 17
1:07 P.M.

"How do you feel, kiddo?"

Nikki kissed Kim's cheek before helping her into the rental car. The first thing she planned to do when her Mercedes got out of the police compound (they were checking it for fibers) was trade it in for a new one. She couldn't stand the idea of driving around in a vehicle *he* had been in.

"I feel like a woman with a black eye and a sprained ankle." Kim smiled. "But grateful to leave the hospital. Thanks for giving me a ride home, hon."

Nikki smiled back before closing the door. She resumed their conversation once she had settled into the driver's side.

"I'll check that ankle before I go to work—"

"Work?" Kim blinked. "You plan to go to work tonight?"

"I don't want to." Nikki sighed. "But I haven't missed a day in years. If I call in, there will be questions—questions I'd rather not answer. Right now the only one who knows what's going on is the chief of staff. I'd prefer to keep it that way."

Kim blew out a breath. "I don't blame you for that. Good lord, the things this could do to your career. You're lucky that the chief of staff is a woman, and that's she's not judgmental." She turned a speculative glance toward Nikki. "Hey, speaking of not telling people things . . ."

Nikki choked out a laugh. "Well it was hardly the kind of thing one brings up over crêpes!"

Kim got a smile out of that. "True. But, Nik," she said, her expression turning serious, "you can tell me anything. Even sexual fantasies. You know that."

Nikki sighed. "I know," she whispered. "I guess I was just a little embarrassed." She turned her head from watching the road long enough to flash Kim a grin. "Now I'm only mildly mortified."

"Don't be," Kim said earnestly. "I can see the appeal to fantasies like that. I've had them myself. Both kinds."

"Both kinds?"

Kim grinned impishly. "You know, being ravished and being the ravisher."

"Ah." Nikki smiled. "In D/s circles we aficionados call that being a switch." She winked. "Someday I'll enlighten ya, little girl."

Kim got a mild chuckle out of that.

They were silent for a minute, and then Kim said, "You know, this is amazing."

Nikki raised an eyebrow. "I don't follow. What do you mean?"

"I mean that less than two days after surviving what is arguably the worst night of our respective lives, we are able to smile. Laugh, even. I think that's amazing."

"I think it's called coping." Nikki sighed. "I can't speak for you, but I've been trying not to think about it. Right now it still feels surreal. Almost like it happened to someone else."

"I know what you mean," Kim replied, her gaze thoughtful.

"Of course, the two cops camped out next door to my apartment are a good reminder of who it did actually happen to."

"Yeah, I'll just bet."

They turned the topic, opting to discuss other things for the remainder of the ride to Kim's house. By the time the colonial-style brick mansion loomed into view, both of them were feeling hungry.

"Let's make something light," Nikki said as she helped Kim from the rental car. "I'm ravenous, but my stomach is still feeling the effects of . . . well, you know."

"Yeah," Kim sighed. "Mine, too."

They decided on tuna salad sandwiches and pretzel sticks with soda—or "pop," as they call soda in Northeastern Ohio. An hour later, they had eaten, gotten Kim propped up in bed surrounded by all the latest and greatest romance-novel releases, and Nikki had checked her ankle. Satisfied that it wasn't swollen, she stood up, preparing to go to work.

"I don't like the idea of you being here alone," Nikki said, her gaze seeking out Kim's.

"I'll be fine. Really."

"Uh huh." Nikki frowned. "Seems to me that's what all the heroines in the movies say right before they get a pickax through the heart."

Kim rolled her eyes. "You're the heroine in this movie, babe. I'm just the boring secondary character."

"Ah. Even better!" Nikki folded her arms under her breasts. "The secondary characters get killed off for sure. Only instead of the pickax going through their heart, they get it in the forehead."

Kim's eyes widened. "Gee wiz. Thanks for the pep talk. Do you work at a suicide hotline in your spare time, by chance? If not, you've missed your calling."

"I'm being serious."

"I know. And you're scaring the shit out of me, okay?" She swallowed roughly, waving a hand over her leg. "I'm kind of at a disadvantage here if Lucifer decides to come calling. The last thing I need is to be freaked out about it."

Nikki sighed. The police had assured her that "Richard" couldn't possibly know who Kim was or where she lived. Only the CPD was aware of those facts. That was no doubt true. From "Richard's" standpoint, Kim had probably just seemed like a passing-by do-gooder. And if he had given who she was any thought, he'd assume she lived in Cleveland, not Hudson. But still . . .

"I have to go to work," Nikki murmured. "I can't afford for people to start asking questions. But I really, really, *big-time* really do not want you here alone."

Kim sighed, looking every inch the martyr. "I know where this conversation is going, and I won't do it. Besides, the cops drive by on the hour to make sure I'm okay."

"And the other fifty-five minutes of each hour? You have to."

"No!"

"*Kim . . .*"

"All right!" she huffed. "All right, you win. I'll phone my stepmother." Her look promised retribution. "But if she shows up here drunk . . ."

"It's still better than being alone."

"Oh yeah, I can see how she'd be a big help," Kim said sarcastically. "If the killer shows up maybe he'll think she's pulling Jedi mind tricks on him when all she's doing is slurring her words. Hey, at least it gives me time to hobble out of here."

Nikki grinned. "Kimmie, you're positively funny when you're on edge."

She grumbled something incoherent under her breath. "Go to work."

"He's very uncomfortable around women," Dr. Sydney Horace said, her spectacles perched on the end of her nose. She glanced up from the paperwork she was shuffling through on her desk. "In fact, it's a safe bet that he's more than uncomfortable. I'd say he's downright afraid of them. Growing up, he probably had an abusive mother or mother figure that he regarded as omnipotent, godlike, if you will. A normal vantage point from any child. A viewpoint that can turn into something deadly if that power is abused."

Thomas absently glanced around the forensic psychologist's minimalist office before turning his head to frown at her. "That's hardly an excuse, Syd," he growled.

Her eyebrows shot up. "Hey, big guy," the older woman said. "You and I have been colleagues for years. Friends, too. You know me better than to suggest I'm excuse-making for this sicko."

He sighed. "I'm sorry," he muttered. "It's been a long couple of days."

"I'll just bet. You look like shit."

"Gee, thanks."

She smiled. "Here's the thing, Thomas. Richard and Nikki spent an entire month emailing back and forth. I hold no doubt but that Lucifer fell in love with her during that time period. And yet, in love as he probably was, once he revealed himself to her he didn't have the courage to so much as carry on a face to face conversation before striking. That's telling, I think."

Thomas nodded. "True. Plus it's easier to regard a victim as an *it* instead of as a *person* when you don't actually speak to them face to face."

"There is that." Dr. Horace sighed as she ran a hand through her short, fashionably cropped silver hair. "Let's see, what else . . ."

He snorted. "Been a long couple of days for you, too, I see."

She winked before glancing back down at her paperwork. "He's highly intelligent, but probably doesn't perform well in life, your classic underachiever." She glanced up. "He might have difficulty holding down a job, or if he's held a steady job for years, he probably hasn't moved up much from the position he first started in."

Thomas filed that away for future reference. "Anything else?"

Dr. Horace removed her spectacles and placed them on the desk. "Based upon the rudimentary physical descriptions given by both living victims at the latest crime scene, and some of the phraseologies 'Richard' repeatedly used in his emails, I'd put him at, oh . . . mid-thirties to very early forties at best."

"Can you pinpoint what type of a job or jobs he might work at?"

She frowned. "Statistically speaking, men like him tend to work at menial labor because they can only hold down odd jobs. You don't find odd jobs in the white-collar labor force. Not to the extent you do in the blue-collar world at any rate."

"From your tone of voice, I sense a but coming on here."

The forensic psychologist shook her head and sighed. "His writing is terribly educated, Thomas. Almost pompous. I have to wonder if someone as arrogant as Lucifer here would think menial labor beneath him."

Thomas chewed that over for a protracted moment before nodding. "Thanks, Syd." He slowly rose to his feet, tugging at his necktie. "Is there anything else, or does that cover it?"

"Only what you've probably already guessed, my friend." She rose to her feet and handed him a copy of the report she would be submitting. She waited for him to meet her gaze before continuing. "The prey got away, Thomas. He's feeling very anxious right now and very much like a failure. He's going to need his ego soothed—soon."

They held each other's gaze in silence for a long pause.

"How soon?" Thomas murmured.

Dr. Horace shrugged. "That's anyone's guess, you know that. Early in his 'career' he struck once every few years. Now the ante has been upped to once every eleven or twelve months. All I can say for sure is that it'll happen way before a calendar year comes and goes. Sexual sadists tend to be very ritualistic, Thomas. You've screwed up his pattern. You can best believe the need for release has got him wound tighter than a drum."

An uneasy feeling settled in his gut. "You don't suppose he'd try for the same prey twice, do you?" Nikki's place was under constant surveillance even though, realistically speaking, serial killers don't tend to fixate on lost prey. They simply move on, finding someone a bit more vulnerable to attack. Then again, most serial killers didn't put the amount of effort into luring victims as Lucifer did. They tended to be too disorganized for that. This one was more organized and selective than most.

"I don't know," Sydney said honestly. Her eyebrows drew together. "It's a distinct possibility that shouldn't be overlooked. With this UNSUB, you simply never know."

Work had been a true respite from the horror of her personal life. Nikki had been given no time to think about Tuesday night or the aftermath that resulted from it. No time to think about all of the obscene, blood-chilling things Richard had planned to do to her. No time to think about the Mercedes she needed to trade in, the two undercover cops camping out in the unfinished apartment next to hers, or whether or not Richard would try to finish the job he had started.

No time to think about Detective Thomas Cavanah. And the fact that, by now, he had probably read most, if not all, of those embarrassing emails.

She blushed. She'd never be able to look him in the eye again.

Thankfully, however, she probably wouldn't have occasion to come face to face with the gruff-looking cop again. Unless Richard made another move or more evidence surfaced.

She didn't know why she was so mortified by the idea of Thomas reading those emails when that knowledge didn't particularly affect her one way or another where the other detectives were concerned. Perhaps because, if she was honest with herself, she had been aware of Thomas Cavanah as a man in those few brief minutes they had spent together. Aware of him in a way in which she hadn't been aware of the others.

She sighed, telling herself there was no use in thinking about that glimmer of attraction let alone mentally admitting to it. Even if he had been aware of her as a woman, which she doubted, their relationship was strictly professional.

"Leaving for the night, Doctor?"

Nikki's head shot up. She smiled at the young nurse whose face she recognized, but whose name she couldn't recall. "As soon as I change into my street clothes, I'm out of here. Page me if you need me."

"Will do."

"Same with me," a male voice muttered. "I'm leaving for the night."

Nikki's body stiffened. She recognized Dr. Sorenson's voice, of course, but pretended obliviousness to it. She didn't know why the man had it out for her, but she conceded that he did. Mentally speaking, she wasn't up for any of his crap tonight. Putting up with the sniveling whiner was difficult on a normal evening. These days she felt anything but normal.

The rivalry between them, at least in Dr. Sorenson's mind, had begun several months ago when the chief of staff had overlooked the senior surgeon in lieu of Nikki for a promotion. Sorenson had been at Cleveland General longer, but Nikki now was, for all intents and purposes, his superior.

The perceived insult had never been forgotten. Every time Nikki turned around he was making insinuations about her lack of ability, or lack of moral character, to the chief of staff. Once, when she and a fellow physician in a different department had been dating, Sorenson had seen them holding hands in the hallway. He had become indignant, complaining to their mutual boss that Nikki's brazen public behavior was not befitting a surgeon.

Nikki had shrugged the complaint off, feeling it was ludicrous. Luckily, the chief of staff had agreed.

There had been other, similar complaints against Nikki put forth by Dr. Sorenson in the past year. She knew her boss didn't take them seriously, but Nikki was intelligent enough to be cautious wherever her alleged rival was concerned. She couldn't understand how or why her fellow surgeon had held a grudge for so long, but she supposed it didn't matter. The point was, he did.

Finished scribbling out her notes on the last patient she'd seen, Nikki filed them away in the proper folder. She turned on her heel to leave.

"Good night to you, too, Dr. Adenike," she heard Dr. Sorenson sarcastically mumble under his breath.

She came to an immediate halt, her back still to the other doctor. Her nostrils flaring, she took a deep breath, reminding herself that he wasn't worth getting upset over.

Nikki slowly turned around, cocking her head to regard him. Michael Sorenson was a tall man, a big man, with a well-honed musculature that bespoke of athleticism. He was also, she begrudgingly admitted, a rather handsome man. Quiet. Socially withdrawn. But still handsome. It was too bad the fates had wasted such superior physical attributes on a venomous man.

Their gazes clashed. He immediately glanced away, unable to hold her stare. No surprise there, she thought acerbically. He might be tall, muscular, and hate-filled, but he was also a wimp.

"Good night, Dr. Sorenson," Nikki calmly replied. She inclined her head. "Have a good evening."

"Here's the report you requested, Detective."

Thomas glanced up from where he'd been going over notes at his desk. His gaze absently raked over the plump female file clerk who'd been employed by the CPD for thirty and some-odd years. He'd always rather liked Nan. She was an overly serious type, but kind, pretty, and efficient. "Oh good. You found it. I was afraid the original report my partner filed on the Pinoza case was lost forever."

Nan's arms folded under her breasts. "It is. Luckily, it turns out I made a backup copy before we switched filing systems four years ago."

His forehead wrinkled.

"Strangest thing," she said, frowning. "I never lose a record. I suppose," she said grudgingly, "that with thirty-three years under my belt, I was bound to mess up at some point."

He winked at her. "You made a backup. Your record remains intact."

She nodded before turning to exit the office. "I'm leaving for the night. If you need anything else, send a message downstairs and I'll see to it as soon as I come in tomorrow."

"Thanks, Nan."

The file clerk was gone a moment later. Thomas turned his attention to the report she'd brought in, the one his partner, James, had filed four years ago after speaking with Vincent Pinoza.

He scanned it quickly, looking for the important part. Vincent's name, Vincent's height and weight, Vincent's occupation and drug habits . . .

Vincent's statement. Here we go, he thought.

Although it was originally believed by CPD that Lisa Pinoza had left home to meet with a lover on the night of her death, Vincent Pinoza remains convinced of his wife's fidelity, referencing how happy the couple had been clear up until the night she was murdered.

Thomas stilled. He reread the statement, frowning. This couldn't be right, he thought.

His gaze raked over the document, coming to settle at the very bottom. The signature:

June 7, Detective James Merdino, Homicide.

Chapter 13

Saturday, July 19
11:07 P.M.

Monica Baker-Evans had led a difficult but wonderful life. She had worked her way up from nothingness after the divorce from Craig, earned her master's degree on the side while holding down a full-time job, and by the age of thirty-three had managed to make Senior Vice-President at the international consulting firm where she was employed.

Life couldn't have been better. Just next week the CEO of World Visions was scheduled to fly in from New York City and announce her as the next president of the Cleveland division, starting in a month when her boss vacated the position to begin his new career at a rival firm. The goal she had worked toward all of these years had been within her grasp.

Almost . . .

"Please, Kevin," she said shakily, her entire body shivering despite the heat. "Please let me go."

Nothing. He said nothing.

She closed her eyes briefly, hope at war with resignation. Hope because a small part of her still wanted to survive. Resignation because she realized he had no intention of letting her go. She was a realist, a pragmatist, and she knew that the end was almost here.

Work had always been rewarding to Monica—very rewarding—but she'd grown a bit lonely in the process of becoming a professional woman to be reckoned with, and she had wanted to meet a man she had a chance at settling down with. If only she could meet Mr. Right and fall in love, she had thought, everything would have been perfect.

But Monica wasn't easy to put up with and she knew it. Emotionally speaking, she was on the needy side and tended to be a bit too clingy a bit too soon where relationships were concerned. Most men were turned off by such displays, so she had pumped tens of thousands of dollars into psychologists in the hopes of miraculously changing.

The change never happened. And as a consequence, Monica had given up on the pursuit of men altogether, deciding she was meant to be alone.

Alone, however, didn't have to mean lonely. She had work, she had her friends, she had her family. All was perfect. Except for one thing: no matter how much she wished it otherwise, a small part of her still held onto that stupid idyllic Cinderella dream that little girls are socially spoon-fed before they can crawl—that dream of being swept off her feet by Prince Charming and finding Happily Ever After.

If only. Life was full of "if onlys."

If only Craig hadn't cheated on her, they'd still be together. If only society at large hadn't spoon-fed her the Cinderella fantasy, she wouldn't have wished for a Prince Charming of her own. If only she hadn't gone looking for her Prince Charming on the Internet . . .

Monica watched through dulled vision as the man she'd met online Wednesday night continued to snap photographs of her naked, spread-eagle body. A body that was quickly growing weaker and weaker from a steady loss of blood. A body that had been slashed with knives in at least fifty different places.

A body she could hardly feel anymore.

He set the camera down, engaged it so that it would take photographs at specified intervals, and then turned to her. His penis was stiff, ready to assault her again. His eyes were glazed over, drunk on a sadistic high. The knife in his hand gleamed, the blood on it beginning to coagulate.

"Tell me you love me," Kevin murmured, his voice thick with a frightening mix of lust and anger. "Tell me Nikki doesn't matter because you love me enough for both of you."

Monica Baker-Evans closed her eyes for a final time. Hope completely deserted her and resignation at last won out. "I love you," she whispered. She swallowed roughly as he resumed the humming of that eerie song, praying the deathblow would come mercifully soon. "I love you enough for both of us."

"How is our little patient doing today?"

Kim distractedly glanced up from the romance novel she had been reading. "Today?" she snorted, closing the book with a thump. "Working nights has really messed up your sense of time. It's one in the morning, hon."

Nikki smiled. "I came as soon as my shift was over." She sighed a bit tiredly as she plopped down on the bed. Her eyes scanned the injury Kim had sustained, easily noticeable since her friend was lying on top of the covers wearing only a thigh-length red robe, her battered leg stretched out. "How's the ankle? Did your mom take you to the doctor today?"

"Step-mom," she muttered. "And yes, she did."

Nikki stared at her best friend for a long moment, her expression mulling. "You know, Kimmie . . ."

"Oh, God, not again." She sighed. "Please. Nik, I'm not up for another of your speeches tonight, okay?"

"Then give her a chance." Nikki frowned. "Megan has been here for two days, and I haven't smelled a drop of alcohol on her breath."

Kim rolled her eyes. "Oh wow. Two whole days. Let's call the *Guinness Book of World Records*."

"You're not being fair," Nikki murmured. "You are all Megan has left. You could at least try—"

"You mean my money is all she has left." Kim picked up the romance novel she'd thrown aside when Nikki first arrived and absently thumbed through it. "She's already gone through all of hers. Time to cozy up to Kim."

Nikki grunted, too exhausted to plead Megan's case tonight, but not willing to let the subject drop without one more solid punch. "I don't think that's true. And what's more, I don't think you think that's true, either."

Kim's nostrils flared as their eyes met, but she said nothing.

"Look, Kim," Nikki said, her smile tired. "I'll let this go for now, but think about this."

One of Kim's blonde eyebrows slowly inched up.

"I'm not excusing Megan's past alcoholism. Not by any stretch of the imagination. But if I had been married to your father," Nikki said calmly but ruthlessly, "I would have been a drunk, too."

Silence.

Kim half snorted and half laughed. "Touché." She shook her head and sighed, setting down the book again. "Enough about me and Megan for tonight. Tell me about you. Has everything been okay at work?" She frowned. "Sorenson causing any more trouble?"

"Not since Thursday. But, lucky me, he was off tonight."

Kim nodded. "And Richard?" she quietly asked. "Any word?"

Nikki shook her head. "Not a thing," she murmured. "I almost wish he'd make a move. Sad, isn't it?"

"Not at all. Very understandable, in fact. At least then you wouldn't have to live in constant fear of a phantom. You'd know exactly what his intentions are."

"That's what he feels like to me," Nikki whispered, her expression faraway. "Like a phantom with deadly intentions. You never know where it will strike, when it will strike, or how it will strike, but you know it's coming."

Kim reached out and placed her hand over Nikki's. "You don't know that for a fact, hon," she said gently. "Don't let him do this to you. You've got him built up in your mind as a larger-than-life demon, when in fact, he is only a man. A sick and twisted man, but still just a man."

Nikki inclined her head. "Now it's my turn to say touché."

"Besides," Kim reminded her. "The police told you that serial killers very rarely stalk the same victim twice. He's probably moved on by now."

"I wish that made me feel better." Nikki briefly closed her eyes, drawing in a calming breath as she did so. "But I'm not one of those people who can think, 'Hey, better her than me.' " She shook her head. "If it's not me it's still someone else, and that doesn't make me feel okay at all. In fact, I doubt I'll ever feel better, at least not until he's caught. Or dead."

"I wish I could help," Kim muttered. "Damn! A week ago I'd have given away my last dollar to stop those dreams. Now I'd give anything for them to come back."

Nikki studied her face. "Do you suppose the images were so strong because they were about me?"

"Definitely."

"But why?" Her nose wrinkled. "I don't get this whole premonition business."

"Me, neither." Kim sighed. "If I understood how it worked I'd be a millionaire."

Nikki slowly smiled. "You are a millionaire."

Kim chuckled. "Touché."

"What the fuck . . ."

Thomas's nostrils flared as he threw Vincent Pinoza up against the brick wall outside the bar from which he'd retrieved him. "Why did you lie?" he ground out, his muscles bulging as he grabbed Lisa's husband by the neck. "Why!" he barked.

"Okay, so I drink on weekends when my parents watch the kids," Vincent blithered out. "I never touch drugs, though. I swear it!"

"I'm not talking about the drugs," Thomas hissed. His jaw clenched. "I'm talking about your dead wife."

Vincent blinked. His face scrunched up. "Either I'm drunk or you're making no sense."

Thomas tightened his hold on Vincent's trachea, letting the man's eyes bulge a little, his throat gurgling from the lack of air. Completely against procedure. Totally illegal.

Oh goddamn well.

"Don't you care who killed her?" he bellowed. "Don't you want the fucker caught?" Thomas knew he was letting his anger get the best of him, knew too his obsession with Lucifer was driving him to lows he'd just as soon not know he had in him.

Vincent gasped when the detective released the pressure on his throat muscle. "Of course I care!" he rasped. "What the fuck are you assaulting me for? This is illegal, don't you know! I could have your fucking badge!"

Thomas rolled his eyes. "Why," he bit out, trying to rein in his barely controlled temper, "did you tamper with a police investigation?"

Vincent looked confused. Convincingly confused. A fact that didn't sit well with the detective.

"Look, man," Lisa's widower muttered, calming down and sobering up a bit. "I honestly don't know what you're talking about. If you care to explain it—without mauling me!—then I'll answer any questions you got. Otherwise, I'm leaving this alley now and going back inside."

A ludicrous statement coming from someone pinned against a brick wall and dangling six inches off the ground, but one that had to be taken seriously if he didn't want to lose his badge. Thomas's nostrils flared as he stared the other man down. Angry, but not sure at whom, he released Vincent Pinoza, letting him collapse to the ground.

"All right, talk," Thomas growled. "I want to know when you were lying. To Detective Merdino four years ago or to me when I came and paid you a visit last week?"

"I don't know what you are talking about!" Vincent shouted, his tone sounding frustrated. "I haven't lied to anybody! Jesus H. Christ!"

"Four years ago you told Detective Merdino you didn't think Lisa was cheating on you," Thomas said in a calmed if angry tone. "Last week you thought she *was* cheating on you. Which is it?"

Vincent shook his head. "My story hasn't changed. And I don't *think* Lisa was cheating on me . . . I *know* Lisa was cheating on me. She told me she was, which I told both you and that other cop four years ago."

An uneasy feeling began to knot in Thomas's stomach. He was good at reading people. Very good. And he was about ninety-percent sure that Vincent Pinoza was telling the truth as he knew it. A fact Thomas didn't know how to feel about. "Were you stoned when Detective Merdino interviewed you?" he asked, his gravelly voice low. "Had you been taking drugs?"

"Taking drugs?" Vincent asked incredulously. "In a one-man holding cell? Yeah right!"

Thomas stilled. In his anger and confusion he had forgotten that fact.

Vincent Pinoza had been interviewed from county lockup. Drugs were always a possibility, even in jail, but the chances in Vincent's case were so remote as to be implausible. Unable to control him while in the throes of a high, the police who'd arrested him had thrown Pinoza into a one-man cell. He'd still been in that cell, and totally sober, by the time James had interviewed him. But if Lisa's widower was telling the truth, then that meant . . .

No. There had to be another explanation. James Merdino was a damn good cop and a damn good friend. To even consider for one moment that his partner would tamper with evidence—that made no damn sense. Fuck.

"I'm sorry about the rough shit," Thomas absently muttered, his thoughts in chaos. He ran a hand over his jaw. "Thanks for the info, bud."

"Any time." Vincent snorted, shaking his head. "Bud."

Sitting in his parked car outside Detective James Merdino's house, Thomas read and reread the report his partner had filed, not knowing what to think or how to feel. Logic dictated that someone was lying. Gut instinct told him Vincent was telling the truth. Or the truth as he knew it.

But James's story was the polar opposite, and the idea that James would purposely tamper with evidence was as illogical as it was unbelievable. Any other cop? Maybe. Who was Thomas to say? But James?

"This makes no sense," Thomas muttered.

He glanced up at the house that belonged to his partner. It was small, colonial, brick—the same as three quarters of the houses in this and many other Ohio neighborhoods. James was a regular guy who led a regular life. It's all he'd ever aspired to and all he'd ever wanted. Some people dreamt of fame and glory—James Merdino's dreams revolved around normalcy and permanence.

Growing up, James's life had been anything but regular. He didn't talk about his childhood much, but Thomas knew from bits and pieces of conversations they'd had over the years that James's father had been an officer in the Marines—and a mean alcoholic to boot. William Merdino had moved his family around a great deal, base to base, city to city. James had never known stability, had never been given the chance to form close relationships with friends. Making friends made no sense when he knew he'd be torn away from them a few months later.

Where many kids of military men in similar situations find a saving grace in their mothers, James did not. Lavina Merdino had started out in life wanting to be a good wife and mother, but somewhere along the line, most likely due to her husband's drinking and philandering ways, her spirit had been broken and she had gone off the deep end. Before she finally committed suicide on James's tenth birthday, she had been institutionalized five times.

Thomas sighed as he alighted from the Cadillac. His eyes flicked over the small, modest brick house—a house his partner could have afforded to abandon in favor of a better neighborhood years ago, but one James had held onto for what Thomas suspected to be sentimental reasons—it had been his first real home. His first sense of security and permanency.

The lights were off inside, which Thomas found a bit odd. James rarely, if ever, went out, and he hadn't known his partner to ever crash for the night before three in the morning. He was a workaholic—and one who got his best work done late at night.

Thomas rapped on the wood door, expecting the lights to come on at any moment. He frowned when they failed to. "James!" he called out as he knocked again.

Nothing.

He rapped two more times, but still, nothing.

"Shit," he muttered.

Turning on his heel, Thomas made his way back to the Cadillac. As he strode toward the car, he couldn't shake a bizarre feeling that plagued him: a feeling that told him he was being watched. He frowned.

He'd let it go for the night, he decided. But tomorrow he would find his partner and get this situation straightened out.

Nikki trudged into her apartment, her body feeling as heavy as lead but her mind sharp and alert. She supposed, given the circumstances, it was to be expected. It was something of a consolation to know that two police officers were always a scream away and could easily bust down her front door, but that knowledge didn't do much to lessen her anxiety.

The things Kim had said to her were true. Her frightened mind really had bestowed superhuman, godlike qualities upon Richard. A fact her would-be murderer would probably enjoy knowing. A fact that mightily irritated her.

Because Kim was right about something else, too. Namely, that no matter how terrified of Richard Nikki might be, he was, in fact, only a man. He couldn't walk through walls or elude two police officers camped out next door like a supernatural villain in a movie. He was just a man . . . *just a damn man.*

She would do well to remember that fact. She would give anything to make her heart rate and overactive imagination understand that fact.

If her maddeningly quick pulse or the perspiration glistening on her forehead were any indication, however, those facts weren't likely to be understood by her various organs until the man was caught—dead or alive.

Swallowing past the lump of anxiety in her throat that felt the size of a watermelon, Nikki quickly flicked on all the lights in the apartment, then proceeded to check out the kitchen. She breathed a bit easier when all the knives—potential weapons—were as they should be, nothing looking undisturbed. Three big butcher knives and ten small carving knives. A gift from Kim three Christmases ago.

She picked up a butcher knife, wielding it like a weapon, then commenced a thorough inspection of all closets and potential hiding places in the apartment. When she was finished, she worried that Richard might have run from one hiding spot to another while she had been busy checking them, so she checked them a second time.

Nothing. Everything was as it should be.

Clutching the butcher knife so tightly her knuckles turned white, Nikki backed herself up against the nearest wall. She hadn't cried, not even once, since this entire ordeal began, but she could feel the emotion getting the best of her and knew she wouldn't be able to stop it this time.

"I can't live like this," she whispered, her voice catching in the back of her throat. "Oh God, *I can't live like this.*"

Her back slid down the wall. She tightly wrapped her arms around her knees and rocked back and forth. When the tears finally came, it would be another hour before they stopped. Another hour before she had the strength to pick herself up off of the floor and fall, exhausted, into bed.

She slept with the lights on.

Chapter 14

Sunday, July 20
2:07 p.m.

"He took time off?" Thomas frowned as he listened to the police chief's explanation as to James's whereabouts. After calling his partner's house a dozen times, and his cell at least a dozen more, he'd had no choice but to go to the boss. "That's weird. He never said anything to me about going to see his old man."

"The bastard got drunk and fell down some steps, split his head open. He was rushed into the E.R., can't recall which one. Oh wait, I scribbled it down—New York Methodist Hospital. In Brooklyn, I think."

"Yeah, that's Brooklyn. Huh."

"He was rushed for time, Cavanah. I'm sure he'll phone you when things settle down a bit and his old man gets released."

Well, at least that explained why James hadn't answered his cell phone. Cells are forbidden in E.R. waiting rooms. Sensible or not, however, everything seemed to be playing out a bit too conveniently. The missing report. Conflicting stories. And now James's dad had taken a spill down the stairs.

The last one would have plausibly explained his partner's untimely absence were it not for the fact that William Merdino had taken a dozen or so tumbles down the stairs in the years Thomas had known James—this was the first time James had felt obliged to go be with his old man following a drunken episode.

"Thanks, Chief," Thomas muttered into the phone. "I'll keep trying his cell."

*Nikki woke up the next morning feeling sick as a dog. She sup*posed she had the crash coming to her, given that she'd existed on pure adrenaline, nerves, and little else for days now. She felt sick to her stomach and had a mild headache to boot, but had still planned to go to work tonight. It wasn't until she took her temperature and found that she was running a mild fever that she decided it was better to stay home.

She knew physicians showed up to work sick all the time, but she had personally never condoned the practice. It made little sense to her for an infected person to try to cure infected people.

"Are you sure you're okay? I can send someone over or come check you out myself if need be."

Nikki smiled into the phone. "I'm a doctor, too, Kelly," she said to the chief of staff. "Remember?"

"That's little comfort," her boss said wryly. "We tend to think of ourselves as invincible and conveniently overlook our own symptoms."

"True. But I'm sure all I need is some solid rest and then I'll be fine." Or as fine as she could be given the circumstances, she mentally qualified. "I'll call you if I get any worse, but I think I'm just experiencing a system crash is all."

"Little wonder," Kelly sighed. "Look, Nik. I know you don't want to discuss what happened Tuesday night, so I won't ask you questions. But please know this: your job is secure. You have no worries here. So if you need to take some time off, do it. Please. Okay?"

"Thanks, Kelly," Nikki murmured. "I'm lucky to have a boss like you."

"Lucky my ass," Kelly returned, making Nikki smile. "Cleveland General is lucky to have you. Now go get some sleep and feel better."

A knock at the door startled Nikki, causing her to jump. She gritted her teeth at her ridiculous reaction, reminding herself that she could not and would not live like this. "That's the door, Kelly. I better go answer it so I can get some sleep."

"All right. Hang in there, kiddo. And remember, call me if you need anything."

"Will do. Thanks, Kel."

"Anytime."

She switched off the cordless and set it down on the kitchen counter before padding out to the living room to answer the door. She was about to throw the door wide open to prove to herself she wasn't a chicken, when she recalled that there was a fine line between living in constant paranoid fear and acting like a reckless idiot. She pressed her eye to the peephole instead, her heart—damn it, anyway—drumming faster than a Mötley Crüe track.

It was the postman, she thought, sighing in relief. Just the postman.

"Hey, John," she said with a welcoming smile as she opened the front door. "What brings you upstairs?"

"Nikki," he said, smiling back on a nod. He was an older man, probably in his late sixties and getting close to the age of retirement. Then again, he was also in excellent physical shape for a man his age and seemed to enjoy his job. "A package for you that wouldn't fit in your box. Figured I'd walk it upstairs myself."

"That was sweet. You didn't have to do that. You could have left it in the office."

"Hey, I gotta keep this old body in practice somehow!"

"You're doing a fine job of it." She grinned. "Thanks, John. You have a great day."

"You, too." He winked before turning on his heel and disappearing downstairs.

Nikki closed the door behind him and locked it. Glancing down at the package, she noted that it had a return address she didn't recognize. That uneasy feeling swamped her again, and again her teeth ground together because of it.

"Stop it," she seethed, chastising herself. "You will not live like this. Serial killers don't put return addresses on packages unless they are too stupid to live!"

Richard, unfortunately, was not too stupid to live. She sighed as she traipsed back into the kitchen, set the package down on the counter, and carefully unwrapped it.

Nikki slowly smiled as she opened the box. "Five pounds of pistachios," she murmured.

She had a feeling she knew who they were from. When she opened the accompanying card and realized her feeling had been right on target, her heart started thumping just as wildly as it was prone to do these past five days, albeit this time in a pleasurable way.

I had to go to five stores to find just the right kind. You damn well better eat them.

Thomas

Her eyes twinkled as she read and reread the card. His words were just like him: clipped, brash, and surly . . . yet strangely comforting.

Nikki grinned as she picked up the pistachios. Suddenly she was in the mood for pudding.

Between trying to track down his partner, different cases he had to give equal time to, and a million other things, Thomas hadn't had a spare moment to finish reading all of the emails exchanged between Lucifer and Nikki. It had been four days since he'd gotten through the first half of them. He was impatient to get to the second half.

Dr. Adenike had been on his mind a lot lately—far too much, in fact. The evening of her attack they had shared a nice sort of truce, albeit under horrible circumstances. She'd even begrudgingly given him her pistachios, he thought with a small smile. He wondered if the truce would last were he to approach her off the record.

Sighing, Thomas slid the CD of the emails into the proper drive. If he were honest with himself, he would have to admit that he hadn't been quite as eager to read the remainder of the emails as he'd like to think he was. Any good cop would want to get as much information as possible when trying to solve a case. Thomas was a good cop. Yet he didn't like reading these emails.

There were three reasons. First of all, Lucifer was lacking many things, but intelligence wasn't among them. The emails would give hints to his personality, perhaps even suggest possible motivations if motivations even existed, but they would not lead the CPD to him. He would have thought that out, taken it under consideration with every word that he typed out.

Secondly, stupid and Neanderthal-like as it sounded, the email exchanges were getting Thomas damn jealous. The reaction was an insane one given that he and Nikki had never even dated, but there it was. He didn't like reading about sexual fantasies and emotional needs she'd revealed to another man. He wanted her to reveal those things to him.

But the fact was, Nikki had never given off even the smallest vibe of interest in Thomas. He supposed he was acting like an ass, feeling territorial over her when the only gesture of niceness, let alone interest, she'd thrown his way was a partially eaten carton of pistachios. He frowned. And she'd given up the pistachios during a vulnerable moment. So not even that counted.

There was also a third reason why Thomas didn't like reading the emails. Namely, because they gave him a hint of the sort of smooth lines and caring pretense that had been thrown Amy's way before her death. Lines that had been used to draw her into a deadly, carefully spun web from which there was no escape.

She'd been gone for six years now, Amy. Tortured—just like the others. Raped—just like the others. He'd never forget the day her body—or what was left of it—had been found.

Thomas had worked Lucifer's case from the beginning, when the sadistic killer had first begun his "career" nine years ago. A hotshot detective hailing originally from Georgia, Thomas had been more than eager to prove himself within the CPD, and had taken the case on with the help of his new partner, James Merdino.

Problem being, Lucifer had been smart from the beginning. Too smart. He never left trails, never left DNA behind at a crime scene, never left anything other than maimed, tortured, bludgeoned bodies. And so, hotshot detective or not, the serial killer had eluded him from day one.

Amy had been the light of Thomas's life, his reason for being. He'd worked his ass off to give her the best that a cop's salary could, wanting her to be happy. And she had been happy. But work kept Thomas away a lot, and left her feeling lonely. Before he knew what she'd been up to, Amy was found dead.

Her body had been badly mauled, most of the torture occurring while she'd still been alive. She'd suffered hundreds of lacerations and a dozen rapes before she'd finally been put out of her misery.

Lucifer had kept her alive, barely, for four days. That was the hardest part for Thomas to deal with. Knowing that she had been alive, praying he'd come and rescue her, for four long, excruciatingly painful days.

Thomas had sunk into a bitter depression after that, a depression it had taken the better part of a year to crawl out of. He had loved Amy with his entire being, and when she'd been murdered, a piece of him had been killed right along with her.

Which had probably been the demon's intent.

After Amy's death, Thomas's work evolved into obsession. And so here he sat, six known victims later, seven if you counted Dr. Adenike, once again trying to unravel the clues that would lead him to a monster.

Somehow, he knew that he was closer. Knew too that Lucifer could feel it as surely as Thomas could.

He clicked on the e: drive and waited for the files to load.

Dear Richard,

I had a grueling day at work, but finding your emails waiting for me when I came home somehow made the day better. You have that effect on me, you do realize. Just seeing your screen name makes me smile . . . .

Thomas frowned throughout the remainder of the email, then clicked open another one to read it. The next exchange Lucifer received from Nikki was teasing and light, almost giddy. Unlike the other emails she'd sent up until now, which all read like dreamy, sometimes erotic Shakespearean sonnets, this one gave the impression of a giggly teenage girl.

*I can't believe I did this—ohmygod! I hope you like the photograph. I made it five minutes ago, just for you. *grins* If you don't like it, I'll probably die of mortification!!!!!!!!!!!!!!!*

Thomas's eyebrows slowly drew together. Curious, he clicked on the attached photograph Nikki had sent and waited for it to load on his screen. When it did, when Dr. Adenike's bare-breasted image appeared right there before him, he was so surprised his jaw literally dropped.

"Shit," he muttered, falling back a bit in his chair. He shifted in the seat, his erection instantaneous and uncontrollable.

Her breasts were gorgeous, he thought, his dark gaze unapologetically studying them. Large, full, soft-looking. And they were capped off by two of the plumpest, pinkest nipples he'd ever seen. He drew in closer, slowly ran his index finger over one, and then the other. His finger stilled. He squinted his eyes a bit as he noticed something else . . . .

Thomas swallowed. Hard.

"Her nipples are pierced," he said thickly, his cock so stiff it was painful. "Jesus Christ."

Apparently the surgeon was full of surprises. In his wildest, most wicked dreams, and he'd had a lot of those revolving around Nikki lately, he'd never envisioned such an upright (and uptight) citizen as her having pierced nipples. But there they were. A delicate gold hoop surrounding each pink, plump nipple.

He blew out a breath as he sat back in the chair. Telling himself he had no business reacting this way—with the desire to drive to her house and ride her for about ten solid hours—he shook off the arousal and told himself to get back to the task of reading the emails.

Thomas grunted. He was a good cop, but he'd never claimed to be a saint. Muttering to himself about what an ass he was, he nevertheless kept the bare-breasted photograph opened on the top right-hand side of the screen as he worked, his gaze repeatedly flicking up to it at whim.

"You've got mail."

Nikki distractedly glanced up from where she stood in the kitchen putting plastic wrap over the tub of pistachio pudding she'd just made. She carried the bowl to the refrigerator, set it on the second shelf, and then walked over to the computer to check her email.

She grinned as she sat down, an email from Kim with the subject heading "Oh My God Get Over Here Before I Murder Megan" filling her screen. She chuckled as she read the email, then typed out a reply and whizzed it off.

Nikki hoped that stepmother and daughter worked their problems out soon. She knew what it was like to have a mother die on you, leaving you with the feeling that there were words left unsaid and hugs left unclaimed. She didn't want that for Kim. Especially not when it had been apparent to Nikki since meeting Megan sixteen years ago that Mrs. Cox would have given her right arm to have a relationship with the only child she'd ever had. That Megan hadn't been the woman to give birth to Kim had never signified.

Due to Megan's alcoholism, Nikki could understand Kim shying away from her stepmother's overtures at a relationship in the past. But all these years later, when Megan was clean as a whistle? That she didn't get. She just hoped they worked it out soon.

Nikki wasn't sure what made her do it, probably habit born of a month of the same routine, but as soon as she sent off the email to Kim, she unthinkingly clicked on an icon that would allow her to see if there was any new email at her *submissivegrrrl* account.

Nikki's breathing hitched when she saw that there was.

Her hand shaking, her heart rate over the top, she clicked onto the account and switched over to it, telling herself not to freak out. "It's probably just junk email," she said shakily. These days, she knew, junk email online was even more common than junk mail in one's real mailbox.

There were twelve new messages. She visually scanned them, relaxing more and more when it looked as if they were all, as she had supposed, junk. But when she arrived at the last email, the twelfth and final one, her eyes widened and her stomach dropped.

The sender of the twelfth email: *FallenAngel*.

"Oh God," Nikki breathed out, her entire body shaking. "Oh no."

She sat there for what felt like hours but was probably only a few seconds, staring at the screen, feeling as stunned and semi-delirious as a deer caught in headlights. Eventually, however, sanity returned and she knew that she had to open it. She blinked, then clicked the mouse on the email from Richard.

My sweet, submissive Nikki,

I'm gravely disappointed in you, darling. I thought we understood each other. I thought you loved me as much as I love you, but you have failed to prove it. You have failed to give me your heart.

Perspiration beaded at her temples. Her stomach knotted and clenched.

I won't let that stop me, my love. I'll wait until the moment is right, then bring you home where you belong. Next time I'll leave nothing to chance. I already feel as though I've been waiting forever to have you, but I suppose forever will have to go on just a bit longer. I don't know how much longer I can wait . . . but I promise you that your homecoming will be sublime.

Yours,

Richard

P.S. Why didn't you go into work tonight, darling? I wanted tonight to be our night.

Nikki gasped, bile churning in her stomach. She reread the last sentence, ice-cold fear lancing through her.

P.S. Why didn't you go into work tonight, darling? I wanted tonight to be our night.

He knew who she was, she thought, her hand flying up and clamping over her mouth. He knew who she was and he knew where she worked.

Oh my God.

She surged to her feet and stumbled toward the phone.

Chapter 15

Sunday, July 20
8:07 P.M.

"It's about time I heard from you, bud. Where the hell you been?" Thomas shut down the computer, wanting to give his partner his full attention.

"Didn't Chief Williams tell you I caught a plane to JFK?" James said through the phone connection. "He said he'd pass the message along."

"Yeah," Thomas confirmed, leaning back in the chair, "he told me."

Silence.

"We need to talk, bro," Thomas said softly.

James was quiet for a moment, and then, "What about?"

"Vincent Pinoza," he drawled.

"Vincent Pinoza? What is it you want to know?"

Thomas considered his words, choosing them carefully. "According to the report you filed, you stated that four years ago Vincent claimed he believed Lisa to have been a faithful wife. I had a little chat with Vincent last week, and he claims that not only was Lisa unfaithful, but that he has maintained that very thing all along." He stared unblinking at the powered-off computer. "Care to shed a little light on the situation for me?"

Silence.

"Just what the fuck are you accusing me of?" James finally bellowed.

Thomas's eyebrows rose. "I'm not accusing you of anything, bro. I need some answers is all."

"Answers? What answers? Vincent is a druggie and a liar. What more of an explanation do you need?"

"Good point. Do you think he was wired the night you interviewed him?"

"I doubt it," James said, calming down. "He was in a one-man holding cell the night I interviewed him."

Thomas mentally blew out a breath. His partner had just passed that part of the test with flying colors.

"Oh, right. I hadn't thought of that. Well, why do you suppose he lied, bro? I can understand him being angry at his wife. I mean, the lady was a whore. But—"

"I doubt Lisa was a whore," James interjected. "Vincent probably made that little story up to you because he felt like fucking with us. He doesn't have anything better to do with his time, so why not bother the cops?"

"Definitely possible," Thomas said, relaxing. He had purposely thrown the slander against Lisa out there to see if his partner would react to it. He'd merely sounded explanatory, not defensive. Thank God.

"Happens all the time. You know that."

"Yeah, it does. Sorry to have bothered you with it, bud," he replied. "Hey, go take care of your dad and I'll see you when you get back."

"It'll be a few days yet."

"I've got your back."

"Thanks, bro."

Thomas ran a hand across his jaw after he clicked off the phone. He closed his eyes, inhaling deeply. There were still too many coincidences for his peace of mind: a missing report, conflicting stories, and James racing off to Brooklyn to care for a father he didn't get on with.

In such a situation, however, Thomas had only two choices available to him: believe the word of James, a man who was not only his partner but his best friend as well; or believe the word of Vincent, a convicted felon, drug addict, and lord knows what else.

"No contest," he muttered, his eyes flicking open. "No damn contest."

Thomas would remain vigilant. He would check out a few things behind the scenes. But for now, at least, he would also give James the benefit of the doubt.

*Seated on the couch, her legs beneath her, Nikki stared un*blinking at the wall across from her while five cops rifled through her apartment trying to ascertain whether or not it was possible that Richard had broken into it at some point prior. So many extreme emotions had assaulted her in the past two hours that she'd eventually gone numb. Fear. Revulsion. Anger . . .

Richard was, it seemed, steadily ruining her life. It was bad enough that she found herself constantly looking over her shoulder. It was worse still that she could no longer relax in her own home. Now the police were telling her she couldn't go to work without an escort. She wasn't about to argue with them, for she knew it was the smart thing to do, but the very necessity of it was depressing and frightening.

Nikki had gotten away from Richard once, but his phantom continued to haunt her.

Sighing, she glanced over to where Thomas Cavanah stood behind Leon Walker, the CPD's resident computer-crimes guru. Judging from the disgruntled look on both men's faces, she thought as she wound her long curls into a topknot on her head, it looked as though Richard had proved cunning once again and left no residual traces of his location behind.

Surprise, surprise.

"My God, are you okay?"

Nikki glanced up at the sound of Kim's voice. She offered her best friend an attempt at a smile as she watched her limp into the living room on crutches, Megan in tow.

"As good as you'd expect, I suppose. How's the ankle?" she asked, her green gaze flicking first over Kim and then Megan.

"To hell with my ankle," Kim grumbled. "Good lord, Nik, I about had a heart attack when the police called me."

Nikki's eyebrows slowly drew together. "You know, I've been so out of it I hadn't thought to phone. Who called you?"

"Detective Cavanah," Kim announced as she made her way over. "He thinks you better come stay with Megan and me for a while. I agree."

Nikki's gaze shot over to where the detective stood. His concentration was on whatever Leon Walker was doing, so he didn't notice her stare. He'd been off duty when Richard's email had arrived and was therefore in his street clothes, snug jeans and a nondescript black T-shirt. The biceps-length T-shirt really showed off those vein-roped arms, she thought with a small swallow. The gun holster added another level of danger and intrigue to him. "Thomas?" she murmured. "Really?"

Kim glanced at Detective Cavanah, then back at her best friend.

Her smile came slowly. "Uh huh." She wiggled her eyebrows. "Yes, *Thomas,*" she said breathily, giving a dramatically sensual imitation of how Nikki had said his name.

Nikki frowned. "I didn't say it like that, brat," she muttered. She felt her cheeks growing hot under the *yeah-right* look Kim threw her way. "Oh, stop it." She decided to ignore her for the time being. "So Megan," she said, turning her attention to the beautiful woman in her early fifties who was standing behind Kim. "How's your mean daughter been treating you?" she said on a wink. She ignored Kim's sigh.

Megan Cox was and always had been a classic beauty that age never managed to get the upper hand over. At fifty-three, her blue eyes were lined with a couple of crinkles at the corners and her face had a mature, sculpted look to it, but she was still as beautiful as ever. Perhaps more so.

Kim's stepmother had married Roger Cox three days shy of her thirty-fourth birthday, putting her stepdaughter at fifteen at the time. Tall, blonde, tan, and statuesque, Megan had made for the perfect trophy wife. Her personality, unlike Kim's, had always been on the quiet, demure side. Megan had never had an easy time of standing up to Roger Cox, so five years later she took to alcohol for comfort instead.

Kim, Nikki knew, had loved her father dearly. And yet she had also hated him. Roger had been a true asshole in every sense of the word. From cheating on Megan, to verbally abusing Kim whenever something inane set him off, to leaving his family alone on the holidays so he wouldn't have to be bothered by them—he'd done it all and then some.

Nikki had always wondered at the animosity Kim harbored toward Megan over the years. She supposed it probably had something to do with Megan's inability to put Roger in his place—

something the young Kim had probably hoped for when the couple had first married. What Kim seemed unable to accept was the fact that nobody could have put Roger Cox in his place. If he didn't like something, he removed it from his life as though it had never been—a fact of which Megan had no doubt been aware.

"She's treating me just fine," Megan said in a quiet, demure voice. She smiled sweetly down to Nikki. "How are you feeling, honey?"

Nikki was given no time to answer the question, for Kim was growling before she could even open her mouth.

"I've been treating you like shit," Kim snapped, causing Megan to blush. Nikki frowned, the urge to swat her best friend a good one barely controlled. "When someone is treating you like shit, Megan, you don't tell the world they are treating you kindly."

"Kim," Nikki murmured. "That's enough."

"Would you quit protecting her?" Kim screeched, causing a few heads, Thomas's included, to turn.

Nikki's nostrils flared. "Would you quit acting like a spoiled little bitch!" she snapped, her voice kept low. "What the hell is wrong with you?"

Kim closed her eyes briefly, sighing. "I'm sorry." She sighed again. "You, too, Megan. I'm sorry."

Megan's blue eyes went so wide Nikki became convinced it was the first kindness Kim had shown to her stepmother since she'd arrived.

"It's okay," Megan whispered. She smiled, a bit unsure of herself. "Kimmie has been under a great deal of stress worrying about you, Nikki."

"And then you defend me," Kim muttered. She sighed, throwing up her hands.

Nikki shot Kim a scathing look. She had always liked Megan, regardless of everything. She might have had a drinking problem in the past, but a more loyal person didn't exist. When the chips were down, Megan Cox could be counted on. Her presence might have irritated Kim, but it gave Nikki security in knowing that Kim was being watched over when Nikki couldn't be there to do so herself.

"I guess both of you are about to be put under a great deal more. Unfortunately, I have to agree that I can no longer stay here. Not until Richard is caught."

Kim smiled, momentarily forgetting her one-sided argument with her stepmother. "Hey," she said softly, "it'll be just like Cambridge. We'll have a blast."

"Are you sure you are up to this, Kim?" Nikki shook her head as she glanced at her. "This is serious stuff, babe. I'm not staying with you while my house is painted or something innocuous like that. I'm staying with you because a sadistic serial killer is trying to hunt me down. A serial killer! Things could get ugly. Maybe I should go somewhere else."

"I'm well aware of what could happen," Kim said quietly, but firmly. "And no way am I letting you go someplace else."

"I've already taken the liberty of hiring around-the-clock security at the house," Megan said in that small, breathy tone of hers. "Plus, there will always be officers in and out. We'll be fine."

Kim's eyebrows shot up. "How generous of you to spend my money for me," she said sarcastically. "Not that I wouldn't have done the same thing," she quickly assured Nikki.

"I used my own money, Kimberly," Megan said, the color in her cheeks rising. "I don't use people," she added pointedly. "I'm not your father."

Well, score one for the Megan-meister, Nikki thought, amused.

She'd finally stood up to her stepdaughter. Apparently that hadn't been lost on said stepdaughter, either, for Nikki saw a glimmer of something—respect, maybe?—shimmer in her eyes.

"Oh," Kim grumbled. "Well . . . thank you, then."

Thomas strolled over, interrupting the conversation. His dark gaze lingered briefly over Nikki before honing in on Kim and Megan. "Thanks for getting here so quickly, Dr. Cox—and Mrs. Cox," he drawled in that raspy, gravelly voice of his. "Why don't you go into Nikki's room and get a suitcase together. I'll drive the three of you home when you're ready to go."

Nikki's eyebrows shot up. "Hey, since when did I become incapacitated?" she mumbled. "I think I can pack my own suitcase."

Thomas frowned. His hands rested on his hips in that stance football players often assume while watching the game from the sidelines. "Quit giving me lip. I never said you couldn't pack your suitcase, Doc. I asked them to do it because I need to go over a few things with you."

"You could have just said so," Nikki sniffed.

He grunted.

Kim was grinning far too fully for Nikki's peace of mind. "Well," she said, clapping her hands together once, "Megan and I will go pack Nik's stuff up, then. We'll leave you two kids to talk." Her blonde eyebrows rose. "Try not to kill each other. Oh and Detective," Kim threw from over her shoulder as she strolled away, "there's a pistachio pudding Nik made in the fridge. You might want to pack that up while you two are 'going over things.' "

Nikki rolled her eyes at Kim.

Thomas watched the schoolteacher walk away. When Kim and Megan had disappeared into the bedroom, he turned to Nikki. "You made pudding out of my nuts?"

Nikki's face colored when four police officers' heads turned.

Her nostrils flared as she regarded Detective Cavanah. "Apparently not the nuts I wanted to make pudding out of," she seethed.

Thomas winced. "Damn, girl, anyone ever told you you're a grouch?"

"I'm rubber, you're glue," she sniffed.

"Ah," Thomas drawled. His intense gaze raked over Nikki's breasts, making her heart race. "I see we've now graduated from the fourth grade."

"So how long you been into that hocus-pocus voodoo junk?" Detective Ben O'Rourke asked Kim before shoving a piece of gum between his lips. "I thought only people in the movies did shit like that."

Amused, Nikki watched the exchange from her position next to Megan in the backseat of the unmarked car. "It is not voodoo," Kim retorted. "It is called ESP." Her eyes narrowed. "And why in the hell are you driving us, anyway?"

Nikki's expression grew thoughtful as she considered that question. Thomas had seemed hell-bent on being the one who would escort them back to the Cox estate, but changed his mind after a call had come in on his cell phone. He hadn't said who the caller was, but Nikki had found herself wondering if it was a girlfriend. Or a wife.

She would never admit it aloud, but both thoughts left her feeling a bit sunken. Dismal, even. She frowned, reminding herself that she and the brash detective didn't have anything besides a mutual disdain of Lucifer and a mutual love of pistachios in common. This did not a potential future make.

"Jesus!" Ben snapped back on a growl. "Is that the mouth you kiss your mother with?"

"Oh, shut up!"

Nikki shook her head, sighing, as Ben and Kim went to verbal war in the front seat. She couldn't blame her best friend for disliking Detective O'Rourke after the way he'd treated her in Thomas's office. Thomas . . .

Her thoughts returned to him.

Nikki'd caught Thomas staring at her strangely a few times since he'd arrived on the scene tonight. She didn't really know how to describe the looks he'd been sneaking of her when he thought her attention was turned, but there was something searching about his black gaze.

A small part of her had thought maybe, just maybe, he might be the smallest bit attracted to her because he kept sneaking peeks at her breasts. She'd discarded that notion entirely, however, when it had occurred to her that he'd been looking right through her. Or looking for something on her . . .

Huh. Interesting. What *did* that mean? she asked herself. What could he possibly have been—

She stilled. Her breathing hitched.

Oh, damn, she thought, her cheeks going up in flames. *Oh, damn! Oh, damn! Oh, damn!*

Nikki felt like groaning with mortification when it at last dawned on her that he had probably come across that topless photo of her when he'd been going through the email exchanges between her and Richard.

"Has anyone ever told you what a jerk you are!" Kim seethed.

"Funny, I was wondering the same thing about you!" Ben bellowed.

Oh, damn, Nikki thought, wanting to bury her head in the nearest sand dune. Thomas knew about her pierced nipples. *Nobody* knew about that except Kim. She'd just had them done six months ago. A secret way for her to feel privately sensual since scrubs and face masks left her feeling anything but.

"Go to hell!" Kim shot back.

"It beats the shit out of spending another second with you!" Ben yelled.

Nikki would never be able to look Thomas in the eye again, she thought dramatically. Oh lord, not ever, ever again.

"Shut the hell up!" Megan shouted from next to Nikki, drawing everyone's stunned attention toward her. "Both of you!"

They shut up. Kim cocked her head and gawked at her step-mother from over her shoulder. Her eyes squinted. "Did you just tell me to shut up?" she squeaked.

"Yes!" Megan fumed. The color in her face was high. "Yes!"

Kim's eyes widened. "That's what I thought." She stared at her stepmother a suspended moment, then turned around in the seat and remained silent.

One side of Nikki's mouth kicked up into a half-smile.

Well. Chalk two up for the Megan-meister.

"What do you got?" Thomas asked from his cell phone when he climbed into his Cadillac.

"Another dead body," Chief Williams sighed. "Cavanah, you better get out to the crime scene ASAP. This one's a bit different than the others."

"How so?" Thomas murmured. An uneasy feeling settled in the pit of his stomach.

"Just get out there," the chief muttered. "You'll see soon enough."

"I'll be there in thirty," Thomas rasped, his voice even scratchier than normal from fatigue. He needed some sleep, but conceded it would have to wait. "Hey, boss, can you phone Ben's car and ask him to meet me out there after he drops off the ladies?"

"James still in Brooklyn?"

"Yeah," Thomas growled. "I'll call him tomorrow and tell him to get his ass back here."

"No need. I'll do it myself as soon as I radio Ben."

"Much appreciated."

Chapter 16

Monday, July 21
1:01 A.M.

"Her name is Monica Baker-Evans," Ben O'Rourke informed Thomas as he strode with him toward the dumpster from which her body had been retrieved. "Thirty-three, big-busted—same as the others. She was the Vice-President of Marketing at World Visions, Inc. in downtown Cleveland."

"Any noticeable differences from previous victims?"

"He didn't spend very much time with her. Preliminary tests indicate she was disposed of pretty quickly, or at least for Lucifer's standards."

"How quickly?"

Ben shrugged. "A few hours tops."

Thomas frowned, thinking that telling bit of information over. "She was his first kill since losing Dr. Adenike. This was probably a quick fix for him, a way to stroke his own ego."

"Yeah. Probably. Anyway, we're pretty sure he picked her up via the Internet. It's too bad Lucifer answered Miss Baker-Evans's ad instead of one of the fake ones Leon Walker put in." Ben sighed. "And I think that more or less brings you up to speed."

Thomas raked a hand through his hair. "Sorry I'm running behind schedule. It took two cups of coffee and a shower to wake up," he muttered. "Who found her, by the way?"

"Homeless dude. Did the chief tell you Monica was a redhead . . . sort of?"

An eyebrow inched up. He flashed his badge at one of the beat cops securing the scene as he walked between two squad cars. "Sort of? What the hell do you mean, 'sort of'?"

Ben sighed. "You're not gonna like this, Cavanah. You're not gonna like it one damn bit."

"Cavanah!" a male voice boomed out, interrupting the conversation.

Thomas's head cocked to the left. His eyes narrowed inquiringly. "What are you doing here, boss?" he drawled as the police chief jogged toward him and Ben.

Chief Williams came to a halt in front of the detectives, his breath coming out in short pants. "Jesus, I'm outta shape," he muttered. "Desk work does that to a man."

Thomas snorted.

"We've got another lady missing," Chief Williams informed him, coming straight to the point. "Normally we don't respond to missing persons reports for twenty-four hours, but in lieu of that sick-ass warning Lucifer left behind for you, I'm taking all missing reports of any women like goddamn DEFCON 1—"

"Whoa! Back up." Thomas frowned. "Lucifer left me a message?"

The chief's bald head wrinkled.

"He just got here," Ben muttered. "He hasn't seen the victim yet."

An ice-cold feeling lodged itself in Thomas's spine. He began walking fast toward the dumpster, not waiting for any more explanations. He had no idea what it was he was about to see, but if Chief Williams was responding to every missing-persons report that came in, then . . .

He came to a halt before the dumpster, bile churning in his stomach in the way it had when he'd found Amy's body six years ago. "Jesus Christ," Thomas murmured, his eyes rounding in shock. "Holy son of God."

Monica Baker-Evans had died as grotesquely as the others, the torture she'd undergone evident. But that wasn't what had thrown Thomas for a loop. That wasn't what was making his blood run cold.

The victim had sustained the same injuries, defacements, and brutalizations as the others before her had. She'd been slashed across the torso and legs hundreds of times. She'd been raped, most likely with use of a condom so no semen traces would be found. Her heart had been removed, probably while she was still alive. Same everything. Almost.

Ben had said that Monica Baker-Evans had once been a redhead—sort of. Now Thomas understood what the younger detective had meant by "sort of." Her red pubic hair was still intact, but Lucifer had shaved her head bald, then used the long fiery tresses to tie the victim's hands above her head. Taking the place of her natural hair was a very obvious light brown wig—a wig that resembled Nikki's hair almost to a tee.

If that didn't make the killer's deadly intentions obvious enough, he had left two more calling cards behind. The first was a photograph of Nikki's face. It had been sewn over Monica's face with needle and thread, like he wanted to pretend that the victim was a different woman. Thomas could only pray that had been done to the victim postmortem, that she hadn't had to live through that agony. (He would find out later that that had been the case.)

As if Lucifer had wanted to make certain that his messages

weren't somehow being misinterpreted, he had left behind a third and final calling card: A name badge had been pinned to Monica's left breast, a badge that bore the name "Dr. Nicole Adenike."

Thomas turned away from the corpse, unable to look at it any longer. "I'm taking Nikki away," he rasped out to the chief. "Do you hear me? I'm taking her away."

He came to her in the middle of the night, rousing her from a deep sleep. She'd been given a sedative to help calm her nerves, so she was having a difficult time opening her eyes.

"Nikki," Thomas murmured. "Wake up, sweetheart. We're leaving."

"Nik," Kim whispered, shaking her, trying to wake her. "You have to go now. Listen to me! Wake up!"

Nikki softly moaned, trying her damnedest to open her eyes. But she was so tired . . .

"Shit," she heard Thomas mutter under his breath. "Have your stepmother carry down her bag," he ordered Kim. "I'll carry Nikki to the car."

A moment later, two warm, powerful hands picked her up and cradled her against a steely chest. She fell back into a deep sleep, lulled by the steady, secure beat of Thomas's heart.

*Nikki groaned as she slowly came to. Her mouth was dry as cot*ton, her brain fuzzy like a cobweb. She opened her eyes against what felt to be terribly bright light, blinking a few times in rapid succession to keep them from watering.

"Where am I?" she said in a groggy tone as she carefully sat up.

Her forehead wrinkled as it occurred to her that she was in the backseat of a station wagon. She stilled when her gaze came into contact with the back of Thomas's head. "Detective?" she croaked, her voice sounding a bit guttural from sleep.

Their gazes met in the rearview mirror. "'Bout time," he muttered.

Nikki's eyes darted about, taking in the scenery of cornfields and hilly highway all around them. "Where are we going?" she asked. She was about to climb into the front seat, then stopped, noticing that she still had on her bedclothes. Her heartbeat went into overdrive. She glanced up, frowning at Thomas's amused expression visible in the rearview mirror.

"I already saw your outfit when I carried you to the car," he drawled. "No use going all shy on me now."

She flushed, regardless of the fact that her bedclothes weren't exactly risqué. The white and red striped cotton pajama bottoms she wore were loose-fitting and cinched together at the waist by a drawstring. That didn't bother her.

What made her self-conscious of her body was the leaves-little-to-the-imagination spaghetti-strap top that went with the bottoms. It was made of sheer white cotton, came down to her waist, and clung to her braless bosom in a way she'd rather it didn't. Making matters that much worse was the fact that her nipples weren't in the mood to cooperate and go soft. They were standing as stiff as two embarrassingly awake soldiers wearing flashing neon signs around their necks that screamed, "Look at me! Look at me!"

She frowned as she glanced around for something to cover herself with.

"The suitcases," Thomas murmured, drawing her attention back to the rearview mirror, "are on top of the car." He grinned, the first time she could recall seeing him do that.

Nikki harrumphed, and decided she wouldn't let him goad her. Decided, too, to ignore the way her heartbeat had kicked up at that grin.

"So," she said in a professional, to-the-point tone, "care to explain just what in the hell is going on here?"

Fifteen minutes later, a clingy top no longer registered as significant to Nikki's horrified mind. Then again, there was very little that registered as significant after listening to the disturbing facts Thomas had laid out for her.

"I think I'm too shocked to speak," Nikki whispered, now seated next to the detective in the front seat. "I can't believe this is happening. I don't understand . . ." She blinked, turning her face to Thomas. "Why me?" she asked. "I want to understand—"

"Nikki," he interrupted. Thomas sighed as he watched the road. "Damn near every victim of a sex crime on earth has asked herself that question. Don't look for a logical answer. You won't find one."

"But . . ." She swallowed, getting her salivary glands to start working again. "There has to be a reason. Do I remind him of somebody or something, do you suppose?"

"Maybe," Thomas replied. "Maybe not. What you have to understand is that what's logical to you and me won't necessarily be logical to him, and vice versa. And sometimes, as hard as it is to fathom, there aren't any reasons. Sometimes wackos like him do what they do simply because it gets their dicks hard, excuse my bluntness."

Nikki blew out a breath as she settled back against the seat. "I feel like I'm living a nightmare," she murmured. "My life went from wonderful to horrible in the blink of an eye."

"But you're still alive," Thomas said softly. "That's what's important here."

Something about the way he'd said that awakened a suspicion in Nikki. Not in a bad way, like he'd harm her or anything, but in a way that made her think perhaps the detective wasn't as much a bystander in all this as he let on.

"Yes," she whispered, "I'm still alive." She cleared her throat. "And what's more, I intend to stay that way."

Silence ensued for the next ten minutes. Thomas watched the road, Nikki watched cornfields. Millions of thoughts pounded away at her brain, all of them competing for attention.

What was going to happen now? Would she be forced into hiding for the rest of her life? What about her apartment? Her job? Would she be allowed to see Kim? Were Kim and Megan safe back at the Cox estate?

But more than anything else, she thought about Richard. Who was he? Nikki asked herself for the hundredth time. And why was he so obsessed with her in particular?

She forced herself to relive the night she'd been attacked. She hated reliving it, but she knew she had to. If she could just remember something significant . . . there had to be *something* there. But it had been so dark out that night, and the shadows had been pitch black. She hadn't been able to make out much about Richard except . . .

"Those eyes," she murmured.

"Huh?" Thomas looked from the road long enough to glance at her. "You say something, Doc?"

"His eyes." She cocked her head and looked at Thomas. "They were so blue. Too blue. Feral, almost."

The detective's body seemed to still. He chewed that information over for a moment, looking lost in his own thoughts. "Too blue," he slowly repeated. "Interesting."

"I feel like a trapped rat." Kim sighed as she stared absently at Megan, her stepmother's hands wringing in her lap, where she was seated in a chair across from Kim's bed. "I doubt he wants either of us, but I'm still freaked out."

"As am I, dear," Megan agreed tremulously. "Detective Cavanah is fairly certain Lucifer couldn't have followed Ben when he brought us here, but 'fairly certain' isn't precisely what I wanted to hear. Unfortunately, having officers parked outside isn't lessening my anxiety, either."

Kim snorted at that. "If we leave Ohio, we give up police protection. If we stay, we give up sanity. This sucks."

"Yes," Megan agreed. "It's like being married to your father all over again." Her blue eyes widened. "Oh goodness. I'm sorry, Kimmie. What I meant was—"

"Megan," Kim said softly. "Quit apologizing. Okay?" She blew out a breath as she flopped back down onto the duvet. "He was an asshole and we both know it."

"Well," Megan said in that soft, demure voice of hers. "That was one of his better points, dear."

Before she knew what came over her, Kim found herself laughing. "That was almost, well . . . that was downright funny, Megan."

Megan blushed, but grinned back. She watched Kim for a drawn-out moment, her eyes twinkling. Her smile slowly faded as she stared at her stepdaughter, her expression serious. "I'm sorry I wasn't a good mother," she whispered. "I should have grown a backbone and learned how to protect both of us from Roger. I should have left him and took you with me."

Kim's nostrils flared. She flipped over onto her side, giving Megan her back. "You and I were getting along just fine for once," she bit out. "Why bring this up now?"

Megan was quiet for a long while. So long, in fact, that Kim had begun to wonder if she'd left the room. But then she spoke, her voice even softer than normal.

"I wasn't able to have children of my own," she said reflectively. "Like you, I was raised in a wealthy household, but back in my day the women's movement was barely off the ground. I wasn't pushed toward a career or finding an identity outside of a man. Not being able to have children . . ." She sighed. "It was like wearing a scarlet letter. When I wasn't able to conceive after ten years of trying, my first husband, Frank, divorced me for a younger woman who could. After that, my parents pushed me toward the first wealthy man that wanted me."

Kim listened, but said nothing.

"When I met Roger," Megan continued, her voice sounding wistful, "he was very kind to me. Very charming, very handsome and elegant." Kim could hear the smile in her voice. "And when he introduced me to you, this blonde-haired, blue-eyed beauty who looked like the little girl I'd always dreamed of having . . . I was lost forever."

Kim closed her eyes, swallowing against the lump of emotion in her throat.

"You had just turned fifteen, but you were so small back then you looked more like ten. Do you remember?" Megan didn't expect her to respond, so she kept talking. "I knew you were older, so I could never replace your dead mother in your eyes, God rest her soul, but I wanted so much for us to be close."

She paused for a moment before continuing.

"I don't think Roger wanted that, though," Megan murmured.

"In his childish mind, if you and I were close, it took away attention from him, made him no longer the center of the universe or something." Her voice sounded far away. "I'd never been obliged to deal with a man so overwhelming as Roger before," she quietly admitted. "I might have been thirty-four, but I was a naïve thirty-four. When he was abusive, or took to other women's beds, or any of his other various activities, I blamed myself. I thought it was something I was doing wrong. If I were thinner, or younger, or prettier, or could have babies . . ."

Kim took a deep breath and exhaled slowly. She blinked back tears, understanding only too well how good her father had been at laying blame.

Megan rose to her feet. "I'll leave you alone now," she said softly. She sighed as she stared at Kim's back. "I know that you're angry with me, as you have every right to be, but I'd like you to consider giving me another chance."

Kim's teeth sank into her lower lip.

"I'd like to be a part of your life, if even only a small part. I'll take anything you're willing to give." Megan paused. When next she spoke, her voice sounded a bit shaky. "I love you," she breathed out. "If you never believe anything else I say, please believe me when I say that I love you."

Kim closed her eyes as she drew in a tug of air. She waited until she heard the door click shut before she let the tears flow freely.

Chapter 17

Monday, July 21
7:15 A.M.

By the time they made it to Cincinnati, Thomas was exhausted. The drive was only four and a half hours, but given how sleep-deprived he was it felt a lot longer. And yet despite the extreme fatigue, his thoughts had become plagued by Nikki's mention of too-blue eyes. He knew he'd have to check into some things before he could collapse.

"Cincinnati," Nikki said, bemused. "I was expecting us to hole up in some ramshackle cabin in the Ozarks."

He grinned. "Cops only do stupid things like that in the movies. In real life, we like to have other cops within spitting distance." He turned his head long enough to wink. "Not to mention running water, multiple phone lines, and food you can order in rather than having to hunt it for yourself."

Nikki chuckled at that, her eyes taking in the semicrowded streets as the nondescript Taurus station wagon made a left-hand turn. "I've never been here before," she admitted. "Hey, maybe we can go ride the roller coasters at King's Island while we're here? I'd pay for it," she said quickly when he frowned. "I wouldn't expect the CPD to pick up the tab or anything."

"It's not the budget issue," Thomas muttered. "It's the safety issue."

"Oh. I see." She took a deep breath and blew it out. "In other words, we might as well be in the Ozarks."

Thomas pulled the station wagon into a high-rise complex, bypassed the main door, and headed directly toward the back. "Hey," he said softly. "Let me catch this guy, then I'll take you on any roller coaster ride you want. All right, Doc?"

Nikki's gaze darted over to stare at his chiseled profile. She smiled. "Thank you," she murmured. "You're pretty okay, Cavanah."

"You're pretty okay too," Thomas drawled. His eyebrows shot up. "For a pistachio thief."

"Fuck," Thomas swore under his breath, "are you sure?"

"Yeah, man," Ben O'Rourke said on a sigh through the phone line. "I confirmed it with Chief Williams himself. I'm sorry, buddy."

Thomas closed his eyes, pain ripping through his gut. He glanced over to where Nikki stood two rooms away emptying their groceries into the refrigerator. He kept his voice low.

"This doesn't make James guilty," he rasped out, "but between that report turning up missing, the conflicting stories between him and Vincent Pinoza, the feral-blue eyes, and now this . . ." He ran a punishing hand through his hair. "Shit, O'Rourke, I feel like I'm gonna be sick."

"I'm having a hell of a time taking it all in myself."

"Amy," Thomas choked out. "She trusted him. I trusted him near her. *Christ.*"

"Don't do this to yourself, man. Do you hear me? We don't know the full story yet. Although I have to admit it's starting to look pretty grim."

Thomas ran a hand over his stubbly chin. "One more time, bro. For my peace of mind . . ." He inhaled deeply, then exhaled slowly. "You are positive—one hundred percent without any shadow of doubt *positive*—that William Merdino was never hospitalized?"

Ben sighed. "I'm holding the fax from the hospital in my hands," he said softly. "What's more, I took the fax straight out of the boss man's hands. I'm sorry, Cavanah, but yes, I'm positive. What do you want me to do?"

Thomas closed his eyes. His partner. His own goddamn partner. "Put out an APB on his license plate," he said, his stomach muscles clenching. "Then go to Judge Johnson with what we've got and get a search warrant. I'll phone Chief Williams and bring him up to speed."

"You coming back or staying put?"

Thomas's intense gaze flicked over to where Dr. Adenike stood. "I'm staying here," he murmured, his jaw tightening. "I failed Amy. I'll be damned if I fail Nikki, too."

Thomas hadn't been exaggerating, Nikki thought as she stood in the kitchen peeling potatoes. They were holed up in Cincinnati in an apartment the police department owned, but as secluded as they were from the rest of the world, they might as well have been in the Ozarks. She sighed as her gaze sought out Thomas.

He'd been acting somewhat strangely for a few hours now, but extremely strangely ever since he'd hung up the phone. She knew he had to be exhausted, but he still hadn't gone to rest in one of the two bedrooms. He'd been sitting in a chair in the living room instead, staring at nothing for the better part of an hour.

"Hey," Nikki said, her eyebrows drawing together. She set down the potato peeler, wiped her hands on a towel, and slung it over her shoulder. "Why don't you go get some sleep?" she suggested as she padded out into the living room. She came to a halt in front of the chair in which he was seated. "If you're hungry, I'll wake you up when dinner's ready."

Thomas's dark gaze slowly inched up, lingering at her breasts. Her cheeks suffused with heat, having forgotten she was wearing the same tell-all top.

"I'm not tired," he muttered, his gaze moving up to her face. He ran a hand over his jaw when she frowned. "Okay, I'm a little tired. But I think I'll wait until we eat."

"Are you all right?" she asked, her eyes searching his face.

His jaw clenched. "Just go cook," he growled, settling back in the chair.

Her nostrils flared. "Fine," she bit out, turning away from him. "Excuse me for caring."

An hour later they sat down to eat in the small but functional kitchen. Nikki pretended obliviousness to Thomas's presence as he wolfed down three hamburgers and enough fried potatoes to feed a small country. She picked at her food, not particularly hungry, her feelings still smarting from earlier. She didn't think he'd noticed, so was surprised when he sighed and offered an apology.

"I shouldn't have snapped at you," Thomas admitted. "It's just been one hell of a shitty day."

Nikki nodded. She rose up to her feet and started carrying dishes to the sink. "It's okay," she said. "I guess my feelings get hurt a little too easily." She smiled from over her shoulder, then turned back to the sink. "Go ahead and get some sleep," she said as she lowered the dishes into the awaiting soapy water. "You look like you could use some—"

"I think Lucifer is my partner, James," he murmured.

"What?" Wide-eyed, Nikki whirled around on her barefoot heel. "Your partner?" she breathed out. "Oh my God. No wonder you're . . . oh my God."

Thomas sighed, his eyes briefly closing. "We don't know for sure, but let's just say the evidence is strong enough to get a search warrant for his place."

She studied his haggard face. "He killed someone you loved, didn't he?" she whispered.

He didn't say anything, but then he didn't need to. His expression said it all.

"I'm so sorry," she said softly. "Do you want to talk about it?"

Thomas shook his head. "I can't," he answered, his gravelly voice low. "I'm sorry."

That feeling she could understand all too well. Everyone from Kim to Megan to the chief of staff at the hospital had been trying to get Nikki to open up and spill her guts since the night of the attack, but all she had wanted to do was retreat and be alone with her wounds.

She walked over to where he sat, her expression concerned. "Come on," she said, holding out her hand. "Let me help you up. You need to get some sleep."

His gaze flicked up to her breasts again. Only this time, against her volition, her nipples stiffened in reaction. She blushed and glanced away.

Thomas's hands found her hips and drew her in closer. Her eyes rounded, her heartbeat kicking up. "What are you doing?" she breathed out.

"Just looking," he said thickly, his eyes heavy-lidded. "Can I touch?"

Nikki swallowed. Impossibly, her nipples tightened even further. "They're not much to look at," she said dumbly, arousal at war with nervousness.

He settled his hard, callused hands at her neck just below the throat. "I disagree," he said, his voice hoarse.

Her breathing hitched as Thomas's hands slowly, ever so slowly, pressed against her upper body and began feeling their way down. Down below her throat, over the swell of her breasts, then lower. By the time his palms ran over her aching nipples, she was so aroused that she gasped.

"So sexy," he said thickly. "So damn sexy."

His hands continued their slow journey until they found her belly. Nikki shuddered as he ran his palms under the edge of her top. He pushed the cotton garment up, inch by anticipatory inch, slowly revealing her naked breasts to his intense dark gaze.

Resting the bottom of her shirt over the swell of her bosom, Thomas was able to let go of it without it falling back down to shield her. He stared at her naked breasts for a long moment, his gaze flicking back and forth from one pierced nipple to the other.

"Your nipples are long and thick," he murmured, his heavy-lidded eyes narrowing a bit more. "My favorite. And these gold rings have got to be the sexiest things I've ever seen."

Her breathing grew more and more labored as she watched him watch her, then hitched once again as he palmed her breasts. "Oh, wow," Nikki said shakily.

His tongue snaked out and latched around one jutting pink nipple. She gasped, shuddering as he drew it into the warmth of his mouth. She instinctively threaded her fingers though his short, dark hair as he closed his eyes and sucked on it.

Thomas took his time with the nipple, rolling it around in his mouth, flicking the tip with his tongue, working her up into a fevered pitch of arousal. By the time he released it with a small popping sound and latched his mouth around the other one to repeat the process, her knees felt ready to give out.

She wanted him so badly. Her head lulled back against her neck as her eyes closed. She pulled his face in closer to her breasts, a slight moan escaping from between her lips as he sucked on her nipples like candy.

Thomas licked them, sucked them, flicked them back and forth with his tongue, made her moan and gasp as his large hands palmed her buttocks and squeezed. And then he did something she'd been hoping he wouldn't do. He stopped.

"I'm so tired I can barely see straight," he rasped out, his dark head rising from between her breasts. His gaze found hers. "When I take you, I want to take you right. I want it to last all night long."

Nikki swallowed, roughly, her breasts still heaving a bit from the arousal as he pulled down her top and recovered them. "Go get some sleep," she said, her voice slightly shaky. "I'll be here when you wake up."

Chapter 18

Tuesday, July 22
10:10 A.M.

Thomas awoke the next morning feeling rejuvenated. An hour, a breakfast, and a shower later, he was ready to search for more facts, ready to hypothesize and analyze. But for the first time in his career as a detective, that wasn't to be. He had to play bodyguard instead.

Not that he minded guarding Nikki's sexy body. In fact, he thought with a frown, he could get rather used to having her, and it, around. He didn't want to feel that way about her, though, because he was fairly certain that when this was all over she'd ditch him faster than a bad attitude.

A detective and a surgeon. He'd heard of stranger couplings, he supposed. Then again, he mentally grumbled, thinking it over, he hadn't.

Unfortunately, telling himself to keep an emotional distance from the object of his affection, lust, and admiration was working about as effectively as a screen door in a submarine. The door might want to keep the ocean out, but in the end there was no stopping the torrent of water.

Problem being, he'd been attracted to Dr. Adenike from the moment she'd glared daggers at him in his office. Stealing his nuts had made her only that much more appealing. Spending time with her and finding out that she was as wonderful as he'd imagined her to be was only adding to it.

He sighed as he ran a hand over his freshly shaved jaw. He really needed to concentrate on work. Call it avoidance, call it whatever—he needed it. Switching on the cell phone, he pounded out the chief's number.

It took a whopping five minutes to ascertain that there had been no strange goings-on at the Cox estate, James still hadn't been located, and the search of his partner's house hadn't rendered anything in the way of evidence—yet. "I'll keep you posted," the chief had said. "Until then, hang tight and watch Dr. Adenike like her life depends on it. Because guess what, it probably does."

As if watching Nikki were a hardship, Thomas thought, scowling. He had an iron-poker erection ninety-nine percent of the time and he wanted to mount her more than he wanted to breathe, but being with her wasn't exactly a hardship. A *hard-on-ship,* but not a hardship.

Women. Ah, who was he kidding? The problem here wasn't women, per se. The problem here was woman, as in singular.

"I made some pistachio ice cream," Nikki said on a smile as she breezed into the living room. "I figured we had it coming to us."

Thomas frowned.

Her face fell. "You don't like pistachio ice cream?" Her cheeks colored a bit. A damn adorable habit she had whenever she got to feeling unsure of herself. "I didn't know," she said, turning around and walking back into the kitchen. "Well, I guess that leaves more for me, then."

He grunted, then stood up. "Give me a damn spoon," he muttered, following her into the kitchen.

Her eyes lit up as she whirled around to face him. "You like pistachio ice cream, too?"

And that was another thing. Most women got their feelings hurt when he snapped and growled at them. It had taken Nikki all of twelve hours to accept that he was just a bit gruff by nature so not to take his attitude personally. She was getting under his skin, he thought grimly.

"Yes, I like pistachio ice cream," he growled. "Do I look like a communist to you?"

Nikki grinned. "Hey, it's your turn to make dinner tonight," she said as she turned around and started scooping out heaping helpings of one of his favorite desserts. "I'm game for just about anything."

How about being ridden hard for about ten solid hours? He shook his head and sighed, plopping down into one of the two kitchen seats. He needed to distract himself. Otherwise he was going to end up making a fool of himself here.

She was wearing jeans and a Cleveland General T-shirt this morning, her recently shampooed hair in a topknot on her head. No bra again, he thought with an inner smile. Then again he'd seen to it that none had been packed. Probably a dumb move on his part because every time they jiggled, a certain part of his anatomy saluted them.

Sucking on her nipples last night had been . . .

He blew out a breath as he dug into his ice cream. Best not to think about that, he conceded, shifting in his chair.

"I want to talk about the emails you exchanged with Lucifer," Thomas said gruffly.

She shifted her gaze from him as she sat down in the chair across from him. "Oh," she mumbled. He could tell she was a bit embarrassed. "What about them?"

His eyebrows drew together. "I want to understand," he said honestly.

She cleared her throat, still not making eye contact. "The attraction to him or the attraction he feels toward the women he verbally seduces?"

"The attraction to him." Thomas was quiet for a moment as he considered things. "I understand—I think—why he chose the women that he did. He likes to bring down strong women. Powerful, professional women."

One of her eyebrows rose as she looked at him. "I thought I recalled reading somewhere that not all of his victims had been career women." She shook her head. "I must have been wrong."

"There were two," he confirmed, "that weren't high-powered career women. Two out of seven—eight, if we count you."

Nikki blew out a breath. "I'd rather not count me," she mumbled before shoving a spoonful of ice cream between her lips.

"Understandable."

"So how do you account for the two?" she asked, putting her spoon down. "When I talked to Dr. Horace she mentioned that organized serial killers tend toward the ritualistic. Lucifer is definitely organized. Why break his own pattern?"

Thomas sighed. "Lisa Pinoza . . . I still don't know. She remains the one mystery victim, the one I can't figure out the why to." His jaw tightened. "I feel like this case would break wide open if I could answer that damn question."

Nikki was quiet for a moment as she studied his face. "And the second victim?" she asked softly, fairly certain she already knew the answer.

His nostrils flared as he looked away. "To get to me. She was a toy to him, a way to punish me for working his case. A way to fuck with me."

"I'm sorry," she said quietly.

Thomas's faraway gaze was reflective for a moment. He shook his head and sighed. "Anyway, back to you and the letters . . ."

She picked up her spoon. "All right. For the record, I find this conversation embarrassing and uncomfortable. But," she muttered, "if you think it'll help, then I'm willing to talk."

He didn't know if it would or wouldn't. Thomas mentally convinced himself that it could, not wanting to deal with the fact that his true motivation was a desire to know more about Nikki.

"Why him?" he asked softly, his dark gaze raking over her features. "You're a beautiful, intelligent woman," he said, inducing her cheeks to color just a bit, "so why go looking for someone online?"

"You've read the emails," she mumbled, shoving her spoon into the ice cream. "You know what I was looking for."

"Fair enough. But why?"

Nikki sighed. She left the spoon suspended in the ice cream as her green gaze found his. "There were lots of reasons."

"Like . . ."

"Like career pressure." She smiled a bit, trying to make him understand. "I love my job, I really do, but it's a job that requires an extreme amount of self-discipline and control. If I have a headache, or an upset stomach, or am feeling a bit down over a petty argument with a friend . . . none of these things matter. I have to detach and completely block them from my mind as if they don't exist."

Thomas slowly nodded. "I'm in touch with that feeling."

Her eyes slightly widened. "I hadn't thought about that, but I guess you would be." She threw a hand toward him. "You know what it's like to play God in people's lives. You decide whether or not they will live as free men and women or go to jail and spend their lives behind bars. I have it a bit worse in that I decide if they will live or die."

"Gotcha," he murmured.

Nikki shrugged. "Don't you ever get tired of being in control? Don't you ever fantasize about letting go of the power and giving it up, if even for a few minutes, to a person you can trust?"

His gaze locked with hers. "No."

Her eyes rounded. She chuckled. "Somehow, coming from you, that does not surprise me." She shook her head and grinned.

Thomas found himself grinning back. "Okay, so career pressure. We've established that. What else?"

Apparently this was the harder part, for Nikki got that flustered, red-cheeked look about her again. He really did find that adorable, he decided.

"It's just . . ." She sighed. "Emotional vulnerability, I suppose."

His eyebrow quirked. "Emotional vulnerability. What does that mean?"

Nikki shrugged, glancing away. "I'm afraid this will sound a bit corny. Childish even, maybe."

"Hey, we've all got aspects like that about us. There's no such thing as perfect except for in books or movies, sweetheart," he growled. "Go on."

She smiled. "True."

"Then go on," he again prodded, though gentler this time.

"I wanted, just once in my life . . ." Nikki looked away again, a reflective expression on her face. "I wanted to be everything to a man. The center of his universe. Just once."

Thomas listened but said nothing.

"Growing up, I never had a father. He died when I was fairly young, so it was just me and Mom. Mom . . . she loved me, I know she did, but she was very . . . how do I put it? Stoic, I guess. She was a stoic, emotionally withdrawn person."

"Didn't show much affection?" he asked softly.

Nikki shook her head. "No. Never." She forced a smile as she met his gaze. "But she loved me and I loved her. She didn't have to tell me for me to know, but it would have helped, if that makes sense."

He inclined his head.

"I think," she said in the way of self-analysis, "that as a result of that and various other events, I stored up all of these incredible feelings that I didn't know how to show others. Feelings that have all been laying in wait for that one lucky guy"—she wiggled her eyebrows—"or unfortunate guy, depending on how you look at it."

Nikki chuckled, trying to keep the conversation light. "It's funny, too, because I can't count how many men I dated when I was younger—before I gave up!—who described me postrelationship as a cold fish, an ice queen. Little did they know I had all of these intense emotions buried beneath the ice that I was waiting and hoping a man would care enough to crack and claim."

Thomas's gaze flicked over her facial features, studying them, memorizing them.

She glanced away, her smile fading. "But that never happened," she said quietly. "And before I knew it, I quit hoping." Nikki sighed. "Anyway, I don't really remember how or when I happened upon my first e-book that revolved around Domination/submission situations, but I do recall being hooked as soon as I read one."

Something in Thomas stilled. "E-books?" he softly asked.

Her eyebrows drew together. "That's an electronic book," she explained.

"I know," he said, running a hand over his jaw. "Was it one publisher in particular you read?"

Nikki's eyes rounded when she realized the direction his thoughts were going in. "Yes," she whispered. "Do you suppose there could be a correlation?"

Thomas shoved away from the table and stood up. "I don't know," he said, the adrenaline kicking in. "Let's go find out."

*"I want you to see if the e-book publisher will willingly cooper-*ate and hand over their records first," Thomas said to Ben through the cell connection. "If not, then we try to get a warrant." He ran a hand over his jaw. "Shit, I hope it doesn't come to that. We don't have enough to go on to obtain one." He frowned. "Nah, it's just a hunch. Well, not even a hunch, really. Just something worth looking into."

Nikki watched Thomas pace back and forth, her gaze mesmerized by the sight of him. Certainly more enthralled than she wanted it to be. Especially considering the fact that he hadn't made any mention today of last night or even behaved as though anything noteworthy had transpired between them. A thought that depressed her more than it probably should have.

Here she was, holed up in an apartment in downtown Cincinnati, where she could be another anonymous face in a crowd, in hiding from a sadistic serial killer who fantasized about raping, torturing, and murdering her in particular, and all Nikki could think about was whether or not Thomas was as attracted to her as she was to him. The irony was not lost on her.

Having Thomas as her bodyguard made her feel invulnerable to attack, which no doubt explained why she hadn't given Lucifer as much thought as the sicko probably hoped she'd been giving him. The detective had a solid, loyal quality about him, a dependability most men, and most people for that matter, lack.

Nikki couldn't decide if he was more handsome clean-shaven, as he was now, or sporting the five-o'clock shadow that partially concealed the lower half of his face most of the time. He looked a bit sinister either way, she supposed. He looked undeniably masculine and handsome either way, too. Even wearing jeans and a T-shirt as he was today, he personified rugged, elemental masculinity.

"Well," Thomas said, making her blink, "Ben's on the case. Now all we can do is sit back and wait to see if anything comes of it."

She nodded. "I'm not sure I understand what it is you're hoping to find, but whatever it is, I obviously hope you find it."

"I'm not looking for anything in particular," he said as he strolled into the kitchen. "And very well might not find anything. That's the best way, if you ask me. If you look for something in particular, you tend to overlook the million other things staring you right in the face."

"Good point."

He grunted. "Well, for both our sakes I hope Ben finds something. I'd like to get the hell out of here and go back to Cleveland to work."

Nikki's heart fell, something she conceded it had no right to do. "Yes," she said quietly, "I can understand that."

Thomas's head poked through the kitchen door. "Hey." He waited for her to look at him before continuing. "Don't go reading shit into things I say." He frowned. "I say what I mean and I mean what I say," he grumbled before disappearing back into the kitchen. "There ain't any lines there for you to read between, Doc."

She held back a smile. In more words or less he had just salvaged her pride, letting her know he wanted to return to Cleveland so it was easier to work, not so he wouldn't be obliged to spend more time with her. Nikki blew out a breath. If Detective Grouch kept doing nice things like that, she was going to be head over heels in love with him before they left Cincinnati.

"I was thinking," Nikki said a bit loudly to make sure Thomas heard her from the kitchen.

"Oh, great," he muttered. "Three words no man wants to hear from a woman's lips."

"Knock it off, I'm being serious."

He grunted. "So am I."

Nikki rolled her eyes to the ceiling. "Anyway," she said pointedly, standing up and walking into the kitchen. "You have a laptop, right?" she asked, leaning against the doorframe.

Thomas glanced up from where he was making sandwiches. "Yeah. You like pastrami?"

"Yes," she said absently. "With mustard, please. Anyway, if you have a laptop, why don't we . . . I don't know . . . try to catch Lucifer ourselves?"

He stilled for a moment. He glanced up at her. "I have to admit the thought did cross my mind."

"But?"

He shrugged. "Leon Walker, our computer expert over at the CPD, already put approximately ten dummy ads in. So far he hasn't even gotten a nibble. There are thousands of ads on Dom4me.com. What are the chances of Lucifer reading the one we put in when he hasn't taken any of Leon's bait?"

"A bit more mustard, please." Nikki considered that. "Well, have you thought about the possibility that Lucifer can smell a trap? Or that Leon isn't using the right trigger words? He is a man after all."

Thomas frowned. "Yes, I've considered that. But Dr. Horace is a woman, and she helped him create the ads. Do you like pickles?"

"What am I, a communist? Okay, granted Dr. Horace is a woman, and a brilliant one at that, but perhaps she is missing that element of vulnerability Lucifer's victims, myself included, shared in common. I bet if we created a fictional ad for a woman in the Cleveland area who has the same professional and *emotional* attributes as me . . ."

He was quiet for a long moment, a thoughtful look etched into his profile. "Go boot up the laptop," Thomas muttered. "I'll get us some chips and pops."

Chapter 19

Tuesday, July 22
6:22 P.M.

"Well, here we go." Nikki blew out a breath as she typed in Dom4me.com and waited for the site to load on the screen of the laptop. Seated on the floor, she and Thomas had set up shop on the living room table, the portable computer, various printouts, and their dinner scattered all over it.

When the site finally loaded, she felt embarrassed inside, realizing as she did that Thomas knew from her email exchange with Richard that she fantasized about the sorts of activities and situations Dom4me.com purported. On the main menu there was a photographic image of a naked woman, her head bowed, kneeling before a man—her Master. The next page contained a photographic image of a naked woman tied up and blindfolded while her Master administered to her sexually.

Oh yes, Nikki was embarrassed. Mortified, more like. But she pretended as though they were looking at nothing more provocative or unusual than a weather-reporting news site.

One of Thomas's eyebrows rose as he watched her navigate Dom4me.com. "I see we know our way around in here," he grumbled.

She blushed and ignored him. "Okay. This is where we set up our ad. I think a good title for it would be, hmm let me think . . . I know!" Nikki began typing, repeating the words back to him as she did. "Lonely CEO Searching for Master."

He frowned. "Shouldn't it be, Lonely *Female* CEO Searching for Master?"

She shook her head. "It's redundant. You can tell by the gender we put in that she, or *we,* rather, are a woman."

"I concede to your finer knowledge of this site," he growled.

Nikki ignored the way her heart was thumping at his obvious jealousy, telling herself she could savor that memory later in private. "Okay, first things first, we need to decide what we look like." Her eyes squinted as she read the selections. "We'll be thirty-four, have dark blonde hair, and green—no, too obvious—blue eyes. What should our, uh . . ." She cleared her throat. "What should our bra size be?"

His eyebrows shot up. "Big. I want to have big tits."

She frowned at him. "I'm being serious."

"So am I." He sighed. "Okay, I was kind of teasing, but actually Lucifer does have a thing for big breasts."

Nikki flushed, quickly looking back down to the screen. "How about 34D, then?"

Thomas's gaze slowly raked over her chest. "That your size?" he softly drawled.

Her heart was beating so dramatically she could hear it better than she could hear him. "That's for me to know and for you to find out."

Thomas snorted at that. "I see we've now passed the fifth grade."

She grinned, but didn't look up.

Fifteen minutes later, Nikki leaned against the couch, chomping on her pastrami and rye sandwich as Thomas checked his email. The ad was done. Together they had created a fictional woman that fit the killer's predilection. Unfortunately, it could take up to forty-eight hours for the ad to post, depending upon how backlogged the site administrators were. All they could do now was sit back and wait—and hope the lure would be too sweet for Lucifer to pass up.

"Why the Master stuff?" Thomas murmured, surprising her.

Nikki's head shot up. She set down the sandwich and swallowed. "What do you mean?"

His dark gaze slowly swept over her, making her belly knot. "Why do you want to call a man *Master* in bed?"

Silence.

She looked away. "I don't know," she quietly admitted. "I guess it's more the symbolism than the word itself."

"Explain what you mean."

She shrugged, her gaze still averted. "Well, sort of like the woman you saw on the Dom4me.com site kneeling before that man. It's not the act of kneeling in and of itself that arouses her enough to do it, it's the symbolism behind the action."

Thomas's heavy-lidded gaze studied her face as he listened.

"She wants to be completely possessed by that man," Nikki said, finding it easier to talk in the third person as if about someone else. "She wants to be owned by him, have him decide her boundaries." She glanced up and grinned. "Probably only in the bedroom. I know there is such a thing as lifestylers who live in those roles twenty-four/seven, but I doubt ninety percent of women who like to be submissive in the bedroom would allow for such goings-on anywhere *but* in bed."

His gaze bore into hers. "You want that, Nikki?" he murmured. "You want a man to own you?"

"Not just any man," she whispered. Nikki drew in a deep tug of air and exhaled slowly. This conversation was arousing her like she didn't know what. "And not just in general. In the bedroom only."

Thomas's intense gaze trailed over her face, down to her lips, up to her eyes. "What if the guy needed to own you outright?" he asked in that low, gravelly voice of his.

She swallowed against the invisible lump in her throat.

"What if he was a jealous bastard who needed to know his woman would never fuck around? Or what if he was worried all the time that something bad might happen to her, so he liked for her to tell him where she was at all times?"

Nikki couldn't help but to wonder if he was speaking of himself—and her. A fact that made her breathing grow a bit heavier. "Well . . ." She blew out a breath. Good lord, she was aroused. Even her nipples were hard as rocks, she thought grimly. "I guess it would depend on what he meant by owning me outright. Would I leave him a note if I needed to dash out unexpectedly or whatever? I think that's mutual respect both parties should demonstrate, not ownership per se."

"What if," he asked softly, "he wanted you to ask his permission before you went anywhere?"

Nikki's smile came slowly. "I'd tell him to go to hell," she whispered.

Thomas grunted. "It was worth a shot," he muttered.

The next several minutes passed in tense silence. She could feel the detective's stare boring into her profile, but nerves kept her from looking back at him. She sat on the floor before the living room table, her back propped against the sofa, feigning an inordinate fascination with the soda she slowly sipped from.

She wanted Thomas Cavanah. More than she'd ever wanted any man. There was no point in denying that reality any longer.

"Richard" had been a fantasy lover, and the affection she'd felt for him based on calculated untruths and castles in the sky—none of it had ever been real. But Thomas, and their burgeoning relationship, was different—both were very real. Her brain knew it. Her aroused body knew it. And now her heart knew it, too. It did not follow, however, that he wanted her back.

Nikki realized he was attracted to her on some level. She bet he'd even have sex with her if she showed the slightest inclination toward sleeping with him. But, she dismally thought, things had gone a bit too far for her to be able to view carnal relations with him as merely casual. She'd never been good at that anyway. With Thomas the effect would be a thousand times worse.

The grouchy, growling man had gotten under her skin in a way no male had ever before accomplished. She liked him as a person, trusted him as a friend, respected him as a detective, and wanted him in the way a woman wants a man. The ice-queen's heart was this close to cracking, and she didn't know how to deal with it. What was worse was the fact that there was nowhere to run, nowhere to hide, for she was as good as glued to Thomas's side until Lucifer was caught.

"I want to be that man," Thomas said, making her blink. She'd been so lost in her thoughts she hadn't heard him get up, let alone walk around the table to stand next to her.

Her head shot up. He looked so strong and powerful standing there before her, his heavily muscled body tensed.

"What man?" Nikki whispered. She nervously met his gaze, her heart pounding in her chest.

His eyes were narrowed, heavy-lidded. "The man who owns you," he said thickly.

Her heart was hammering so hard she could scarcely breathe. She said nothing, couldn't have spoken if her life depended on it, as she sat there and watched him watch her, her breasts rising and falling with her labored breathing.

Thomas reached for her topknot and unwound it, letting curls spill down to the middle of her back. "Can I own you, Nikki?" he softly asked, his callused fingers tucking a curl behind her ear. The feel of his hardened skin raking her softer flesh made her nipples pucker. She glanced down, seeing his erection pressed tight against his jeans, before looking up to meet his gaze again. "Can I?"

Nikki had never felt more nervous, excited, or closer to fainting in her entire life. Everything she'd ever fantasized about, every last wicked fantasy, was suddenly within her grasp. She wanted to live out her desires more than anything, but also conceded that if she said yes to Thomas, the ice-queen might very well be turning over her cracked-open heart to the detective to do with as he would.

Could she chance that? Did she have the guts?

Her chest was heaving so dramatically it was a wonder she could breathe. "Yes," Nikki whispered, her eyes now as intense as Thomas's. "Yes, you can."

His heavy-lidded gaze raked over her breasts, over her face. "Prove it," he commanded. "Get on your knees and tell me that."

Nikki slowly blew out a breath, her hands a bit shaky. She glanced away, suddenly embarrassed about her submissive fantasies. Kneeling before a man had been one thing in thought, while masturbating; it was entirely another thing—a very, very unnerving thing—in reality.

The mortifying thought that Thomas found the situation humorous crossed her mind, made her cheeks redden. But when she looked at his expression, really studied it for the first time, she could tell without reservation that the detective was as aroused by her fantasies as she was. "Okay," she breathed out, more nervous and vulnerable than she'd ever been in her life. She made to get up, climb up to her knees.

"Take your clothes off first," he said hoarsely, backing up a few steps. "Stand up, take off your clothes, and then kneel before me."

His words, coupled with the command itself, were so arousing she could feel her entire body flushing. Taking a deep, steadying breath, Nikki came up on shaky feet and slowly began to peel off her clothing.

"Your shirt first," he instructed.

She glanced down, no longer able to meet his gaze, as she gradually inched the Cleveland General T-shirt above her navel, above her rib cage, above her naked breasts . . .

The sound of his breath sucking in made her nipples harden. "Very nice," he rasped out as the T-shirt went over her neck and then fell to the floor. "There isn't much sexier than a topless, busty woman wearing nothing but jeans."

Nikki blushed, still too nervous to meet his gaze.

"But I want the jeans gone," he said in that gravelly drawl of his. "Take them off."

She blew out another breath, so aroused she felt like squeezing her thighs together. She did as she'd been instructed, her hands shaking just a bit as she raised them to her jeans and unsnapped.

"Faster," Thomas ordered. "I want to see *my* pussy."

Nikki unzipped the jeans and stepped out of them quickly, tossing them aside as she nervously stood before him. She'd never been so turned on in her entire life. Until this moment, she had believed a woman couldn't experience an orgasm with a man with the same intensity as she could through masturbation. She realized she was about to be proved wrong and then some.

"You're not wearing underwear."

She could feel his eyes staring at her. "You didn't pack me any," she whispered, her head still nervously bowed.

"Look at me," Thomas murmured. She sucked in her breath when his callused fingers reached toward her, sifting through her soft pubic hair. "Look at me," he again ordered her.

Nikki's head came up. Her eyes, narrowed with desire, found his. She moaned softly, almost imperceptibly, as the tips of his fingers grazed through the triangle of light brown hair at the apex of her thighs. His eyes, always intense, were blazing. His jaw, always rigid, was tighter than ever.

"Who does this pussy belong to now?" Thomas asked possessively.

Her heart was ready to beat out of her chest. Some women might find words like that offensive. She now realized she wasn't one of them. At least not when Thomas Cavanah was the man using them. "You," she breathed out.

Two of his callused fingers found her clit and started rubbing it. She moaned a bit louder.

"Will you ever let another man touch you here?" he drawled.

She wet her lips, could barely keep her eyes open. "No."

"No, what?" he growled.

It was unnerving how quickly the words came to her lips. "No . . . Master."

Silence. He said nothing as he stroked her clit, his dark gaze boring into hers.

"Good girl," Thomas finally purred.

He rubbed her clit harder, the vein in his bicep bulging. Nikki gasped, one of her hands blindly reaching out to dig into his shoulder so she didn't collapse.

"Oh, god," she groaned, her eyes instinctively closing as he rubbed her clit faster.

"Let it go," he murmured, his voice hoarse. "Come for me, baby."

She couldn't have stopped her inevitable orgasm if she had wanted to. "Thomas," she gasped, the intimate massage growing more and more intense. She moaned long and loud as her fingers dug into his shoulder, her legs ready to collapse. On one last groan she burst, her entire body shuddering, her nipples stiffening to the point of near pain, as she climaxed. *"Oh, god."*

Thomas quickly wrapped an arm around her, catching her before she fell. He allowed her trembling legs to slowly give out, buckling so that she sat on her knees before him panting for breath.

"Tell me," he murmured, his voice thick with arousal. "Say that you want me to own you."

Nikki was so weak from the orgasm it was all she could do to lift her gaze up to his. Her breathing was labored, her breasts methodically rising and falling with the movement.

"I want you to own me," she panted out. "You and only you."

Silence.

"I hope this isn't a game you're playing, sweetheart," Thomas growled as he lifted his shirt up and over his head. She wet her lips as the T-shirt was flung to the ground, revealing a chest that was as heavy with muscle and athletic definition as she'd known it would be. The perfect amount of black hair sprinkled his tanned chest, narrowing into a thin line that disappeared into his jeans. "Because I've never been more serious in my life."

She said nothing as she stared at him, her anticipation of seeing his cock apparent. He lifted one eyebrow as he unzipped his jeans, stepping out of his trousers and boxers at the same time.

Nikki blew out a breath as Thomas stood before her in his naked, erect glory. His penis was, just as she'd hoped, as big and imposing as the rest of him was. It stood swollen and stiff against his belly, a large vein running from root to head.

"Kiss him," Thomas murmured. He threaded his fingers through her hair and wound a few long tresses around his hand. "I want to feel your lips wrapped around my cock, Nikki."

She was so worked up she would have reached for him without prompting. That he'd commanded her to do as much in the tone that guaranteed her arousal only added fuel to the flames already burning inside of her.

Nikki wrapped her hand around his stiff penis and took it into her mouth without ceremony. The sound of his breath catching made her that much more determined to pleasure him as thoroughly as he'd just pleasured her. She moaned from around his cock, letting him know how much she enjoyed sucking on him.

"Shit," Thomas muttered, letting her hair fall to cascade down her back. He palmed either side of her face, his stomach muscles clenching as she repeatedly deep-throated him, taking him in as far as humanly possible and then some. "Faster," he gritted out.

She went faster. Nikki sucked on him hard, taking him in deeper, making him hiss. The sound of lips meeting stiff flesh permeated the small living room, her head ruthlessly bobbing back and forth, as she sucked him off. He moaned as she deep-throated his cock, the guttural sound the headiest she'd ever heard.

She kept up the brisk pace for two solid minutes, determined to make him come. The sound of his moans soon overtook the sound of her lips sucking on the flesh that had been dampened from her mouth. His muscles tensed, his breathing grew labored, and she knew he was about to burst.

But just when he neared the point of climax, that precipice nobody can stop from falling over once reached, Thomas pulled back. He forced his cock from her mouth with a popping sound, his breathing as ragged as hers.

"The first time I come in you," he said hoarsely, bodily pulling her up to her feet, "won't be in your mouth." His dark gaze raked over her swollen lips, swept across her features, as his fingers possessively sifted through her pubic hair. "It'll be in *my* pussy," he growled.

There went her heart again, beating like a rock in her chest. Nikki was given no time to respond to his announcement, for the next thing she knew, her hand was in Thomas's as he quickly led her into the bedroom he'd been using since they had arrived. Once inside, he wasted no time.

"Lay on the bed and spread your legs wide open," he ordered as he strode to the other side of the bedroom. "I'll be there in a second."

Her forehead wrinkled, wondering what he was up to, but she went to the bed anyway and did as instructed. She climbed up on top of it, lying down on her back, her breasts thrust upward and her thighs spread wide apart. Not even five seconds later, she heard the telltale sound of handcuffs being opened up. Her eyes rounded a bit as Thomas turned around and began walking toward where she lay, her suspicion of his intentions confirmed by the gleaming metal in his hands and the fierce erection standing against his belly.

Oh boy, Nikki thought, blowing out a breath. Here it comes. The realization of her most secret, fevered fantasy. She wet her lips, both nervous and turned on.

The anticipation of what was to come was even more arousing than in her fantasies. Because this was Thomas Cavanah. A man she could trust, a man she wasn't afraid to surrender her body to . . .

A man whose handcuffs were real.

She swallowed a bit roughly as she watched him approach the bed, his dark eyes blazing and narrowed. He didn't speak a word as he clasped first one wrist and then the other before stretching her arms over her head. Using what looked to be a necktie, he wound the piece of material around the chain of the handcuffs, looped the other end through a hole in the carved, oak headboard, and made a tight knot. His biceps bulged with the effort, letting Nikki know there was no escape from the impenetrable knot.

Only then did Thomas join her on the bed. She could see how defined and muscled his buttocks were in profile as he made his way to the center of the bed before coming up on his knees between her splayed thighs. He took his sweet time looking his fill at her naked body, his dark eyes penetrating every last inch.

"My pussy is very pretty," he drawled, his voice even gravellier than usual. "I bet it'll feel even better than it looks."

Nikki instinctively wet her lips, praying he'd test the theory quickly.

His callused hands cupped her breasts, causing her to shiver. His thumbs played with the thin gold hoops encircling her nipples, tugging at them just enough to force a moan out of her. He plucked at her nipples then, plumping them up until they stabbed into the air and she was gasping with arousal. He lowered his head, sucking on each one a minute or so, until her body was worked up into a tightly strung, fevered pitch.

She could do nothing but lie there and take it, unable to move, unable to resist. The inability to wiggle away or force his lips from off of her swollen nipples somehow made the arousal more pronounced. Within moments Nikki was groaning, her breathing labored as she watched Thomas lick and suck on her nipples. By the time he raised his dark head from her breasts, she was already close to another orgasm.

"You're being a very good little girl," Thomas murmured, his voice thick, as he once again took to his knees. "Keep it up and Daddy'll give you a big treat."

She took a deep breath and exhaled slowly. He was using words straight from her fantasies to work her up and was succeeding admirably. Yet somehow she realized this was more than a sex game to him. He enjoyed the power exchange, took immense masculine satisfaction in her sexual submission. That only made the situation all the more pleasurable. They weren't two actors playing roles, but a man and a woman doing what came naturally to their individual selves.

Thomas straddled Nikki's face, his powerful, muscled thighs settling at either side of her head. "Open up," he said hoarsely. "Show Master how good his little girl can be."

Her lips immediately parted. They both groaned as he pressed his way into her warm, wet mouth.

"Take him all the way in," he murmured, his hips thrusting back and forth at a leisurely pace. "That's it," he ground out, the head of his cock touching the back of her throat. "Just like that."

Nikki moaned from around his stiff cock. Thomas picked up the pace, plunging in and out of her pliant mouth in faster strokes. She could hear his breathing growing labored, could feel his muscles tensing around her.

And then, just like before, he stopped. Thomas plucked his erection out from between her suctioning lips, the sound again a popping noise.

"Daddy loves how you suck his cock," he rasped, "but now it's my turn. I want to taste my sweet, juicy pussy."

The words made her belly knot. The sight of his dark head disappearing between her splayed thighs made the knot coil tightly.

"Mmmm," Thomas murmured, his mouth making slurping sounds as he sucked on her hole. "You taste so damn good, baby." He swirled his tongue around the opening again before clamping his lips around her clit and sucking it into his mouth. "Mmmm," he

purred from around her clit as her hips instinctively bucked up. *"Mmmmmmm."*

"Oh, god," Nikki groaned.

Her eyes closed and her head fell back on the pillows as he sucked harder. Her legs began to tremble as the knot in her belly threatened to break loose. His fingers dug into the padding of her thighs as he sucked harder and faster and—

"Ohhhh, god!" Nikki screamed, her legs shaking as violently as the orgasm that ripped through her. *"Oh, yes—oh, god!"*

Thomas made a small growling sound as he lapped at her juices, his tongue frenziedly licking her all up. "Please," Nikki gasped, her eyes opening, "I can't wait any longer."

His jaw was tight and his breathing heavy as his face slowly surfaced from between her legs. "Neither can I," he murmured.

Settling himself between Nikki's outstretched thighs, Thomas came down on top of her. His nostrils were flaring as his dark gaze clashed with hers and he palmed her breasts. "I need to know how my pussy feels."

She wet her dry lips.

Poising the tip of his erection at the entrance to her aroused flesh, Thomas groaned as he sank into her, his teeth gritting as he seated himself to the hilt. Nikki moaned, her head falling back and her neck bared to him as he mounted her.

With her arms stretched above her head as he slowly plunged in and out of her, she could only lie there and take it. Every hard inch of him possessed her body as her breasts jiggled with each thrust.

"Oh god," she breathed out, her eyes closing in pleasure. "Oh yes."

"*My* pussy feels so good," he rasped, picking up the pace of their mating. He slammed into her harder, his hands clamped around her breasts in the way her flesh was clamped around his stiff cock. He growled low in his throat as he took her, thrusting deeper and faster into her wet, suctioning depths.

"Thomas," Nikki groaned, her voice guttural. The sound of flesh slapping against flesh filled the bedroom, competing only with the sound of the bed squeaking and Thomas growling.

He rotated his hips and sank fully into her again, then pistoned back and forth in lightning-quick movements that made her moans come louder and last longer. She wrapped her legs around his hips as he took her, her mind in a place beyond ecstasy as he rode her body hard in a series of intense thrusts. His nostrils were flared, his jaw tense.

He took her harder, plunging in and out of her pussy, over and over, again and again and again. *"Mine,"* he rasped. "*My* woman. *My* cunt."

"I'm coming," Nikki cried out, her nipples so stiff they ached. A second and far more intense knot of pleasure coiled in her belly, again threatening to break. The friction against her clit as he repeatedly plunged into her was her undoing. She threw her hips back at him while she moaned, her breasts jiggling.

"Do it, baby," Thomas hoarsely encouraged her. He rode her body without mercy, pounding away inside of her. "Come for me."

"Thomas," she gasped. *"Oh god."*

Nikki came long and loudly, moaning as her orgasm ripped through her insides. Blood rushed to her face to heat it, and to her nipples making them stab up against his palms.

"Good girl," he gritted out, sinking in and out of her flesh in deep, hard strokes. "My god, you feel so damn good."

The intense expression on his face told her he wanted to ride her all night long and then some, but realized that he could only stave off his inevitable climax for so long. Thomas took her impossibly faster, his eyes squeezing shut as if to savor the feel of her pussy convulsing around him, milking his cock for release.

"I'm coming," he rasped out, his hands firmly clamped around her breasts. He stroked into her harder—faster—deeper—once, twice, three times more . . . .

"Nikki," he growled, slamming into her body a final time.

His jaw was clenched, his breathing heavy, as he shuddered on top of her. He groaned as he spurted his cum deep inside of her, his hands instinctively squeezing her breasts.

Thomas collapsed almost immediately, his breathing ragged. With a tired groan, he came down a bit on the bed, then buried his face between her breasts and rested his head there.

Nikki reached out to touch him, to hold him, recalling the handcuffs only when she wasn't able to. She thought to remind him of them so he would release her, but decided against it, not quite ready to give up the languorous, sensual feeling of being submissively splayed out for the pleasure of the dominant male she craved.

A few minutes later, after both of their heart rates had calmed down, Thomas raised his head from her breasts high enough to suck on her nipples. Apparently, she thought as arousal knotted in her belly once more, the dominant male wasn't quite ready to give up the submissive state in which he held her captive, either. Good.

His dark head rose from her breasts as he intimately settled himself between her thighs. "I won't be done with this pussy of mine for a long time," Thomas drawled. Nikki wet her lips, her gaze meeting his. "In fact," he said thickly, sinking into her on a groan, "it'll be tomorrow morning before Daddy'll give his sexy little girl a rest."

She wondered if that was supposed to be a threat. If so, Nikki thought, amused, it was a weak one.

Chapter 20

Wednesday, July 23
10:40 A.M.

Priscilla Harrington-Barnsworth would have been embarrassed to admit her online activities to anyone of her acquaintance. But then, most people of her acquaintance didn't realize she fantasized about the sorts of situations and happenings that she did. Cilla expected that her fantasies would remain behind lock and key forever, for she couldn't chance the public being made privy to her sex life.

Cilla was, after all, a Harrington. If her family hadn't been passengers on the original Mayflower, well, they'd certainly been on the second or third boat to dock at America's shores.

With the Harrington name came more social pressure than most people could imagine. Children of poorer or middle-class families who aspired to have the sort of money Cilla had been born into liked to point out how hard they'd had to work, how ambitious they'd had to be, in order to climb to the top. That was no doubt true, but what most of them failed to realize was that the burden of performance was just as dramatic for the children born to the moneyed. Or, at least, that was how she felt.

Everything Cilla had ever done—from her first date, to her first job, to what napkins she laid out for guests to make use of at holiday parties—was scrutinized and criticized. If the napkins were too dainty, it was proof she was a social snob not in touch with the masses. If the napkins were too plain and blasé, then clearly she had no taste. (Or, worse yet, her family didn't have as much money as they let on.)

No matter what she did, no matter what she said, somebody was always there, waiting to evaluate it and her. That those had been her experiences since she'd been old enough to crawl should have been enough to waylay her from further burdening herself. The deeply seeded desire to serve humankind, to help those less fortunate than herself, had, however, called to her from adolescence onward.

And so Priscilla Harrington-Barnsworth, daughter of former Senator Maxwell Harrington, granddaughter of former Secretary of State Toddsworth Harrington, wife of shipping magnate Otis Barnsworth IV, had announced her candidacy for the House of Representatives on her twenty-fifth birthday. It was no contest. She had won the race, served her constituency from the elite, moneyed Cleveland suburb well, and had been re-elected in every subsequent match.

When Cilla turned thirty-one she turned her attention toward the Senate. That contest had been tougher, a lot tougher, in fact, but again she had emerged the winner. The voting trend in Ohio had been largely Democratic at the time, so it had taken quite a few well-spent campaign dollars to ensure that the wealthy Republican daughter of an even wealthier Republican father came across as an everyday woman worthy of everyday votes. Not an easy feat, but she'd done it.

Truth be told, Priscilla Harrington-Barnsworth considered herself to be neither a Republican nor a Democrat, but unless your name was Jesse "The Body" Ventura, you didn't have a shot at winning a serious race running as an independent. Cilla had, therefore, done the only sane thing she could think to do and run on the very ticket her father had.

Ironically enough, entering the contest as a Republican had been the best choice she, as a woman, could have made. It was Cilla's belief that many moderate voters, the very people whose votes she needed the most, tended to view female Democrats as too liberal and male Republicans as too conservative, even if the exact opposite was true where the individuals themselves were concerned. But a female Republican . . .

So here Cilla was, five years later, a Republican senator from a largely Democratic state, spending grueling hours on the campaign trail in preparation for the election in November. She held no doubts but that she would win. She'd been bred for this her entire life. She would serve in the Senate for four more years, then run for the governorship of Ohio after that. Who knows. Maybe she'd even run for president someday.

It didn't matter. Not really. Not anymore. Because politics, she'd soon learned, wasn't what it was supposed to be. Her father and grandfather had passed on foolishly idyllic notions of what it meant to be a public servant to Cilla as a child, ridiculous flights of fancy that were as far off in the reality department as a nonmedicated schizophrenic's thought processes.

Cilla had thought to use her money and familial influence to effect meaningful changes. She wanted to force deadbeat dads to pay child support, lower the crime rate, feed the hungry, educate the masses, and get tough on terrorism to boot. She wanted to serve humankind, to make a real difference in the lives of those who had little hope left to them.

Her dreams had been smashed to bitter pieces within two weeks of arriving in Washington. She was no public servant, she'd soon learned. The public served her. What she was, she now knew, was a corporate servant. Corporations told her what to do, and she, the mediator, decided how much the public would let said corporations get away with. It was as simple and ugly as that.

It was probably, she mused, little wonder that her sexual fantasies had evolved into the complexly submissive scenarios that they had. Every day, every hour, every minute, *someone* was kissing her ass. From other senators who needed a favor, to oil barons who needed a favor, to the janitor down the hall who needed a favor . . .

Cilla sighed as she logged on to her *SpankMeImA-NaughtyGirl* account. Somebody was always kissing her ass because somebody always needed a favor.

She smiled when she saw that Claude had emailed her again. Claude—

He was sexy, if he looked anything like his photograph. She could have had him checked out, she supposed, but to what purpose? It wasn't like she was *really* going to meet him. Yeah right! Of course, Claude didn't know that. Yet.

Cilla would cyber-play with Claude until he realized she had no intention of meeting in R/T (online lingo for "real time"), then he would "dump" her, and she'd move on to a new online Master. She'd repeated this particular performance more times than she could count, so she already knew how it would play out.

It amused her to talk—or type—dirty things to men online. Sometimes she even giggled, which she never did in real life, when she allowed herself to imagine the dumbfounded expressions that would have been on the men's faces had they realized the one talking dirty to them was a "conservative" Republican senator with more money than Midas and more power than the electric company.

She was, of course, careful not to divulge information that could be traced back to her—very careful. Cilla was even in the habit of making up various physical descriptions for herself every time she hunted for a new play Master. She mostly liked being a redhead with fair skin and blue eyes. She didn't know why, just one of those things, she supposed.

Therefore, she was both amused and stunned by the fact that she'd given her real age and physical description to Claude. She'd even admitted to him that her first name was Priscilla. Truthfully, it didn't matter much. Hair color, eye color, and a first name hardly made her traceable. It was the very fact that she had given him the information to begin with that stupefied her.

Cilla found herself wondering why—why him, why now? In the three years she'd been playing D/s games online, she had met some terrific men. Men she would have liked to get to know in real life, perhaps even had real sex with. If she were honest with herself, she would have to admit that Claude was at the top of that list. But Senator Priscilla Harrington-Barnsworth could never chance meeting any of them, not even Claude.

Cilla was, after all, a Harrington.

Thomas stared at Nikki through hooded eyes as he watched her prepare bacon and eggs for breakfast. Seated at the tiny kitchen table, he was wearing unzipped jeans and nothing else. The good doctor, on the other hand, was totally naked. Just the way he liked her. Just the way he wanted to keep her.

Nikki had flat-out told him she didn't want to be owned in any way except sexually. Fair enough. He frowned. He'd just have to keep her naked as much as possible to make certain their entire lives revolved around sex, then.

I'm a Neanderthal. So shoot me.

Thomas realized he was a difficult man to put up with. Very difficult. His personality had always tended toward the jealous side with women he was serious about, but with Nikki he felt downright possessive. The mere thought of another man kissing her on the cheek, let alone doing what he'd done to her last night—and what he'd be doing to her again after breakfast—was enough to make his nostrils flare and his jaw clench.

She wielded a power over him and his emotions in a way he suspected she didn't yet realize. The irony was not lost on him. He held all the power over her during sex, but she held that power over him outside of it. All the more reason to keep her busy in the bump-and-grind department, he thought grimly.

"What are you snarling about?" Nikki cheerfully asked as she fried up bacon at the stove.

Thomas frowned. As if he'd admit that aloud. "I'm hungry," he growled. "How long does it take to fry up bacon?"

"As long as it takes to be done," she replied, her good mood undaunted.

Par for the course, he thought with down-turned lips. She now knew him too well to get put off by his surliness. Sweet lord above, what defenses did he have left to him? He sighed as he absently raked a hand over his jaw. At the rate they were moving, he'd be putty in her hands outside of a week. Surly, snapping putty, but still.

"I'm gonna go check to see if that ad posted yet," Thomas muttered, standing up and pushing away from the table.

"Okay. I'll let you know when breakfast is ready."

He grumbled his agreement and stalked off. Putty, he thought gloomily. Putty.

* * *

The e-book publisher was a dead-end, Ben had said. Thomas wasn't surprised and hadn't expected to find anything. He had hoped that because the e-book publisher specialized in erotic *romances* that most customers would be female and a male buyer would stick out like a sore thumb. Wrong. The gender breakdown was about 60/40 favoring females, so men didn't stick out at all.

Furthermore, the name Richard Remington was not in the publisher's customer database. Thomas knew that alias of Lucifer's was a made-up one anyway, that the real Richard Remington was truly a conservative teacher, so it wasn't exactly a surprise to find out he wasn't a customer.

Twenty minutes, a dead-end lead, and no posted ad later, Thomas's head shot up when Nikki's voice floated out from the kitchen to announce breakfast. "Be there in a minute," he told her as he closed down the laptop, wondering how the hell long it would take for the ad to post. He considered simply asking Nikki what the time differential was between posting it and having it go live, but that would only force him to think about the fact she'd put an ad in at Dom4me.com before.

He was having a difficult enough time coming to terms with all the feelings he'd allowed himself to mentally admit to in regards to the surgeon. Adding jealousy into the mix was a bit much a bit soon.

Upon arriving in the kitchen, and more specifically upon viewing the object of his desire and affection serving breakfast in the nude, all thoughts of jealousy, psychos, and anything else that wasn't Nikki flew out the proverbial window. Like the human male version of Pavlov's dog, his eyes immediately grew heavy-lidded, his cock erect. He pulled down his jeans and stepped out of them, raising an eyebrow when she glanced toward him and stilled.

"I see we're hungry," Nikki said with a smile as she dished out bacon and eggs onto the plate before him.

He grunted. Catching the double entendre, he decided to answer like for like. "Come feed me, then," he growled.

Her cheeks reddened a bit, which Thomas found more adorable now than ever before. Especially considering everything he'd done to her last night. He'd taken her three times before letting her go to sleep. He'd sucked on her pussy again, she'd sucked on his cock, he'd taken her from the front, from behind, and every which way his heart desired. Yet after all that she could still blush. Adorable. Too goddamn adorable, he thought grimly.

"Yes, sir," Nikki said after setting the pans back down on the stovetop. She rinsed her hands in the sink, then wiped them dry on a towel. "Let me get a fork."

"Come here," Thomas murmured. His dark eyes trailed over her well-rounded backside, and then, when she turned around to face him, over her pierced nipples and trimmed pubic hair. "Sit on my lap."

She blew out a breath. "Okay," she whispered.

Nikki made to sit down on his knee. He grunted, shaking his head. "Sit on my lap, not my damn knee."

She blushed, grinning, but did what he said. "Like this?" Nikki murmured, straddling his lap. She wrapped her arms around his neck, thrusting her breasts into his line of vision.

His eyelids were so heavy with arousal he could barely keep them open. "Almost," Thomas drawled. "I've got the perfect seat for you. Guaranteed you won't fall off." He smiled at her chuckle. "Sit on him," he said thickly, his expression turning serious. "Please," he rasped.

Nikki's breath caught in the back of her throat as she sank down onto his erect cock and enveloped him inside of her warmth.

His teeth gritted at the exquisite feel of her tight, wet pussy wrapped around him, squeezing him. He could stay like this forever, Thomas thought in a rare moment of unstoppable nostalgia. Buried ten inches deep inside the woman of his dreams.

Bending his head to her breasts, he drew one plump nipple into his mouth and leisurely sucked on it. She shivered, a small breathy moan escaping from between her lips.

Thomas raised his dark head. "Feed me," he murmured, his gaze snagging hers.

Nikki blinked. She took a deep breath and exhaled. Moving her hips, she slowly began undulating them back and forth, riding up and down the length of him as she stabbed the fork into a pile of eggs. "I think this requires more coordination than I've got," she gasped.

He grunted. "A skill any devoted sex slave should acquire," he informed her.

She stopped riding him. Her eyes narrowed almost imperceptibly. "There's been one before me?" she asked a bit shrilly, making his heart thump.

His eyes widened just a bit, the knowledge that Nikki was jealous somehow making him feel good. She didn't want another woman touching him. Good.

"No," Thomas admitted, his gaze boring into hers. "You're the first and you'd better be the last," he growled. That was as much of an emotional confession as he was up to, so he was glad and more than a little relieved when she smiled, let the subject go, and continued riding him.

She shoved a forkful of eggs into his mouth. He tried to concentrate on chewing and then swallowing them, knowing they both needed to eat, but all he wanted to do was take her back into the bedroom and ride her like there was no tomorrow.

Thomas blew out a breath. "You eat some of those eggs, too," he murmured. His eyebrow quirked. "You'll need the energy."

But Nikki had other plans. Apparently she had gotten as worked up as he currently was, for the next thing Thomas heard was the sound of a fork clanging against a plate. A second later, her arms were wrapped around his neck, her head was thrown back, and she was moaning and groaning as she bounced away on top of him.

He about came just watching her big breasts jiggle. The sound of her pussy repeatedly suctioning him inside her made beads of sweat break out on his forehead.

Thomas's jaw clenched. His fingers found her waist and dug into the flesh there. "I guess the goddamn eggs can wait," he gritted out.

Chapter 21

Wednesday, July 23
2:07 P.M.

Thomas stared at nothing as he listened to Ben spill out the facts to him over the cell connection. The things Detective O'Rourke was saying to him felt surreal, as if they couldn't possibly be true. Thomas's body had gone numb, though he could feel his stomach knotting up and his heart dropping into it.

"You're sure?" he quietly asked.

"Yeah." Ben sighed. "We can't be one hundred percent positive until the DNA results come in, but the blood type is a definite match." He paused, his tone sympathetic. "I'm sorry, man. I've never been sorrier about anything in my whole fucking life."

Thomas closed his eyes against the pain. The search of James's house was still in the discovery phase, but the CPD had already recovered a few items from it, such as hair and fibers, that his partner would have a hard time explaining away. The most difficult discovery from Thomas's vantage point, however, was the blood-soaked shirt that had been found wedged between two books in a closet.

More horrific still, it was a blood-soaked shirt that had belonged to his sweet, dead Amy.

"I feel like I'm gonna be sick," Thomas rasped out.

Ben was silent for a moment. "I know this is hard, but we need to focus here for a minute. I'm doing my damnedest to locate James, but right now the chief wants it kept quiet. Until we know for sure—"

"Amy's shirt is a pretty good sign," Thomas snarled. "What the fuck else does he need?"

"I agree. I think he's just having a hard time accepting it. A part of him is still searching for another explanation."

Thomas briefly closed his eyes, understanding that feeling all too well. "Is he giving you the kind of help you need?"

"Yeah—yeah!" Ben quickly assured him. "It's just, well, they ain't you, buddy. I sure could do with an experienced set of eyes."

"I can't." Thomas sighed. "I want to come back and help you, goddamn, you must know I want to come back and help you—"

"But Dr. Adenike."

"Exactly," Thomas murmured, running a hand over his jaw. "You saw Monica Baker-Evans postmortem. I can't let that happen to her."

Ben sighed. "Look, I'm not trying to be a dick here . . ."

"But?"

"What if we never find James?" he asked reasonably. "I mean, you can't stay in hiding with her forever. The chief will allow you only so long. You know that."

And Thomas had already considered that. "I'll take personal time if I need to," he said firmly.

"And when that runs out?"

Thomas frowned. "Hell, I don't know." He sighed. "I haven't got that far along in my plans. Look, hang tight, O'Rourke. Keep searching. In the mean time, let's wait and see what happens with the ad Nikki and I put in at Dom4me.com. It might be the break we need."

"Will do."

"I need to go," Thomas said, his voice uncharacteristically subdued. "I've got . . . a lot of things to come to terms with."

"You don't need to explain, man." Ben sighed. "You don't need to explain a damn thing."

"Ohio Senator Priscilla Harrington-Barnsworth will return home to Cleveland next week for a four-day respite with her husband and son before resuming her duties in Washington. Speculation has arisen suggesting that November's campaign is the last reelection she will seek in the Senate, and that she will, in fact, run for the governor's office in four years. The senator's spokesman has declined comment, citing that the Harrington-Barnsworth camp can only focus on one race at a time."

Kim absently watched the midday news, her thoughts scattered. She sighed as she flicked off the TV by remote, then stood up and slowly made her way toward her bedroom window. Her ankle was doing a lot better and seemed to get stronger with each passing day. Thank god, too, because she was due to head back to Eastern Academy to teach in a few short weeks.

Her blue eyes flicked beyond the window to where Megan was shooting a gun at a makeshift target. Kim had to squint to see her because Megan was a good ways down the estate in the side yard. *A gun . . .*

Kim shook her head, disbelieving that her stepmother had done something like purchase a revolver, let alone teach herself how to shoot one. It might have been understandable given the current circumstances, but it was still completely out of character for her. Or was it out of character? Kim conceded that she didn't really know because she didn't know her stepmother as well as she'd thought.

The things Megan had said to Kim two days ago had truly thrown her for a loop. She hadn't sought her stepmother out, or even talked to her since then, because in all honesty she didn't know what to say. A part of her wanted to try, to give Megan another chance, but another part of her couldn't help but to remember all those embarrassing occasions she'd brought friends home only to find Megan drunk as a skunk, passed out on various pieces of furniture.

"Oh, how adorable," she could still hear Cilla Harrington (now Harrington-Barnsworth) saying in that pompous, contemptuous tone of hers, "is this part of Laura Ashley's latest collection?"

Not that she really cared what Cilla Harrington and others like her thought. But still . . .

Kim's hopes had been so high when her father had remarried. In the beginning things between her and Megan had been good, too. Kim had needed a mother and Megan had seemed to want a daughter. But the longer Roger and Megan Cox were married, the more withdrawn her stepmother had become. After that, the drinking began. Before Kim knew it, Megan was as estranged from her as Roger had always been.

Megan. She sighed. She couldn't think about her stepmother right now. Even if she wanted to, she still couldn't, for her mind as of late had been plagued with other things.

Kim couldn't pinpoint exactly what it was, but something didn't feel . . . *right.* It wasn't ESP or anything like that in so far as she knew, yet she'd been harboring a strange feeling in her gut ever since the night Ben had driven her, Megan, and Nikki back to the Cox estate. Actually, she'd been harboring that feeling ever since the day she had first met Ben in Detective Cavanah's office, but since she hadn't come into contact with him again until Nikki had received that email from Lucifer, the feeling had lain dormant.

The feeling, unfortunately, was back. Something wasn't right.

Kim sighed, having no idea what it was about Ben that made the tiny hairs at the nape of her neck stir. She frowned, hating it when things like that happened. It was like trying to recall a name or telephone number when your memory didn't feel like cooperating. The more she tried to figure it out, the fuzzier the impressions got.

Her absent gaze went back to Megan. She shrugged her shoulders, deciding to let the worry go for the time being. It wasn't like there was much choice.

Nikki's concern for Thomas grew more and more acute as the evening wore on. He'd been like this for hours now, drinking liquor and staring at nothing, his gaze absent. His five-o'clock shadow had already come back, which added an even more dangerous level to his appearance.

She wished she knew what was upsetting him. Unfortunately, he had refused to open up to her after he'd gotten off the phone earlier today and had locked himself in the bedroom for about two solid hours following that conversation. When he finally emerged, his breath reeked of alcohol and his speech, what little he'd granted her with, was slurred.

The drinking had only escalated from there. She had no idea how one man could hold down so much liquor without acquiring alcohol poisoning, but there it was.

Finally, unable to take any more, and totally worried about

Thomas, Nikki walked over to the couch and snatched the bottle of Jack Daniels from his hand. His eyebrows slowly drew together.

"Why the hell'd ya do that?" he slurred.

Her nostrils flared. "I think you've had more than enough. You need to go lie down. Try to sleep it off."

Thomas frowned. "I'm not tired."

"Yes, you are," she snapped.

"Has anyone ever told you what a meanie you are?"

"Every drunk the police have ever escorted into the hospital." She sighed, her eyes briefly closing. "Just go to bed, please."

"No." He glanced around. "Truthfully, I don't think I can walk."

Her jaw clenched. Surprise, surprise. "Will you go if I walk with you?"

His dark gaze flicked over her breasts before landing on her face. "Will you go to bed with me?" he asked thickly.

Nikki rolled her eyes. "Hate to break the news to you, Detective, but I'm a doctor. And as a doctor I am willing to wager you couldn't get it up right now if your life depended on it. Come on," she said, tugging at his arm, "let's go."

Thomas muttered something imperceptible under his breath, but allowed her to help him up. He leaned on her enough to stay upright, but even inebriated was careful not to give her his full weight. The last thing he needed was to topple her over. Lord knows if she fell on the floor, he'd go down with her. Then they'd both be stuck there for who knows how long, because he was pretty damn certain he wouldn't be able to get back up.

"I'm sorry," he groaned as Nikki led him into one of the bedrooms. "I don't ever do this. Really I don't."

Nikki said nothing. She could sense he meant his words. He was having a difficult time speaking, yet he'd wanted her to hear him say that. "Hey, the only one here you're hurting is yourself. Apologize to the mirror, because I'm not the one who's going to have the headache from hell when I wake up."

Thomas frowned. "You're right about that," he mumbled as she led him the rest of the way into the bedroom.

"Maybe next time you'll talk to me instead of drowning your sorrows in drink," Nikki said ruthlessly. She figured he was learning his lesson, because without a doubt he would be sick as a dog when he woke up. He was already heading that way quickly.

He half groaned and half whimpered as he plopped down onto the bed. "You're a big meanie, Dr. Cavanah."

Nikki's eyes widened when he called her by his last name. Her heart began beating rapidly. "Get some sleep," she whispered, reminding herself he'd been drinking. "I'll come check on you throughout the night."

Thomas rolled over onto his back and flung an arm over his head. "Nikki," he mumbled as he closed his eyes.

"Yes?" she quietly asked, still reeling from his reference to her as Dr. Cavanah.

"Come here."

She blinked, then did as he'd asked. Quietly padding back over to the bed, she came to a stop next to it.

"Come here," he growled without opening his eyes.

"I'm here."

He frowned, his dark eyes slowly opening. "Closer," he grumbled.

Nikki didn't know what he wanted, but figured he probably didn't either. What made sense to a man who had been drinking often made little or no sense to anybody else. Still, she leaned in closer, her breasts dangling next to his face. "Yes?" she whispered.

Thomas reached up and began gently massaging her nipples through the fabric of the T-shirt she wore. She swallowed a bit roughly, but didn't stop him. He played with them about thirty seconds or so, arousing her beyond belief, before his hands fell to his sides and his eyes closed again.

She blew out a breath and, with some effort, straightened up.

"I know what name I called you by," he muttered, as if reading her thoughts.

She stilled. "Get some rest," Nikki said softly. "You need it."

Thomas ignored her. "Freud once said the only time people tell the truth is when they are tired or drunk." He opened his eyes long enough to rake his gaze over her. "I'm both."

Nikki checked on Thomas countless times throughout the night. She could tell he was in a great deal of pain. Being a doctor, and worried to boot, she encouraged him to try and vomit just in case he did have alcohol poisoning. But even when she held out a garbage can for him to relieve himself in, he wouldn't do it. Too stubborn to show a weakness, she supposed.

Every time she went in the bedroom to check on Thomas, he didn't want her to leave. He would mutter for her to lie down beside him, which she did for the few minutes it would take for him to fall back to sleep.

She enjoyed those stolen moments more than she cared to admit. She doubted he'd remember the way she ran her fingers through his sweat-soaked hair, or whispered encouraging words to him as she kissed him on the forehead. She let herself indulge in those acts, reminding herself that it was now or never, for when he awoke he might still be upset and not want her around him at all.

Nikki thought back on Thomas's mumbled words about Freud, softly smiling as she did so. Inebriated as he was, the detective had more or less confessed that he harbored feelings toward her, feelings he was unlikely to admit to sober. If that was the case, any hopes at a future with him would be like the deaf leading the blind. He was too stubborn to admit to caring about her, and she was too wracked with self-doubt to admit to caring about him.

In some ways—for example, professionally—Nikki had a lot of confidence, but where relationships were concerned, and men in general, she possessed enough ego to fill the head of a pin, if that. Still, she hoped those mumbled words had been true. Even if nothing ever resulted from that confession, she'd always hug the memory close to her heart.

The next time Nikki entered the bedroom to check on Thomas, she could tell he was having nightmares. His forehead was sweating profusely, his body was shaking slightly, and he kept mumbling incoherently in a sad, broken voice that left her wondering more than ever before just what Detective O'Rourke had said to him on the phone to cause this.

"Amy," Thomas muttered, a pained expression on his face even in slumber, "my sweet Amy."

Nikki closed her eyes, hating herself for feeling jealousy. He was obviously speaking about a woman who had meant a great deal to him, a woman who had been killed at Lucifer's hands. She was dead, this woman, and yet Nikki was jealous of her. She hated admitting to it, but knew it was true.

Thomas's labored breathing told her his heart rate was over the top, a fact that made her forget her jealousy long enough to run to the bed and sit down beside him. "Shhh . . . you're okay, big guy," she whispered, running a soothing hand over his perspiration-drenched forehead. "It's just a dream."

"Amy," he whimpered, the first vulnerable sound she'd ever heard him make. He flung an arm over his head. "I love you."

Nikki closed her eyes against the pain, reminding herself that the woman was dead. *Don't be jealous of a ghost. That's not right.*

Right or not, the jealousy she felt in regards to Amy clawed at her gut, made her want to run as far and as fast as she could. It made her want to quit loving Thomas . . . .

Love him? She sighed. She just didn't know. But what she was certain of was the fact that she cared very deeply for him, apparently deeply enough to even experience jealousy she had no right to feel. And because she cared for him, the rest shouldn't matter. She needed to help him get through this night, if nothing else. When he had recovered, she would deal with the rest.

"Amy's okay," she whispered, tears welling in her eyes. She hated the pain he was going through and hated herself for the jealous way she'd reacted to it. "She's in a safe place now. Get some sleep, Thomas." She leaned over and kissed his forehead. "Get some sleep."

"I'm so sorry," Thomas rasped out before he finally collapsed and fell back to sleep. "Amy . . . so damn sorry."

Nikki inhaled deeply, then exhaled slowly. "She loves you, too," she whispered, her voice catching. "Go to sleep."

Chapter 22

Thursday, July 24
1:08 P.M.

Nikki's bags had been packed and ready to go since six o'clock in the morning. She hadn't gotten very much restful sleep last night, so as the day wore on she felt more and more fatigued. She had come this close to calling a cab and returning to Cleveland without telling Thomas in person, but in the end decided that as much as he had gone out of his way to protect her, she at least owed him something in the way of an explanation.

Not that she could tell him the truth about why she was leaving. The truth was too embarrassing . . . and didn't reflect well on her as a person.

What would she say to him if he pressed for the total truth? How could she ever look herself in the mirror again if she heard herself say the words aloud: *I am jealous of a dead woman. Yes, a serial killer is stalking me, but I'd rather face him than these feelings I have for you. No, I did not pass the sixth grade . . . .*

Nikki sighed as she placed her bags next to the front door, then stood there and stared at them. She knew Thomas was going to think she was an idiot for leaving, but in the end what could he do to stop her?

And would he even try? She morosely considered the fact that he might be just as eager to see her go. Maybe he was as uncomfortable being locked away with her in a world that boasted a population of two as she now was with him.

"Going somewhere, Doc?"

Nikki spun around on her heel, her eyes rounding. "I didn't realize you'd woken up yet."

Thomas frowned. "Apparently not," he muttered as he slowly walked toward her. "I've been awake for some time. Recovering."

Nikki's heart began rapidly palpitating, the same way it generally did in the detective's presence. Wearing only jeans, jeans that were slightly unzipped at that, he looked as masculinely beautiful as ever. She glanced down, absently noting the black hair that tapered off into a thin line that trailed down into his jeans and disappeared, before glancing back up to his face.

"I wasn't going to leave without telling you," she whispered.

His eyes narrowed. "You aren't going to leave period," he growled.

"Thomas . . ."

"What the hell is this about?" His nostrils flared. "Tell me."

She inclined her head, preparing to spew out her well-rehearsed speech. "I appreciate everything you've done to protect me," Nikki began, "but I need to get back to work before I don't have a work left to go to. I'll stay with Kim and Megan," she said quickly when his eyes further narrowed. "I'll have a well-trained guard with me at all times." She tentatively smiled, glad that she'd managed to get the entire speech out so well despite the fact that she felt like she was dying on the inside.

"Bullshit," he ground out, making her smile fade. "You'll have a well-trained guard with you at all times, true. I know that's true because I'm him." His jaw clenched. "Otherwise, everything you said is bullshit and we both know it."

Her chin went up a notch. "I'm leaving and that's that." Nikki sighed, rubbing her temples. "Look, Thomas, I don't want to argue. You and I both know it's illegal to hold me here against my will. There's no point in going through this. I'm leaving and I'm not changing my mind. Would you like to return to Cleveland with me, or should I call a cab and catch a flight?"

Thomas smiled—something he rarely did, so it immediately put her on guard. "Did you notice the deadbolt?" he murmured.

Nikki's eyebrows drew together. "Yes, what about it?"

"Did you notice it's been engaged, and won't open without a key?"

She stilled. She swiveled her neck around far enough to see what he was talking about. Sure enough, there it was. A tiny padlock she hadn't noticed before. A tiny padlock she was certain hadn't been there before. She whirled around to face him. "What kind of a game are you playing here? Give me the damn key!"

His eyebrows shot up. "Finders keepers, losers weepers."

She gritted her teeth. "What you are doing is illegal, immoral, and . . . and . . . arrg! Just give me the damn key!"

"Nope."

"I want to go home!" she screeched. "Thomas Cavanah—give me that key!"

"No." Thomas turned on his heel and strode toward the kitchen.

Nikki felt like screaming with frustration. Instead, she stomped off into the next room, following him. "What is the big deal if someone protects me here or in Cleveland? As to that, what's to stop Lucifer from finding me in Cincinnati if he wants me badly enough? What the hell is wrong with you? I want to leave!"

Thomas turned around and glared down at her. "Why?" he barked. "Tell me the truth or this conversation is over."

"I did tell you the truth!"

He frowned. "You might as well go to the bedroom and take a load off, Doc," he muttered. "Because this conversation is officially over."

Nikki's eyes turned a bit desperate. "You can't just keep me here like this," she breathed. "I want to leave. Don't force me to call the police on you, Thomas."

He sighed as he opened up the refrigerator. "You'll leave when I say so and not a moment before then," he told her in a monotone. "Would you like something to eat?"

Her nostrils flared. "Then you leave me no choice. I'm calling the police," she informed him as she spun around and made her way toward the living room.

Thomas slammed the refrigerator door shut and stomped off behind her. "Good luck," he growled, "because I've taken care of that situation too."

Nikki ignored him as she scooped the phone up off of its cradle.

"I knew you were packing, Doc. I saw you this morning when I got up to shower!"

She gasped when she realized the phone line had been disabled. "This is really smart!" she fumed as she slammed the phone down and spun around on her heel to face off with him. "What if something should happen and we needed to call out!"

"I'll use my cell!" he bellowed. His hand slashed through the air. "You're staying put, and that is that!"

"Thomas!" Nikki took a deep breath and blew it out. "Why are you doing this?" she asked more quietly, the fight slowly draining out of her. "Why?"

His jaw was clenched so tightly it looked like it might crack.

"Because I don't want you to leave me," he snarled. "There. I said it. Happy?"

Silence.

Yes, she was happy, she thought, swallowing. More than she cared to admit.

Nikki steeled herself against her emotions, feeling like she'd go mad if she didn't get some time away to sort through her confused thoughts. She hated herself right now, but she needed to leave.

"I can't stay," she said softly, glancing away. She shook her head, sounding as defeated as she looked. "I just can't."

"Is it because I'm a cop?" he asked roughly. "You decided that fucking me is akin to slumming it?"

"No!" How could he think that? "That's not true at all!"

His expression didn't gentle. "Then why?" Thomas demanded. "Make me understand."

"Because . . ." she began. Her mouth worked up and down to give him the truth, but nothing came out. "Because," she quietly reiterated.

"You're going to have to do better than that," he gritted out. "WHY?"

She closed her eyes. "Because maybe I don't want to be a replacement," she softly admitted, ignoring the anger in his voice.

Thomas blinked. "A what?" he frowned.

"A replacement." Her eyes opened.

"I heard you. But what the hell are you talking about?"

Her nostrils flared. Fine. He wanted to know the truth? Well then she'd give it to him! "Amy," she snapped. "She's all you talked about in your sleep last night, Detective."

Nikki felt like a trapped animal. She needed to get out of here—out and far away. Before she said anything else to make herself look like a bigger jerk. She marched toward the door, picking up her bags. "There! Now I've admitted what an asshole I am to be jealous of a dead woman! Now will you open the goddamn door!" she screeched, her face turning red.

"I don't believe this," Thomas muttered, shaking his head. His hands took to his hips in the football stance he favored. "Put down your bags and sit down. *Please*."

"Open. The. Door," she bit out, seething. "Now!"

"Sit down!" he bellowed.

"Open the door!" Nikki whirled around and began beating at the door. "Somebody help me! Call the police!"

Thomas was at the door in two big steps. He seized her by the shoulders and spun her around. "Stop it!" he raged, shaking her. "Goddamn it!"

Nikki wanted to cry. All she wanted to do was leave. She hadn't wanted to admit to her irrational jealousy, nor did she want to cause him further upset by going on about it. "*Please* . . . I know I don't have any right to feel this way," she said, her voice catching, "but I just need some time—"

"Amy was my daughter," Thomas said hoarsely, his dark gaze searching her face.

Nikki stilled. Her heart stopped beating for a moment. "Oh my God," she whispered.

Thomas's hands dropped from her shoulders. He turned around and slowly walked away a few paces. "Her mom—we were young," he said quietly. "Young and reckless. Eileen was fifteen when she got pregnant, and I was sixteen." He sighed, his back still to her, his hands finding his hips again. "She died giving birth," he murmured, inducing Nikki's hand to clamp over her mouth. "She lived about an hour, long enough to name our daughter Amy, and then she was gone."

Nikki slowly lowered her hand and balled it into a fist. "I . . . oh, Thomas," she said, her voice shaking.

"I don't remember much of Eileen," he admitted. "We'd only been going together a few months when she got pregnant. But Amy . . . well, she was the love of my life."

"I'm sure she was," she whispered.

"Amy was special," Thomas murmured. She could hear the pride in his voice. "She loved everybody, trusted everybody, always smiling. I don't think I ever saw that girl frown." He shook his head and sighed, his muscled back still to her. "I've never been real on the sunny side personality-wise, but my girl, she was like this bright shining light that never dimmed. An angel on earth I got to have for sixteen years. When she died . . ."

Nikki's eyes briefly closed as she choked back her tears. She knew how Amy'd died. At Richard's—Lucifer's—hands. "I'm so sorry."

Thomas turned around and faced her. Tears were gathered in his eyes, but they didn't fall. "She was raped and tortured for four days," he rasped out. "It's hard to live with myself, knowing that for four long days she spent every moment wondering why Daddy wasn't coming in to make the bad man stop hurting her."

"Oh, Thomas." Nikki felt like she was going to be sick. "Don't blame yourself. Amy must have known you did everything you could—"

"Let me show you a picture of my Amy," Thomas interrupted as he reached into his jeans pocket and pulled out his wallet. "I think you'll understand why I know that can't be true."

Nikki stilled, not certain what he meant. When he placed the worn photograph in her hand, a photograph she could tell he'd looked at countless times, her gaze slowly flicked down to Amy. She stopped breathing altogether, her eyes widening.

It was a photograph of Thomas and his daughter together at Christmas. They were both smiling, looking so happy. Thomas was holding on his lap a gorgeous sixteen-year-old girl with dark hair so much like his own. Amy's eyes, unlike her father's eyes however, were green and . . . severely sloped.

Nikki felt her heart freeze at the realization. "Your daughter had Down's syndrome?"

He nodded, closing his eyes.

"Oh my God."

"Amy was severely retarded. She wouldn't have understood what he was doing to her," he said hoarsely, his eyes filled with pain. "She just understood that he was hurting her and that Daddy wasn't stopping him."

Nikki's bottom lip trembled.

"When I found her body," he gasped, his voice breaking, "I just wanted to die, Nikki. I wanted to die so I could see Amy, so I could hold her again and tell her how damn sorry Daddy was."

Tears streamed down Nikki's face as she stared at him, her body simultaneously shivering and numb. "Thomas," she said shakily. "I'm so sorry."

He closed his eyes and took a deep breath. When he opened them, he turned around, giving her his back again. His head drooped down. "So that's who Amy is, Doc. I'm sorry I didn't tell you before, but it's hard for me to talk about my daughter."

Nikki had never felt lower in her life. Worse yet, she didn't know what to do, didn't know what to say, to atone for actions that had been born of what she now understood to be the worst possible kind of jealousy. Thomas looked so broken. So defeated and empty. And it was all because she'd more or less pressed him to relive the memories he'd tried so hard to forget.

"Thomas," she whispered, her voice catching. She slowly walked toward him and laid one shaking palm on his back. "I . . ."

Nikki's face scrunched up, the pain she felt for him and Amy tearing at her insides and making her weep. "I'm such a jerk," she gasped, burying her face into his back. "I am so incredibly sorry for taking you through that."

His body tensed. "It's okay, Doc. I wanted you to know."

Thomas slowly turned around and drew Nikki's crying form into his arms. He sighed as he held her, resting his chin on top of her head while she clung to him and quietly sobbed. "I hope now you understand why I don't have it in me to let you walk out that door," he murmured.

She nodded as she cried, too emotional to speak.

"I care about you very much, Nikki. I don't want to lose you when I've finally found you," he whispered.

Nikki's head rose from his chest. Her eyes were red and puffy, her face tear-streaked as she searched his gaze. "I care about you, too," she admitted, her voice still shaky. "That's why I wanted to leave."

He frowned, releasing her so he could use the pads of his thumbs to wipe at her tears. "Leaving me's a funny way to show it," he grumbled.

She half laughed and half groaned. Her eyes gentled as she looked at him. "I deserve for you to hate me."

He searched her face. "Nah, I could never hate you," he murmured. He took a deep breath and blew it out as his gaze shot up and absently raked the ceiling. "You and I have got some things we need to discuss, Doc."

She realized he wanted to back away from the subject of Amy as much as possible, which she could hardly blame him for. The moment, and his memories, had become too emotionally raw. "Such as?"

"Such as the fact that you can't leave."

She glanced away. "I know that now," she acknowledged. "I won't ask again."

Silence.

"Detective O'Rourke found a blood-stained shirt at my partner's house," Thomas finally said.

Nikki stilled. She briefly closed her eyes, sighing. "That was what the phone call was about yesterday? The one that led to your drinking binge?"

He nodded, his gaze finding hers. "It belonged to my daughter," he quietly admitted.

She blew out a breath, feeling as though she might be sick. Pushing away from Thomas, she ran a hand through her hair. "I'm against the death penalty, you know. But in this instance I could flip the switch without remorse," she gritted out. "Remorse?" She snorted. "Who am I kidding? Hell, I'd probably enjoy it. Pretty sick, huh?"

Thomas sighed. "If it is, we're both sickos."

Nikki was quiet for a long moment, her expression mulling. When finally she looked up at him, her anger had been replaced by sorrow.

"I won't ask you to tell me how you feel," she whispered. "I can't pretend to know what it is you are going through. Finding out your partner is responsible for Amy's death would be as devastating as if I found out Kim was the one who'd tried to kill me." She shook her head. "Just know I'm here if you feel like venting, okay?"

He stared at her. "Thank you," he said softly.

She nodded. Her forehead wrinkled when something occurred to her. "Wait a minute. If we know who Lucifer is, why are we staying here in Cincinnati?"

Thomas frowned as he turned to stroll into the kitchen. "Because he's on the loose. We know who did it, but James—Lucifer—hasn't been apprehended yet."

Nikki followed him with her gaze. "You making something to eat?"

"Yeah," he called out. "Truthfully my appetite is nil, but my stomach is growling something fierce. Figured I'd better eat so I don't get sick."

"I'll take whatever it is you're making, too," she said absently, her gaze going toward the living room table where the laptop sat. "I'm going to sign on and see if our ad posted yet."

"Let me know if it did."

"Will do."

Kim sat at the kitchen table as she watched Megan chop up salad greens for dinner. Her stepmother had a flushed look about her, indicating she'd been in the sun a bit too long today. It seems she was taking target practice in the side yard very seriously. And, Kim begrudgingly conceded, she was getting good at it, too.

"Megan?"

"Yes, dear?"

Kim sighed, her hand running through her long, blonde hair. She stood up and pushed away from the table, gaining Megan's full, wide-eyed attention. "I just wanted to say . . ."

Her stepmother seemed to swallow quickly. "Yes?"

"I . . ." Kim frowned. She wasn't quite ready to let bygones be bygones, but she realized that carrying on in the childish way she had been wasn't getting them anywhere, either. "You, uh, you make great salad," she grumbled.

Her stepmother's face seemed to fall a bit. "Oh." Megan cleared her throat. "Well, thank you, dear." She turned back to the counter and continued chopping up vegetables.

Kim briefly closed her eyes, then opened them to focus at her stepmother's back. "I love you, too," she softly admitted. "But we've got a lot of water under the bridge between us." Megan's back tensed, but she didn't look up from her work. "Let's give our relationship some time and see where we go from here. Okay?"

Her stepmother slowly turned her head to study her face. Tears that didn't fall were gathered in her eyes. "I—I'd like that," she said shakily.

Kim nodded. "Me, too." Afraid she might cry, and determined not to, she took a deep breath and wobbled out of the room, leaving Megan to stare after her.

It took five minutes to ascertain that the ad had been posted at Dom4me.com. It took only another minute to realize that the fictional female CEO Nikki and Thomas had created together had yet to receive any responses from would-be suitors.

"The ad could have been live for only ten minutes for all we know," Nikki assured Thomas as he plopped down beside her on the living room floor and handed her a plate with a hotdog and chips on it. "I know it's difficult, but we need to be patient."

"Difficult is a good word," he muttered. "There is also exasperating, irritating, frustrating, and *pissing-me-off*." He frowned. "I just hope he takes the damn bait."

Nikki gave that some thought as she bit down into the hotdog. "He will," she said from around a mouthful of meat and bun. She snuggled in closer to Thomas, laying her head against his chest when he wrapped a solid, muscled arm around her. “He will.”

Ten minutes later, both of their heads shot up when the computer announced that they had an email.

Chapter 23

Thursday, July 24
11:31 P.M.

Seated next to Thomas in the Ford Taurus, Nikki sat in silence as they steadily made their way back to Cleveland. It was over. The nightmare had ended. For her. She knew it was just the beginning, however, for the man seated beside her.

No faster had the computer announced an incoming email than a call had come in from Detective Ben O'Rourke announcing that James had been found and that the police were preparing to storm his motel room as they spoke. Sadly, Detective James Merdino had been apprehended while sending an email, leaving no doubts in anyone's mind but that he was the one who had responded to the fake CEO's ad. Nobody could verify that, and it was doubtful anyone ever would. Lucifer was a computer expert well-versed in rerouting emails to dummy servers. Still, James's laptop had been confiscated and Leon Walker was busily sifting through it for evidence.

It didn't matter. Not any longer. Everyone knew the truth.

There were so many things Nikki wanted to say to Thomas, but she realized there were no words to help what he was currently going through. What a bittersweet night for him, she decided. After all these years, he'd finally found his daughter's killer, but at what price? Only to learn that the one man he trusted more than any other, his own partner and best friend, was her murderer. She couldn't begin to imagine how painful that must feel.

Oddly enough, she'd given little thought so far to what this new development meant to her own situation from a personal standpoint. Richard—James—was captured. Life could return to normal. She was grateful it was so, but wished normalcy could have been handed back to her without Thomas getting hurt in the process.

Nikki's head turned. Her gaze lingered at his haggard profile, noting the sternness of his features. The rigidity of his jaw, the stark gaze that was somehow faraway yet intense at the same time.

"Are you okay?" she whispered.

He didn't answer for a long moment. "I've been better," he finally drawled.

"I bet."

Thomas sighed, his eyes never straying from the road. "Look, Doc . . ."

Nikki quirked an eyebrow, but said nothing.

"I know you mean well and all, but—"

"But you need to go through this alone." She sighed, glancing forward to absently stare out the windshield. "I won't pretend to know how you must be feeling, but needing to come to terms with it alone . . . well, that I can understand all too well," she murmured.

His callused hand found her knee and gently squeezed. "Thanks, Nikki," he muttered. "You're a special lady."

Nikki cocked her head enough to smile at him. "You're welcome."

Turning away, she snuggled up as best she could against the passenger side window and attempted to fall asleep. When slumber finally came, it only lasted in short ten-minute spurts here and there. Nikki couldn't say why, but an ominous feeling had settled in her belly, a feeling that told her the situation was about to get a whole lot worse.

Surely one of the first things Thomas would do upon their return would be confront his partner. She could only imagine what would happen from there.

"Hello? Hellooooo?"

Priscilla Harrington-Barnsworth frowned as she impatiently waited for the caller to say something—anything. This was the third phone call she'd received in the past few days during which the aggravating person on the other end of the line said nothing. All three times she'd attempted to trace the call. All three times her secretary had come up with nothing.

She hated to admit it, but something about this situation didn't settle well with her. None of her personal phone lines were supposed to be traceable, and all the other lines were answered by assistants. Had one of her online men managed to track her down against all odds? Did one of them, Claude perhaps, realize who she was?

No—definitely not. It wasn't possible, she assured herself, biting down on her lower lip. She'd been so careful. Discretion should have been her middle name. Priscilla Discretion Harrington-Barnsworth. It was certainly more attractive than her true legal one: Matilda.

"Hello?" Cilla gritted out, now angry. The call seemed to be coming from somewhere heavily populated. A bar perhaps? "Look," Cilla huffed, "either state what it is you want or quit calling. I hold little patience for wimps."

"Priscilla," a male voice breathed into the phone. Apparently the cutting remark had gotten her somewhere. "You sound as sexy as I knew you would."

Her eyes widened. Oh damn. Not just any man would speak to her in that fashion.

"Who are you?" she asked weakly.

He chuckled. "The love of your life, darling. Surely you must know that."

Fuck. "I can't imagine who you are," she lied, her heartbeat thumping like mad. "Don't ever call this number again."

Her hands shaking, Cilla turned off her cell phone and held it against her chest. The caller ID had shown UNKNOWN, meaning she couldn't readily ascertain what number Claude had dialed from. Whenever UNKNOWN popped up on her cell phone, she always assumed the call came from Otis or her father—the two people in her life who made a habit of keeping themselves untraceable. Such was the only reason she'd taken the damn call to begin with.

Cilla didn't move for what felt like an hour, her feet and hazel gaze rooted to the same spot, as her entire future, or lack of it, flashed before her eyes. The election was in a little over three months.

Damn. Damn. Damn.

She closed her eyes and breathed deeply, feeling as though she might be sick. She had to find this man, she thought desperately. She had to find him and either pay him off or . . . or something. Anything—she'd do anything to keep him quiet.

"What the hell's got you looking like that, Cilla?"

Her head shot up at the sound of her father's aging but still authoritative voice. "Oh, Daddy," she cried, her voice catching, "Daddy, help me."

Maxwell Harrington frowned. His forehead wrinkled as he studied her face. "Oh fuck, Cilla. You haven't been messing around online again, have you?" He sighed, her expression telling him all he needed to know. "You're a married woman!" he snapped. "Hell, I don't give a damn about Otis, but Jesus H. Christ, what do you think will happen to your career if word gets out?"

"I'm finished," she mumbled. She couldn't be totally certain the caller had been Claude, but her gut instinct was declaring it so. And, unfortunately, Claude didn't sound like a man who would conveniently disappear into the woodwork. No. He wouldn't, she realized. How could she have been so stupid? "It's over."

Her father thumped his fist on the desk. "Like hell. Tell me what's going on," he demanded as he took her by the elbow and steered her into the adjoining parlor.

It took all of ten minutes to bring him up to speed. She confessed everything, finishing up at the point when she'd hung up, right before Maxwell had entered her suite. She was pacing by the time she'd finished, biting her nails as she wore a hole in the carpet.

"What do I do, Daddy?" Cilla nervously asked before resuming her nail biting.

"For one thing you quit biting your nails. You just had them manicured, and stubby fingers aren't a good look for a senator."

Maxwell sighed, scratching his short salt-and-pepper beard as he gave the situation some thought. "Suddenly I know how all of President Clinton's aides must have felt," he muttered. "Doing everything they could do to clean up his sex-life fiascos." His eyebrows shot up when his daughter threw him a frown. "Well hell, Cilla. Gain a hundred pounds, grow a penis, and you two could be twins. Especially after you voted for that antigun bill." He grunted. "How any self-respecting Republican can vote to stiffen the gun laws is beyond me."

She threw up her hands, exasperated. "Because it's what I believe in! And I won't be voting for any more bills period if you don't help me figure a way out of this goddamn mess!"

Cilla knew that if anyone could turn the situation around it would be Maxwell Harrington. He was a man obsessed when it came to her career. Far more concerned with it than she ever had been, in fact. Where Maxwell hadn't had what it took to advance his career beyond the senate before he retired, his daughter did possess that indefinable something, that cult of personality one shows to the masses to snag votes.

She realized that, vicarious or not, she was her father's only shot at being in the governor's mansion, and quite possibly the White House. Maxwell loved her as any father loves a daughter, perhaps more so, but it wouldn't be love that would drive him to root Claude out. It would be obsession. Nothing would come between Cilla and Maxwell's goals for her if it could be helped.

"I'm thinking. I'm thinking. Are you sure it's this Claude character who's been calling you?"

"No," she slowly admitted. "But the odds are definitely leaning heavily in that direction. Who else could it be?"

"A crank caller?" he said hopefully. Maxwell sighed at her frown. "You do tend toward the dramatic at times, Cilla."

"Okay," she finally conceded, "I suppose there is a chance it could be a crank caller. But I still feel the situation warrants looking into!"

"I'll take care of it," her father announced as he stood up. He ran his hands over his suit jacket, smoothing it out. "In the interim, I want you to return to Cleveland this very moment. Have Beverly cancel whatever it was you were supposed to do tomorrow. Nobody can accuse you of sleeping around if you're in Cleveland with Otis by your side."

Cilla nodded. "Yes. Yes, of course. I want to see my son, anyway."

Maxwell grunted. "You might do well to think of Todd the next time you get it up your ass to do something stupid. Do you have any notion what this will do to him if word gets around what his mother has been up to?"

She winced and took a deep breath. "I know." Cilla had never particularly cared for Otis one way or the other. Any socially presentable man would have done as a husband. But their son was a different story altogether.

For the first time she understood why it was that her father sank to such depths to save her every time she needed saving. It was more than obsession with her career. It was more than a desire to see his flesh and blood achieve what he couldn't. It was something far more primitive and primal. A genetic instinct that drove a person to cut off any threat to the survival and livelihood of one's offspring.

Cilla's eyes followed her father as he made his way from the parlor. "Daddy?"

Maxwell stopped in his tracks long enough to look at her from over his shoulder.

"Thank you."

By the time Nikki and Thomas made it back to Cleveland the next morning, Thomas's entire demeanor had changed. Gone was the passionate lover who couldn't keep his hands off of her, and in his place was a cold, frighteningly aloof man Nikki'd never been introduced to before. Even in the car, his thoughts miles away, the need to touch her had always, at minimum, compelled him to leave a hand resting somewhere on her body. Now it was as though that affection had never been.

Realistically, she knew not to expect more than this from Thomas. Her brain understood, but his coldness still left her feeling rejected. From a mental and emotional standpoint, Thomas was going through more than she could fathom. Intellectually speaking, she understood that he needed to put up the walls to get through what was sure to be a hellish day of reckoning on his part. Now if only her brain would explain that to her wounded heart.

Nikki stared up at the high-rise apartment complex that was her home, somehow feeling disjointed from it now. She'd been gone but a few days, yet it felt like forever since life had been normal here. She sighed, wondering if this place would ever feel like home again.

"Thanks for the lift," Nikki said, her green eyes turning to look at Thomas. "I suppose you need to be going."

"Yeah," he muttered. "I do." He ran a hand over his jaw, never once looking at her. The frostiness of his expression made her feel cold and empty inside. "You want me to walk you up?"

Yes, but she'd never admit that. "No." She shook her head. "I'll be fine. You go do what you need to do." She glanced at the clock in the dashboard. "I better go. I need to call my boss and let her know I'll be coming in tonight."

Thomas nodded, still not looking at her. "Take care of yourself, Doc."

Her stomach muscles clenched. That almost sounded like good-bye. Maybe it was good-bye.

Determined not to show any vulnerability, Nikki opened the passenger side door and climbed out of the Taurus. Making a feeble attempt at a wave, she turned, briskly walking toward the high-rise's entrance.

Chapter 24

Friday, July 25
7:31 P.M.

"Hey, Nita. Mind if I have a seat?"

Juanita Brown's gaze flicked from the TV screen in the hospital cafeteria to Nikki. Her eyes widened. "Hey, girl! Where have you been?"

"Sick," Nikki informed her, deciding that wasn't altogether a lie. She definitely wouldn't be talking about what had really kept her away from Cleveland General for four days. Besides, she *had* been running a fever the first day.

"Oh, I'm sorry to hear that," the O.R. nurse said in the way of sympathy as she waved to the empty seat across from her. "Glad you're back, though."

"Me, too."

The conversation was friendly and light, typical of the way people chat with good work acquaintances they have no relationship with outside of their place of employment. Nikki had always thought highly of Juanita and enjoyed her company, but their personalities were too disparate to have much in common beyond Cleveland General and the occasional after-hours drink. Nita loved Cleveland's late-night scene and enjoyed the party life outside of work. Nothing wrong with that per se—it just wasn't Nikki's cup of tea.

"These political ads are always so syrupy sweet," Juanita snorted, her gaze going back to the TV console. She tucked a springy black curl behind an ear. "I wonder if people really fall for them."

Nikki grinned as she watched the brief and ultra-idyllic Harrington-Barnsworth television campaign ad with her colleague. "Gee, they even have a dog in this one. I didn't know Cilla had a pet. I thought fur gave her allergies!"

"Cilla?" Juanita's eyebrows rose. "You actually know the beanpole senator personally?"

Nikki shrugged. "More like my best friend knows her. They grew up together. Truthfully, I don't much care for her on a personal level. Too condescending for my taste."

Juanita smiled slowly. "I sense a bit of history there."

Nikki sighed. "A bit." Her expression was bemused. "I hate admitting to this now, Nita, but back in college I was a little jealous of her! She seemed to have it all together, if you know what I mean. The perfect woman with the perfect clothes and the perfect car who heralded from the perfect family."

"Uh huh."

"I tried to warm up to her for my best friend's sake, but it was mission impossible. She was always so cutting, so arrogant and rude."

Juanita frowned. "Not that I was before, but now I'm definitely not voting for her."

"Hey now!" Nikki grinned. "She could have changed. It happens."

"Hmmm . . ."

Nikki was about to chuckle when their conversation was interrupted by Dr. Michael Sorenson. She inwardly sighed, not in the mood to deal with him.

Nikki supposed she wouldn't have liked being overlooked for a promotion in lieu of a doctor that had been on staff for a shorter period of time, either, but she would have shrugged off such an event months ago. Not Sorenson. He was determined to prove wrong the chief of staff's decision to promote her.

She could only be grateful for the fact the jerk had no idea why she'd been absent the past four days. If the surgeon ever did learn the details, he'd probably embarrass the hospital into firing her. Indeed, he'd already made at least three flippant remarks tonight about how she couldn't even see fit to show up to work, muttering under his breath about what immoral things she'd probably been doing in lieu of her job.

"I see we finally made it back to work," he said in a pompous tone that grated.

Her smile was as syrupy sweet as the one Cilla favored for the cameras. "Yes," Nikki replied with false cheer. "I'm feeling a lot better. Thanks for your concern."

Dr. Sorenson frowned, his dark eyes trailing over her face. "You look flushed."

God, he was weird. Probably one of those kooky, overly religious types. Granted, Michael Sorenson had no idea why Nikki had been gone the past few days, but neither was it his business, and she'd be damned if she'd enlighten him. Her life was no concern of his, and she planned on keeping it that way. "Recently recovered from a fever."

"I see."

"Hey," Juanita cut in, "dinner time is almost up." She rose from her chair, thankfully saving Nikki from further conversation. "Good to see you, Dr. Sorenson."

Michael inclined his head. "A good evening to you, Nurse Brown."

Nurse Brown. Nikki tamped down on the desire to roll her eyes at the way he'd emphasized the word "Nurse." She had never fallen for that line of bull that a doctor's position was superior to a nurse's. They were a team, all of them performing their own individually vital functions.

"Good evening, Dr. Sorenson," Nikki said, attempting to conceal her irritation. Following Juanita, she nodded before walking away.

"What is with him?" Juanita muttered under her breath once he was out of earshot. "Don't tell me he's still pissed about that promotion?"

"Yep." Nikki sighed. "Don't pay him any attention, Nita. I sure don't."

Work tonight had not been its usual respite. Far from it in fact. Her boss was out with the flu, and Dr. Sorenson was out to get her. . . . No changes there.

Nikki sighed as she finished donning her street clothes. Picking up her duffel bag, she quickly exited the hospital, walking toward her Mercedes in the underground staff-only parking garage. The sound of nearby cars starting up and the noxious smell of gas fumes punctured the air—just like always. Everything was normal once again. All was as it had been before "Richard."

Except for one thing, she silently admitted. Nothing could ever be the same again. Not after having spent those few days with Thomas.

He'd made her most secret fantasies reality. What's more, he was slowly but surely making her fall in love with him. She wished she could say the latter was due to sex, but she knew it wasn't. Her feelings had been deepening since before they'd slept together. Heck, she'd already been half in love with him the day he sent her those pistachios, she mused.

Opening the trunk of her car, Nikki threw the duffel bag inside and slammed it closed. She wondered what Thomas was doing this very moment, wondered too how he was coming to terms with all that had happened. She hoped that he'd want to see her again, but conceded that so much as looking at her might bring back painful memories he'd rather forget.

She had been with him, after all, when he'd received the bad news. Lucifer was, albeit indirectly, responsible for bringing them together in the first place. Perhaps the detective would have a hard time forgetting all of that.

Nikki frowned as she fumbled with the keys, telling herself she was behaving pathetically. If Thomas didn't want to see her again, that was that, and there was no sense in dwelling on what could have been but would never be. She was stronger than that, she realized. She'd just have to keep reminding herself of that fact.

But it was difficult. Opening herself up to him in the way she had, surrendering total power to him while he handcuffed her to the bed and had his wicked way with her . . .

Well, the books on D/s had been correct. A special, inexplicable bond had been forged with Thomas in those hours. A bond that, for her at least, would never be broken. She didn't know how much of it had to do with their far-from-ordinary sex and how much was due to the overall extreme circumstances they'd found themselves thrust into together, but she suspected it was both.

Opening the driver's side door, Nikki was about to seat herself inside the Mercedes when a funny feeling crept its way up her spine. It was an odd but unmistakable feeling, that eerie chill that alerts a person to the fact that they are being watched. She stilled, her gaze slowly and methodically scanning the parking garage as her heart rate accelerated.

Nothing. Not a damn thing.

She relaxed, deciding she was losing it. "The bastard is in jail," Nikki murmured to herself.

It angered her that even behind bars he wielded this much power over the normalcy of her day-to-day life. At least he did now that she was alone again. When she'd been at Thomas's side, no fear of him had existed.

Nikki shrugged off the bizarre feeling engulfing her. She couldn't and wouldn't live like this. Besides, she mentally grumbled as she fell into the car and slammed the door shut, the man who wanted to kill her was in jail where he belonged.

She sighed. She just hoped Thomas didn't end up in there with him after he got his hands on his alleged best friend.

It was the better part of the day and half the night before Thomas was permitted to see James. Nobody, from the chief of police to Ben O'Rourke to Nan in filing, felt that he should be alone in the same room with his ex-partner. He hated to admit it, but they were right. Rage had never consumed him—cold bitter hatred—in the way that it now did.

Being forcibly kept apart from James, when the desire to tear out the bastard's heart with his bare hands overwhelmed him, felt like punishment. Like a wild animal kept from hunting and killing its prey. He wondered if this was the same uncontrollable rage Lucifer went into during each of his murders. Lord knows this was the closest he'd ever come to understanding it.

Finally, after what felt like forever, Thomas was permitted to speak to James from the other side of the bars in the holding cell.

He had to be patted down first, all keys removed from his possession, so there was no way for him to get past those bars.

Usually the cold steel served the purpose of keeping criminals away from society so they couldn't inflict more damage on anyone. That was still true. But tonight the bars held a dual purpose—they also kept one sicko in particular from getting murdered at the hands of the man he'd once called partner and best friend.

His muscles tense, his jaw tight, Thomas slowly made his way down the hall to the cell where James was held. He came to a stop before it, noting the surprised expression on his ex-partner's face to see him standing there. Apparently he too had thought the chief would never leave them alone together. Not even with impenetrable steel bars between them.

Their gazes clashed and locked. James held his stare a moment longer, then looked away.

Silence consumed the holding-cell area, completely deserted for the moment. Thomas breathed deeply, realizing his questions would never be answered if he couldn't get a handle on his rage.

"Why?" he finally snarled. "Just tell me goddamn why."

James said nothing.

"*Why?*" Thomas bellowed.

James closed his eyes. He sighed, then opened them. "And if I told you I was innocent?" he asked in a monotone, his face averted from Thomas's.

"I'd say you're a liar." His jaw was so tight it felt like it might crack. "Don't give me this bullshit, James. Tell me. Off the record." His hands balled and unballed at his sides. The tentative control he'd held over his raw emotions was quickly evaporating. "O'Rourke found Amy's bloody shirt in your house," he gasped. "Why?" He was torn between wanting to cry, needing to vomit, and wanting to kill. "*Tell me.*"

"I didn't do it!" James bellowed as he shot to his feet. He began to pace from within the small confines of the holding cell, a tiny area that boasted a small bed and a toilet. "*Christ,*" he ground out. "I can't fucking explain that shirt, Cavanah. I don't know how it got there unless Lucifer put it there. All I know is I didn't kill her, *could never kill her*."

His ex-partner's eyes were wild, naked with upset and revulsion. Revulsion of himself perhaps? Or just revulsion that he'd finally been beaten at his game?

"I know you don't believe me," James muttered, running a punishing hand through his short light brown hair. "Shit, I wouldn't either. I fucked up when I lied to you about Lisa Pinoza. I know that! But this . . . my God, it's making my stomach turn."

Thomas closed his eyes and took a deep, steadying breath. Every man ever arrested said the same damn thing. It wasn't him. It couldn't be him. No way could he do something like that to another person. It was always the same line. In this case Thomas wanted to believe the line, but realized that he couldn't. His daughter's bloody shirt—there was no way to explain that away. No way in hell.

"I see this conversation is going nowhere," Thomas said, opening his eyes. "I asked for the answer to one question and you wouldn't even give me that."

"You want me to make something up?" James snapped. "Because that's what any alleged confession would amount to—lies!"

"How the fuck did my daughter's shirt get in your house?" Thomas bellowed, his hand slicing wildly through the air. His heartbeat was accelerating, perspiration breaking out on his forehead. "She trusted you, you sick fuck!" he raged, his teeth gritting as he grabbed the steel bars so tightly his knuckles turned white. Tears stung the backs of his eyes—whether from anger, sorrow, betrayal, or all three, he couldn't say. "She trusted you," he said hoarsely.

A pained expression crossed James's features. "I lied about Lisa. I don't deny it," he said softly. His voice caught. "But God in heaven, I could never have hurt Amy."

Thomas shook the bars once, his fury escalating. He wanted to believe him. Sweet lord how he wanted to. "Talk to me. Now. *Tell me*."

James was quiet a long, tense moment. "I was sleeping with Lisa," he finally muttered. "When she turned up dead . . . I don't know. I freaked out. All I can say is I freaked out! You were in Savannah visiting your mom, I didn't have you around to bounce my guilt and fear off of. I made the wrong decision, and it's been eating me up ever since! Shit!"

He began to pace again. "I had no alibi for the time frame of her death. *None,*" he said, slashing his hand through the air. "I freaked out. I just lost it."

"Lack of an alibi wouldn't have automatically made you look guilty," Thomas growled. "You can—"

"Bullshit!" James shot back. "I was fucking Lisa. I thought I was the only extramarital lover she had. She wound up dead—*dead!*—killed by a man everyone knew she was *willingly* going to meet. I had no alibi whatsoever." His jaw clenched. "That would have been enough and you know it. We've both seen men go to death row with far less 'evidence' to go on!"

Thomas ran a hand over his unshaven jaw, not able to refute that. He didn't know what to believe, and it was tearing him apart. He wanted to believe James more than he wanted to breathe, but the last time he'd put his trust into him he'd been calculatingly lied to.

"I'm not ready for this," Thomas muttered, backing away from the holding cell. "I thought I was, but I'm not."

James grabbed the bars as Thomas began to back away. "If I

had used logic back then," he rasped, "I would have realized I'd get to go free when Lucifer killed again. Because men like him can't stop. They need it like my old man needs a bottle."

Thomas's eyes narrowed. He turned on his heel, giving James his back as he walked away.

"He'll do it again!" James bellowed, rattling the bars. "Do you hear me? He'll do it again! He might stop for a while, feeling lucky that the scent has been thrown off his trail, but in the end the need for a fix will take over and *he will kill*. Listen to me, goddamn you!"

Thomas stilled, his body tense.

"Just watch out for Dr. Adenike," James said to his back, the fight going out of him. "When the house of cards started falling down around me I tried to hunt him like a man possessed. I don't know much more than I started out with, but I know he still wants her.

"I don't know why I thought I could find him alone when me and you together haven't found him after all these years, but then I don't know why I ran scared after Lisa was murdered rather than confide in you either. Call it desperation," he muttered. "A desperate mind grasps at anything."

Thomas said nothing. He hesitated for a long moment, and then left the holding cell.

Seeing Kim again felt so good Nikki about cried. She spent the first five minutes doing nothing but hugging her.

Seated at the kitchen table within the Cox estate, she spent the next half hour or so bringing her best friend up to speed. "I'm so tired," she finally finished, her expression far away, "but the thought of going back into that apartment alone is about as appealing as chewing broken glass."

Kim ran a gentle hand over her back. "Stay here tonight. You can go into work tomorrow directly from here."

"I don't have a work to go to."

Kim's eyes widened. "They fired you?" she asked incredulously.

"No—no!" Nikki shook her head, causing Kim to release a pent-up breath. "Sorry I wasn't clearer. They changed our schedules while I was away is all. I'm off Saturday and Sunday nights now."

"Whoa! That schedule almost fits that of a normal person," Kim teased.

Nikki smiled. "Almost."

Kim absently drummed her fingertips on the kitchen table as she gave that new development some thought. "Why don't we go away for the weekend?" she asked. "Maybe Amish country. Someplace relatively close and extremely noneventful."

"Sounds good," Nikki said with a small chuckle.

She wavered for only a second, long enough to wonder if Thomas would call while she was away, then discarded the possibility altogether. She doubted he'd call. And even if he did, she was not the type of woman who only spared time for her best friend when no available men were around. No matter who that man was. "Why don't we drive down tonight? I recall there being a quaint little Victorian inn close to Sugarcreek."

"Hmm . . . the one in Millersburg?"

"Yep. That's the one."

"Sounds good," Kim said, grinning. She rose up to her feet. "We'll do a little shopping, show off our scantily clad ankles to the yokels . . . it'll be a hoot."

"Scantily clad ankles," Nikki muttered. "Hell, let's just be really brazen and wear shorts. Show them Amish boys a little knee while we're at it."

Kim laughed as she hobbled away. "Let me leave Megan a note, and then we're outta here."

Chapter 25

Saturday, July 26
1:15 P.M.

Thomas paced inside his small office, agitated that Nikki still hadn't answered the phone. He'd called at least a dozen times to check up on her, paged her beeper just as many times, drove over to her apartment twice, and still hadn't located her. The hospital said she was off until Monday afternoon so not to expect her in unless an emergency surgery ensued.

He sighed as he hung up the cell phone, deciding to stop over at the Cox estate after he left headquarters to see if Nikki'd shown up there. He didn't know if he should be worried or jealous.

Unable to sort out how he felt about James, Thomas had decided to play it safe and make sure two cops stuck to Nikki like white on rice. Unfortunately, he'd given the order after she'd left work for the night. Both cops had reported that Nikki never showed up at home after leaving the hospital, so sticking to her like anything wasn't possible.

"He'll do it again! Do you hear me? He'll do it again! . . . Listen to me, goddamn you!"

Thomas had listened. Loud and clear. The rational part of his brain, however, told him Lucifer was behind bars where he belonged. "Face it, buddy," he muttered to himself. "Wanting James to be innocent damn sure don't make him that way."

He picked up some files to rifle through later at home and then left. He needed to talk to Nikki.

Scowling, Thomas read and reread the note Dr. Kimberly Cox had left behind for her stepmother:

> *Megan,*
>
> *As you know, Lucifer has been caught. Nikki and I both need to unwind a bit, so I'm taking her away for the three Fs—food, fun, and *ahem* flirting with handsome men. Call my cell if you need me. I'll see you on Sunday.*
>
> *Kim*

**ahem* flirting with handsome men.* His teeth gritted. Thomas realized that Kimberly Cox was probably only joking—he hoped—but that didn't lessen the intense jealousy coiling in his gut.

"Thanks for letting me know," Thomas muttered as he handed back the note to Megan Cox. "Have you spoken to your daughter recently?"

She nodded. "Both of them. Not even an hour ago. They sounded just fine."

He absently inclined his head.

"Is everything all right?" Mrs. Cox asked, her expression worried. "Should I call Kim on her cell phone?"

No, it sure as hell wasn't all right. The note didn't say where Nikki was, and the curiosity was killing him. There had better be no **ahem** anything, he thought grimly. Still, he didn't want to drag Dr. Cox and her mother into the middle of things. That wasn't Thomas's style, never had been. He'd wait to speak to Nikki until she returned from her weekend getaway—or until she saw fit to answer one of his numerous pages.

And just why wasn't Nikki answering his pages? Had she lied to him that night, saying she wanted to belong to him? Was it all just a bunch of words she used so he'd want to play out her sexual fantasies? She must have known how upset he'd be, that he'd need her after he saw James, yet she'd left him high and dry the moment she got off work.

The thought that he'd been used and tossed aside made his blood boil. But more to the point, it also hurt more than he cared to admit. Anger was easier to own up to, but he'd be a liar if he said his stomach wasn't twisted with hurt. Still, there was no need to worry Kim's mother.

"Everything's fine, ma'am," he assured her. "But if one of them should phone you again, please tell Nikki I'd like her to get in touch with me."

That seemed to lessen her anxiety. "Of course, Detective. Thanks for dropping by."

Thomas inclined his head then left.

"No . . . oh please—noooo!"

"Wake up, Kimmie. Wake up!"

Kim gasped as she bolted upright in the bed, sweat plastering the silk nightgown against her body like a second skin. Panting for air, her eyes wildly darted around the suite until realization dawned and she knew she'd been dreaming.

"Are you okay?" Nikki gently prodded as she brushed Kim's soaking-wet hair back from her forehead. Her eyes widened. "My God, Kim, you're in a cold sweat! That must have been one heck of a nightmare."

"It was," she admitted shakily, her eyes round as moons. Her breasts rose and fell with her labored breathing. "Damn," she muttered, briefly closing her eyes.

"Was it about . . . him?" Nikki softly inquired.

Kim nodded. "Yes. It was awful." Her face scrunched up. *"Awful."*

Nikki sighed but said nothing.

"It was like before," Kim whispered, her eyes opening, "but worse. A dark space. The scent of water. Rape. Torture. Death. And those eyes . . ." She shivered. "There's something strange about his eyes. They are so . . ."

"Blue," Nikki finished for her.

"Yes." Kim frowned. "Yes. So blue. Almost . . . too blue."

Nikki bit her lip. That same thought had gone through her mind before, too. Richard's eyes had seemed almost surreal. Like one of those dogs—Siberian huskies, she thought they were called. Or like a man wearing contacts for Halloween. But it didn't matter anymore. He was locked away. End of story.

"I don't like this," Kim muttered, tearing off the covers. "Something isn't right."

"Kimmie," Nikki gently reminded her as she helped her stand up. "He's in jail now. We're both safe. You've got to let him go."

Their gazes met and held. "Yes," Kim slowly agreed. She sighed.

"Of course, you're right." She smiled in a self-deprecating manner. "I guess my voodoo hocus-pocus hasn't figured that out yet, though."

Nikki chuckled at the reminder of how Detective Ben O'Rourke had referred to Kim's visions. "Go take a bath, kiddo. I'll find you a fresh nightie while you're soaking and bring it in to you in a few."

"Thanks." Kim grinned. "I've had a really fabulous time so far. Well, right up until that dream."

"I'll just bet you have," Nikki said pointedly. "I've seen more horny Amish men this weekend than I care to contemplate. All thanks to you and your ever-so-seductive ankles."

"Hey, when you've got it, might as well flaunt it."

Nikki laughed at that. "Go take a bath, you hussy. I'll make us a midnight snack and fetch that nightie."

"Well?" Priscilla demanded after her father locked the office door behind them. She smoothed out the flowing silk robe she wore, hating to look a mess even in the middle of the night. "Tell me, please, before I expire of curiosity!"

Maxwell Harrington's face looked haggard, defeated even. She searched her father's eyes, knowing no good news would be forthcoming.

"I've blown it forever this time, haven't I?" Priscilla asked fearfully. "I'm so sorry, Daddy. I never meant to disappoint you like this."

"Cilla." Maxwell sighed. "Get a hold of yourself, sweetheart. You know Daddy won't let that little toad come between you and reelection."

Her eyes widened. "You've found him, then?" she said hopefully.

He frowned. "I think so, but we don't know yet. Your secretary and I have got it narrowed down to three." His eyebrows slowly inched together. "You've been keeping that cell phone as well as your private bedroom phone on like I told you to?"

"Yes, Daddy."

"Good girl." Maxwell inclined his head. "Remember to try to keep him talking as long as you can next time he calls."

"I will."

Her father tiredly ran a hand over his cheek. "I need some sleep. Tomorrow morning we all go to church together, smile at the press, etcetera, etcetera. I want you to throw the occasional devoted smile up to Otis, make it look real convincing. You know what I'm talking about."

The senator nodded.

"Go get some sleep, Cilla," Maxwell muttered. "You've got bags under your eyes and you know how sallow that makes you look on television."

"I know. It's just been so difficult to fall asleep, and you know where I stand on sedatives." The senator stood up on tiptoe to kiss her father's cheek, then turned to leave the office. "Good night, Daddy."

Maxwell watched her walk away. "Cilla," he called out just as she was preparing to open the door. She turned her head to look at him. "Remember that bill you endorsed? The antigun legislation?"

She sighed. "Daddy, I don't feel like going through this right now. I—"

"I'm proud of you," he said softly, making her eyes widen. "I've never believed in giving any fool with a few bucks the right to own a deadly weapon, either. Difference between us being I never had the guts to say so." His eyes shone with pride. If she didn't get out of here soon, she suspected hers would start shining with tears.

"You're a damn good senator, Cilla. I'm proud to call you my daughter."

Their gazes found each other. "Thank you," she said a bit shakily. "You don't know how many years I've been waiting to hear you say that."

"Go to bed before we both start crying like pussies," Maxwell grumbled.

Cilla smiled tremulously. "Will you still love me if my career goes down faster than the *Titanic*?" she whispered.

"Of course. You're my child." Maxwell shook his head. "Anyway, that won't happen. We'll get through this, you and me, just like always." He walked toward the office's opposite door. "Just do me a favor after I take care of your little problem?" he threw out over his shoulder.

Cilla's eyebrows drew together inquiringly.

Maxwell frowned. "Buy a vibrator."

She coughed into her hand, muttered her agreement, and fled the office.

Chapter 26

Sunday, July 27
8:59 P.M.

Nikki had almost decided to stay the night at Kim's house, but a lack of clean clothing had worked as a deterrent. Besides, if she slept over at the Cox residence, she and Kim would end up talking into the wee hours of the morning again and Nikki wouldn't be sufficiently rested for work tomorrow afternoon.

There was also the issue of Thomas. Megan had informed Nikki upon their return that he wanted to speak with her. At first she had wondered why he hadn't simply paged her if he wanted to talk, so out of curiosity she'd checked her beeper. A wince and a panic later, she'd realized it had accidentally been powered off.

Nikki could only be grateful the hospital hadn't tried to contact her while she'd been gone. She never would have forgiven herself had there been an emergency surgery and her O.R. team had unsuccessfully tried to reach her. Not to mention the fact that she probably would have been fired. The only thing she could figure was that the Lucifer situation had rattled her brain a bit loose. Luckily, she was starting to feel like the old Nikki again—in control.

Sinking the key into the lock, Nikki pushed open the door to her apartment with her hip since her arms were full of shopping bags from purchases she'd made in Amish country over the weekend. She didn't particularly care for the country theme, so hadn't bought much in the way of decorations, but their food was too good to not bring home bags filled with it. Cheeses, trail bologna, wines, spiced cider, fudge—yum.

"Well look who finally came home," a male voice drawled.

Nikki yelped, so startled she almost dropped one of her shopping bags. In fact, if Thomas's reflexes hadn't been what they were, the wine probably would have crashed to the floor.

"Thomas," she breathed out as he plucked the wine from her tentative grasp. "My God, you scared me half to death."

"Good," he growled. "I say you deserve it for what you've put me through."

Her forehead wrinkled. "I have no idea what you're talking about," she said as she walked her bags over to the dining room table and set them down. "But I can tell you I'm not in the mood for the third degree."

He followed hot on her heels. "Where have you been?" he demanded, setting the wine down next to the other bags. His nostrils were flaring. "Who have you been with?"

She looked at him like he'd gone crazy. "What is wrong with you?" Nikki snapped. "I've been with Kim!"

His dark eyes narrowed at her. "What happened to all that stuff you said about showing respect to your partner? Leaving me a note when you decide to trot off and all that? I was worried! I haven't heard a goddamn thing from you since I dropped you off when we left Cincinnati!"

She frowned. He had a point, but she was too angry at the way he was interrogating her to concede to it. "If you want the truth," she spat, "I didn't realize I had a partner when I left town!"

"After everything we've gone through together?" he snarled. "Yeah, right!" His jaw tightened. "I think you're *trying* to make me jealous is what's going on here. Rather than flat-out admit you want attention, you punish me for not automatically giving it. I'd only just found out that my partner murdered my daughter—excuse the piss out of me for not being tuned in to your womanly needs!"

"And excuse me for not always thinking rationally!" she screeched back. "I make mistakes too, you know! Or are you the only one allowed to do that?"

Thomas stilled, but said nothing. His breathing was heavy, anger and jealousy still radiating off of him in waves. Yet somehow Nikki realized he was calming down a bit, too.

"Hell," he muttered, glancing away.

She was quiet for a moment. "Thomas, I'm sorry," she said softly. Good god, he had a valid point about trying to make him jealous. She hated admitting it, but it was true. More than once this weekend she'd found herself hoping Thomas had called her apartment only to realize she wasn't at home—her way of letting him know life could go on without him. "I left town because I was afraid you didn't want me anymore and I needed to get away and . . ." She sighed. "I'm sorry," she whispered.

His brooding gaze bore into hers. "Me, too," he rumbled out. He did a little sighing of his own. "I should have just told you I needed to get myself together rather than shutting you out like I did. Hell, I suck at relationships. But I'm trying, Nikki. I promise. I don't want to lose you."

"It's okay," Nikki assured him. "And I'm sorry about not calling you back. Thomas, I only just realized a few minutes ago that my beeper was accidentally turned off. I swear that's the truth."

Silence.

Thomas gently but firmly grabbed her by the shoulders and started backing her toward the sofa. "Just tell me one thing because I need to hear it from you," he rasped. His gaze was intense, his jaw clenched. "Tell me you didn't fuck anyone this weekend. *Tell me.*"

"I swear it," she said quickly. "I don't want another man touching me."

He backed her into the arm of the sofa, his erection pressing against her thigh. "If you ever give away my pussy to another man," he vowed as he ripped open her jeans and pulled them down with her panties, "I swear I'll kill him." His nostrils flared. "You hear me?"

"Yes," Nikki breathed out.

He flipped her over so that her stomach lay across the arm of the sofa. Arousal knotted in her belly as the sound of his zipper coming undone reached her ears. Her jeans were at her ankles, her shirt still on. Only her most intimate part was bared.

"Show me my cunt," Thomas ordered, his voice thick with arousal. "Spread apart your ass cheeks so I can see everything that belongs to me."

She blew out a breath, intensely aroused. Her hands a bit shaky, she grabbed her buttocks and spread the cheeks apart as far as she could so that nothing impeded his view of her bared vagina and anus.

"Good girl," Thomas said thickly. "Now tell Master who this juicy pussy belongs to."

"To you," Nikki gasped, so aroused she could barely stand. Feeling his eyes on her submissively bared center was making her belly knot impossibly tighter. "Only to you."

Thomas stood there for a lingering moment, doing and saying nothing, simply staring at what he'd claimed for his own. The effect was unnerving. Being on sexual display made her nipples harden and her breathing hitch. A few seconds later, Nikki hissed when she felt his index finger slide into her anus.

"I've missed you," she said throatily, wiggling her bottom at him.

"I've missed you, too, baby," Thomas said hoarsely. His index finger slid in and out of her anus, forcing new and pleasurable sensations on her. "One day soon I'm gonna want this ass too. Will you give it to me?"

"Yes."

"You ever had a man here?" he growled.

"No."

"Then I've definitely got to mark it. It's mine."

She swallowed between pants. "Everything is yours."

Thomas played with her anus for several more moments before withdrawing his index finger. "Later for that," he rasped. "Right now I need to be inside my pussy."

"Please," she whimpered. "Quit teasing. Please take me."

He gritted his teeth as he guided his cock to her vagina. "I love it when you beg, baby. You know how hard that gets Daddy."

"Please."

Sinking into her flesh from behind, he impaled himself to the hilt within her. "Goddamn," Thomas groaned. "You're gonna kill me."

He withdrew slightly and sank into her body again. She moaned, her hands leaving her buttocks to rest before her on the sofa. Thomas immediately began to ride her fast and hard, his hips pistoning back and forth with increasing speed as his cock surged in and out of her.

"Oh, Thomas," Nikki gasped as he took her hard from behind. She threw her hips back at him, meeting him thrust for thrust. She could hear the sound of her sticky flesh gripping around his cock and sucking him into her with every outstroke. "Oh," she breathed out, her nipples stabbing out from under her bra. *"Thomas."*

His callused hands reached under the T-shirt she wore and threw her bra up over the swell of her breasts. He palmed them, his thumbs and forefingers clamping around her nipples as he plunged into her flesh from behind. He rode her hard, making her gasp and groan, his tight balls smacking against the back of her as he sank in and out of her like a man obsessed.

"All mine," he growled into her ear. His voice was hoarse. "My nipples. My pussy. My ass. *My woman.*"

Nikki closed her eyes and let the arousal overwhelm her. Her breathing was labored, her heart thumping like mad. Her nipples were so stiff that his hold on them was pleasurable to the point of pain.

He released her breasts, leaving them there to jiggle with each thrust, his hands settling on her raised buttocks. He cupped the cheeks, kneading them with his callused hands, simultaneously pumping in and out of her at a merciless pace.

Whack!

Nikki gasped, the small, stinging smack to her bottom startling. Her eyes widened as she wondered if she and Thomas had read the same books . . . only the detective had never admitted it.

Whack! Whack!

"Ooooh," she groaned.

The books hadn't lied. Making blood rush to her bottom *did* sensitize another, crucial part of her anatomy.

"You like that?" Thomas murmured into her ear, his voice thick. "Can you feel my cock better, baby?"

"Yes," she gasped. "One more time. A bit harder, please."

Whack! Whack! Whack!

"Oooooh!"

He took her impossibly harder, sinking in and out of her flesh like he meant to brand it. *"Thomas,"* she groaned, heat rushing to her face and nipples. *"Oh, god."* Nikki moaned low in her throat, throwing her hips back at him as a violent orgasm ripped through her belly.

He growled as he fucked her, pounding into her harder and deeper and faster. His hands left her buttocks and cupped her breasts again. "I'm coming, too," he gritted out. His muscles tensed, his breathing grew ragged against her ear. His hands squeezed her breasts, reminding her who they belonged to.

"All mine," he rasped, his powerful body shuddering. She could practically hear his jaw clenching. *"Mine."*

Thomas groaned loudly as he came, hot semen spurting from his cock to warm her insides. He kept up the steady pace, pumping away inside of her until his balls were depleted.

When it was over, when they were both exhausted, they didn't move for a long moment. He kept her pinned to the sofa, her buttocks up in the air, his palms tenderly massaging the warm spots.

"I came so hard I damn near passed out," Thomas muttered, finally letting Nikki up. He lifted his T-shirt, using the edge to mop perspiration from his forehead.

She chuckled softly. "Me, too." An eyebrow arched as she turned on her heel to stare at him. She studied his face, a suspicious look in her eye.

He grunted. "What?"

"You read the e-books from my computer, didn't you?"

He grinned.

Her smile came slowly. *"Lady Polly and the Pirate Master?"*

He scratched the stubble on his cheek. "You gotta admit," Thomas drawled. "That scene when Captain Triston spanked Polly after he caught her trying to seduce that dude with the gimp leg was pretty hot."

Nikki shook her head, unable to stop herself from laughing. "So what made you decide to try the spanking on me?" she asked as she pulled off her jeans.

He shrugged. "It came out of nowhere, to be honest. I'm just glad you liked it," he mumbled, "or I would have felt like a real dumb asshole."

Her arms crossed under her breasts. She huffed. "You mean that spanking was for real?"

His face colored slightly. "Only the first whack." He frowned at the look on her face. "I was feeling territorial, okay? I know we made up and all, but I still have a hard time not knowing where the hell you've been all weekend!"

Nikki rolled her eyes as she pulled her T-shirt off. "You really meant it when you said you were the jealous type, didn't you?"

"Yes." He grunted. "So where were you?"

She shook her head and sighed, too amused to be angry. "Millersburg," she answered, squatting down to tug off the jeans pooled around Thomas's ankles. "You know, that notoriously seedy hotbed of Amish party life."

His frown deepened. "You mean to tell me I've been walking around with a broken heart the whole damn weekend when all along you've been hanging out with corn-husking ZZ Top look-alikes?"

Nikki shrugged. "Apparently so. Hey, want some Amish cheese?"

"No," he snapped.

One eyebrow slowly inched up. "Pistachios?" she murmured.

"Maybe later," Thomas sniffed. "I'm not in the mood."

"What are you in the mood for?" she whispered, standing to wrap her arms around his neck.

Thomas bent his head to kiss her. He thrust his tongue in between her lips, groaning into her mouth when she ground her body against his quickly stiffening erection.

He picked Nikki up and carried her into the bedroom, his lips never leaving hers, deciding to show her what he was in the mood for instead of telling her.

"Priscilla," Claude's voice purred from the cell phone. "I don't think you understand what it is I want from you."

Cilla's teeth ground together as she paced back and forth in her bedroom. She could only hope her father was listening in on this conversation. More specifically, she could only pray he was tracing Claude's location.

"Name your price," she said after she blew out a puff of smoke from the cigarette dangling between her lips. "Whatever it is, I'll pay it."

Claude chuckled. "Master doesn't want your money, silly slave girl. He wants your heart."

She rolled her eyes. How utterly sweet and utterly provincial. "Fine. You have it. Does this mean you'll leave me alone now?"

He was quiet for a long moment. Eerily silent. Something about it sent chills down her spine.

"You're a bad girl, Priscilla. You're naughty, just like Lisa. You pretend to be someone you aren't."

"Who doesn't online?" Cilla snapped. "Look! I am growing weary and my patience thin. Either name a price or go to the media. Either way, I refuse to play this game with you a moment longer. Especially since it'll be *my* word against yours!"

"Yes, it will be. But do you really want to take that chance?"

Silence.

"Meet me in an hour in the alleyway next to Jake's down in the Flats. If you're late, or if you bring anyone with you, every major television station will own a copy of our chat transcripts . . . as well as proof that you are in fact the owner of the SpankMeImANaughtyGirl account."

She hysterically wondered if he could be believed. Her career couldn't end like this—not like this! "An hour?" Cilla said shakily. "But what about—"

She cursed under her breath as the line went dead.

Damn it!

Thomas's cell phone rang, the interruption making him frown. He stopped thrusting and bent his neck to kiss the tip of Nikki's nose before reaching for the phone. His eyebrows rose as he pointedly looked at the handcuffs securing her to the bed. "Don't go anywhere," he ordered. She grinned. "Yeah?"

"Cavanah."

"Ben? What's up?"

"You at Dr. Adenike's?"

"Yeah. Why?"

Ben sighed. "I'll send over two cops to watch her place. You better get down here."

Thomas stilled. "What's going on, O'Rourke?"

"James. He escaped."

"*What?*" Thomas noticed the frightened way Nikki was staring at him, so he ran a soothing hand over her belly before sitting up in the bed. "He escaped?" he asked, looking at a wide-eyed Nikki.

"Yes. And it gets worse."

Of course. "I hate to ask, but know I have to. How?"

"A missing woman report just came in," Ben said quietly.

Thomas closed his eyes. "Who?"

"You ready for this?"

"Tell me."

"Priscilla Harrington-Barnsworth."

His eyes flew open and then narrowed. "Why does that name ring a bell?" Thomas muttered.

"Cavanah! Hello! *Senator* Priscilla Harrington-Barnsworth."

"Shit."

"Exactly. And I just had a chat with her dad. It seems the senator has an, um, *interesting* online life."

Thomas took a deep breath and exhaled. "I'll be right there."

Chapter 27

Monday, July 28
1:37 A.M.

"This report just in: Channel One News has learned that Ohio Senator Priscilla Harrington-Barnsworth was reported missing to the Cleveland Police Department. The report was filed a little over thirty minutes ago by her husband and father. Making this news more shocking still is a second report that just came in . . ."

Nikki paced back and forth in her living room, now wondering how idiotic she'd been to decide on staying put rather than going to Kim's. The fact that two policemen were outside offered little in the way of comfort. Especially considering that a police officer, James, had already tried to kill her. If only she had thought of that before Thomas left.

Her eyes flicked back to the television where the shocked anchorman was continuing his report.

"Are you sure?" the anchorman muttered to someone off-camera. He nodded, swallowed, and then looked up into the camera's eye. *"It appears that former police detective James Merdino,*

the man arrested in connection with the brutal rape and slaying murders of nearly ten women in the Cleveland Metropolitan area, escaped from county lockup approximately one to two hours prior to Senator Harrington-Barnsworth's disappearance. Speculation is running rampant as to whether or not there might be a connection between these two cases. The senator's spokesman has declined to comment."

The phone rang, causing Nikki to yelp. Clutching her heart, she briefly closed her eyes and drew in a deep, calming breath. "Hello?" she whispered into the phone.

"Nik . . . my God. Are you watching the news?" Kim breathed out.

Nikki swallowed. "Yeah. I never particularly liked your old friend Cilla on a personal level, but goodness." She clutched her stomach. "I feel like I'm going to be sick."

"Is Thomas there with you?" Kim quickly asked.

"No. But there are two policemen parked outside my window."

"Don't let either of them in," she said desperately. "Please. I'm on my way over to get you."

Nikki's heart was beating so fast she felt like she might vomit. "Did you have another dream?" she asked, her voice catching.

"Just promise me you won't open the door for anybody but me," Kim said. "Promise me!"

"I—I promise," Nikki stuttered. "Kim, I'm frightened. I—"

The phone line went dead. Her eyes widened.

Oh God.

"Where are you going?" Megan asked anxiously. She wrung her hands together in her lap, her eyes big and troubled. "Why don't you call Detective Cavanah and tell him your worries?"

"To get Nikki," Kim muttered as she seized a knife from the cutting block on the kitchen counter. "And I did try to call him. His cell's been busy for the last five minutes. I've got no more time to play with."

"But your ankle—"

"—is fine," Kim cut in. She took a deep breath. "Look, Megan, I know you think my dreams are kooky, but the fact is, they came true before." She felt like she was going to be sick she was so worried. "I have to get to Nik," she said, her voice trembling. "If I lose her . . ."

"I'm going with you," Megan firmly declared, surging up from the chair.

Kim stilled. Her eyes widened. "No," she said softly, zipping up her jacket. "You're not going."

"But Kim—"

"No!" She gentled her severe expression a bit. "You could get hurt and I . . ." Kim cleared her throat, glancing away. "I don't want anything to happen to you."

Her stepmother looked at her as though she'd lost her mind. "And I *do* want something to happen to *you?*" she asked in the loudest, most incredulous tone of voice Kim had ever heard come from her mouth. It did things to her heart she had no time to dwell on.

Megan's lips tightened. "I know how to use that gun. And what's more, I *will* use it if need be. I am so damn sick of being helpless. And I'm sick of men. They all suck!"

Kim blinked. Given the situation, there was little room for amusement, yet a guttural sound ripped from her throat as she tried to stifle a laugh. She'd never seen Megan so angry and determined. Dressed as she was in a white silk blouse and designer black slacks, her hair fashionably pinned back in a high-class coif, her stepmother could have been the pin-up girl for idle, useless rich women. Her demeanor, however, was in stark contrast to her attire.

"I would agree that as a species, men suck," Kim said, amused. "However, I think this situation goes a little beyond that."

Megan's chin notched up. "I'm going with you, Kimberly, and that is that."

"Megan! We're not Cagney and Lacey!" Kim huffed.

"And you are not Xena the Warrior Princess! You lucked out once with a knife. We won't chance twice." Megan inclined her head. "Go start the car. I'll be but a moment. I need to retrieve my gun. Oh, and my black gloves."

Kim's eyebrows drew together. "Black gloves?"

Megan shrugged. "It's what they do in the movies, dear. There must be a reason for it."

"Huh." Kim couldn't think of anything to say to that. She shook her head then hightailed it into the garage.

The lights inside the apartment flickered out, making Nikki gasp. She instinctively stilled, her body shaking. She swallowed roughly as her eyes tried to adjust to the pitch-blackness they'd been engulfed in.

Her heart was beating so dramatically she could hear nothing but its continual *thump-thump-thump* inside her ears. She needed to calm down, she realized, breathing deeply in an effort to do just that. Not being able to hear put her at an extreme disadvantage.

It could be a blown fuse, she reasonably told herself. *Just a fuse.*

The lights flicked back on. Her eyes widened. The sound of breathing coming from somewhere in the room both shocked and frightened her. She whirled around in a circle, stunned when she saw him standing there.

"Oh my God," she exclaimed, her eyes briefly shuttering as she clutched her heart. "You scared me half to death! What are you doing here?"

He said nothing, just stared at her.

Her eyes narrowed in confusion. Why *was* he here? There was something different about him tonight. His expression, his eyes . . .

Realization slowly and horrifically dawned. "Oh no." Nikki shook her head, her voice breaking as she started backing away. She bumped into a bookshelf, ten novels and three magazines raining down on her at impact. "Oh God, not you. Please," she gasped, "you can't be him!"

He was quiet for a moment as he studied her through crazed eyes. "Nikki," he finally whispered in a false voice she recognized all too well. He slowly began walking toward her. "My love . . ."

His arm raised up, a gleaming metal object momentarily visible. Nikki would have screamed, but a blow to the skull sent her plummeting to the floor instead.

Where the hell is she? Thomas thought, his heart racing as the Cadillac sped toward Nikki's apartment. She must know he'd be worried. She'd answer his calls if she could. First James escaped, then Ben up and disappeared, and now he couldn't get a hold of either Nikki or the two cops assigned to her.

Shit.

A panicky, terrified feeling swamped him, much the way he'd felt when Amy had disappeared. Things couldn't end that way again. They just couldn't. He had failed his little girl. He'd be damned if he'd also fail the woman he loved—yes, he loved her.

"Don't let me be too late," Thomas pleaded under his breath to the heavens. Every muscle in his body was tensed, his jaw tight. "Please God, please, don't let me be too late."

* * *

Kim and Megan raced up the stairs toward Nikki's apartment. The jarring movements caused pain to splinter through Kim's ankle, but she gritted her teeth and ignored it. "One more flight," she panted to her stepmother as they rounded another incline in the stairwell.

Megan held the revolver like a pro, not too obvious but ready to be used if it came to that. By the time they reached Nikki's apartment, Kim already knew she was too late. Bile churned in her stomach at the sight of the unlocked, slightly ajar front door. "No," she gasped. "No! No! No! No! No!"

"Maybe she's still inside," Megan said shakily as they let themselves into the apartment and ran in. "Please be inside," she whispered to the walls as she came to a halt in the living room. Her wide blue eyes watched Kim as she dashed into the bedroom, the bathroom, everywhere, looking for Nikki.

"Nikki!" Kim shouted, her voice on the verge of hysteria. "Nikki, please answer me! Please!"

Megan's teeth sank into her lower lip. Her gaze flicked down to the carpet. Her eyes, already wide, bulged. "Oh dear God," she gasped. "Kim—oh no!"

Kim was at her side in a heartbeat. "What?" she shouted, her breasts heaving up and down with her labored breathing. "Megan—what is it?"

Thomas burst his way into the apartment, scaring the life out of Kim. She jumped, then upon realizing who it was, turned haunted blue eyes up to the detective as she watched him stare at her, his breathing even more ragged than hers.

"She's not here," Kim croaked out, her voice catching. "I checked everywhere."

He looked as nauseous as she felt. Nikki was gone and the two cops assigned to protect her had seemingly disappeared into thin air. "I'll go check the grounds and call the station," Thomas rasped. "I'll be right—"

"They are long gone," Megan whispered. She took a deep breath as she pointed to the carpet, but her voice still trembled. "Look."

Her stepmother seemed too shocked, too sick, to say anything else. Following her line of vision, Kim glanced down to the carpet. She stilled.

"Blood," Thomas murmured, having come up behind her.

Kim felt dizzy, everything around her spinning. "Dried blood," she said, the words ripping out of her throat in a guttural, half-insane sound. That meant Lucifer had dragged her out minutes ago—maybe many minutes ago. Perhaps too long to find him. "No! *Oh, god*—Nik, please!"

She felt Thomas's hands rest on the back of her shoulders—felt them but somehow didn't register they were there. She was going to faint, or be sick, or . . .

Not Nikki, Kim hysterically thought. This wasn't happening. She should have stayed with her, should never have let her best friend out of her sight.

"Stay put!" she heard Thomas shout as he ran out of the apartment. The world was spinning. Her ears were ringing from the violent way her heart was pumping. "I'll be right back!"

Chapter 28

Monday, July 28
3:44 A.M.

Nikki awoke slowly, groggily, the top of her head aching so badly it wrenched a soft moan from her. Her eyelids felt heavy, like lead weights she wanted to open but couldn't. She was cold, she thought, her teeth starting to chatter. She needed a blanket—something, anything. So cold.

"Please," she heard a feminine voice softly plead. "I can't take any more."

No answer. Just the sound of a Polaroid snapping photographs and a familiar tune being hummed while . . .

Nikki stilled. She knew that tune. And, she thought, as memories came flooding back, she knew that woman's voice. *Open your eyes,* she commanded herself. *Open them!*

"Please," the feminine voice gasped. "No more—just kill me," she begged. "Please *just kill me.*"

Nikki's heart began slamming in her chest. Her eyes flew open. She stared in horror at the sight that greeted her.

Priscilla Harrington-Barnsworth—naked, spread-eagled, tied down to a folding table. Four tiny but deep cuts on her upper torso kept blood steadily dripping from her body. Her unblinking hazel eyes were dim with pain and empty with resolve.

He walked toward the senator, humming in his throat. *Him.* Oh God—how could it be him? How could she have not known . . .

He was going to rape Priscilla, Nikki thought, perspiration breaking out on her forehead. He was starting to unzip his trousers and—

"No!" Nikki groaned, her head feeling like it was ready to split into two. "Leave her the hell alone, you sadistic asshole!"

He stilled. His head slowly turned toward her.

She hadn't been dreaming, she thought, feeling sick. It *was* him.

"Don't talk to me like that!" he bellowed, stalking toward her, Priscilla forgotten. "Don't ever talk to me like that!" He raised his palm and slapped her across the face, brutally enough to make Nikki taste blood.

Nikki's gaze fell to the senator—the same senator who had managed to work one of her hands loose of the knots. She resisted the urge to let her eyes widen and narrowed them at the man who meant to kill her instead. She smiled at him, confusing him.

Please God! she thought hysterically, her raw emotions in stark contrast to her calm, even cold exterior. *Please let me pull this off.*

"You're a coward," Nikki whispered, watching his body tense and still. "You can rape me. You can kill me. . . ." She smiled fully, showing him white teeth stained by dripping crimson blood. "But you will always fear me."

"Shut up!" He backhanded her again.

Nikki blinked several times in rapid succession, the impact making her vision blurry.

"Shut up!" He grabbed fistfuls of his hair by the roots and closed his eyes. His chest heaved up and down as he worked to calm himself.

The police profiler she'd spoken to had been right, Nikki realized. He did fear women. He feared their power over him, couldn't stand to be taunted by one.

"Shut up!" he bellowed.

The senator was so close to being free. Nikki could see how close in her peripheral vision.

He couldn't. Yet.

Terrified of what his reaction would be, but knowing she had no choice left to her, Nikki went in for the kill. "Just a coward," she murmured, taunting him. *Hurry the hell up, Priscilla!* she frantically thought. If her adrenaline went any higher, she'd pass out. "A coward."

Rage the likes of which she'd never before been the brunt of swept over his features in a way that horrified her. His entire musculature contorted, sweat dripped off his forehead in rivulets.

A gleaming silver knife rose high above his head. Nikki didn't want to show him fear, but couldn't contain it. Her eyes widened when the grim reality that she had pushed him too far clawed at her gut like talons.

There would be no time for Thomas to find her, she realized in ice-cold terror. Unlike Priscilla, Nikki's deathblow would be coming mercifully soon.

Thomas. Oh God, she loved him so much. What would this do to him? He'd wrongly believe he'd failed her. Just like he wrongly believed he'd failed Amy.

Her captor wielded the knife higher above his head, screaming like the lunatic he was, his body shaking.

It was over, Nikki realized, swallowing convulsively. Her time had just run out.

* * *

Kim stared unblinking at nothing as she paced back and forth in Nikki's apartment, police officers seemingly everywhere. Thomas had said to wait for him here, but he was yet to come back. One of the detectives had informed her he'd raced over to the Harrington-Barnsworth campaign headquarters to follow up on a possible lead. The officer didn't know how long it would be until Thomas returned.

Deciding not to wait around like a useless decoration, she walked over to where Megan sat on the sofa. "Let's go," she said softly. At her stepmother's nod, she turned to the closest detective to let him know they were leaving. "My cell will be on at all times. Please have Detective Cavanah phone me as soon as he hears something."

"He wants you to wait here for him, ma'am," the officer politely informed her. "I think you should, too."

Kim closed her eyes and took a deep breath. "I can't," she whispered, the pain she felt unguarded. Her eyes opened and found his. "How can you expect me to stay here where all I can do is stare at my best friend's blood on the carpet?"

He sighed, his expression letting her know he understood. "Go on," he said gently. "I'll radio Thomas to let him know."

She released a shaky breath. "Thank you." She needed to get out of here before she lost it completely. As far away from this apartment as possible. She needed to run, scream, sob, think. Right now she felt numb, disassociated from her body. "Please let me know the second you get any news at all."

The officer nodded. "Will do, ma'am."

Five minutes later, Kim and Megan were in Kim's BMW, Megan at the steering wheel. Kim turned up the air-conditioning as high and cold as it could go, closing her eyes at the sudden blast. It felt good, the icy intensity almost painful. It helped her shake off the feeling of disassociation that had engulfed her.

Think, damn it. Think. . . .

The dreams. Over time many of the little details in them had changed. The vantage point through which she could see Nikki's murder take place, the accompanying sounds, even the method of death. But a few things had always—*always*—stayed the same.

A dark place. The scent of water. Her eyes widened.

"Don't go home," Kim whispered, her head turning to stare at her stepmother. "Go to the Flats."

One of Megan's eyebrows slowly inched up.

"She's still alive," Kim said, her heartbeat picking up enough to give her an adrenaline rush. She felt hope surge inside of her for the first time since finding her best friend's apartment abandoned, blood stains on the carpet. "I know she's still alive."

Thomas paced back and forth. He saw Maxwell Harrington do the same a few feet over. Both men were liable to wear holes into the linoleum floors of the small campaign headquarters the senator kept in the Flats.

The instinct Thomas had to blindly comb the streets was overpowering. It took all of his willpower to talk himself out of it. Nikki was out there somewhere, still alive. Her time was running out. So was the senator's.

There was no efficiency in roaming the streets. Not yet. Not when a very real lead might come of the waiting. Since the phone company hadn't offered much in the way of enlightenment, Thomas needed to hear the communication specialist's results, see if she discovered anything from the last phone call Priscilla

Harrington-Barnsworth had engaged in. He'd give her five more minutes before he started that combing.

Nikki, he thought. *Nikki.*

He'd never loved a woman like he loved her. He couldn't lose her, refused to lose her.

Thomas tried not to dwell on how much trouble Lucifer had gone through to acquire Nikki—he'd knocked out one officer assigned to watch her apartment and slit the throat of the second one. He tried not to let it mess with his focus, but he was all too aware that the more Lucifer craved a victim the longer and more intense the torture he doled out to her was.

He couldn't stand to think of that. It ate at his gut the way it did every time he thought about the four brutal days his daughter had endured.

James. How could James be capable of this. . . .

"The location of the perpetrator when he phoned the senator," Amanda Hibbs, the communications specialist, announced, "was definitely within the Flats."

"That's it?" Maxwell shouted, coming to a standstill to face her. "As much money as I'm paying you, I hope you've got something more to go on than that!"

She frowned. "I'd estimate somewhere within a five-block radius of our current location."

"Five blocks," Maxwell growled. He looked ready to tear the specialist apart. "My daughter is missing and the best you can do is five blocks! Do you know how many fucking buildings there are in a five-block radius?" He turned to say something to Thomas, but stopped when he saw the detective punching out numbers on the phone.

Thomas resumed his pacing as he spoke to the police chief on a landline, bringing him up to speed. He listened to the chief's response, desperate to hang up the phone and begin searching. "Good. I'm going to start combing the streets. Call my cell if any tips come in." He slammed the phone down and began jogging toward the door.

"Detective!" Maxwell shouted. "I want to go with you."

"No," Thomas threw out over his shoulder. "I need you to stay here where you are accessible to the media. Phone me if any leads come in."

"But my daughter—"

"Needs you to stay out of my way," Thomas growled. He was anxious to get moving, his control tenuous at best.

Nikki. He had to find her.

Still, he understood what the old man was going through. He'd lost Amy. No man should have to go through losing a daughter like that. He could see the fear and helplessness etched into Maxwell's face like a mask of pain.

Pausing long enough to quickly bring him up to speed, he told him, "Every available patrol officer in the area is now combing this five-block radius. I need to go be one of them."

Maxwell nodded, his expression frightened but rational.

"Help your daughter," Thomas said softly, "by staying here. The phone number to this place is being plastered all over the media as we speak. If any viewers call in with a lead, however far-fetched, you phone me." At four A.M., he doubted many would be watching, but it helped to give the senator's father some focus.

"Yes," Maxwell whispered. "Yes, I will."

Thomas inclined his head before running out of the building.

Nikki's eyes clashed with his, defiantly meeting his gaze as he prepared to deliver the deathblow. There was no possible way to survive it, she realized. Not with that much force and hatred behind it.

"Son of a fucking bitch!" a male voice snarled, making Nikki blink. She stilled. She recognized that man from TV. Nikki gasped as she watched Detective James Merdino lunge at Lucifer, both men toppling to the ground when their bodies collided. Hope surged in her chest, crashing almost as quickly when she saw that the detective's hands were cuffed together.

He had escaped jail. He had found them. But James Merdino's only weapon, his hands, were chained together.

Nikki struggled with the knots that held her naked body roped down, like the senator, trying to loosen them. Priscilla was feverishly working the knots at her legs, her hands now free. But like Nikki, there were so many of them on either of her legs—intricate bondage knots that kept their ankles and thighs tied together, secured to more knots that roped them down.

James knocked Lucifer into a stone wall with his shoulders, a growl erupting from both of their throats at the force. Lucifer blindly slashed out with the knife in his hand, slicing open James's shoulder in the doing. The pain startled James for only a moment, but it was enough time for Lucifer to lunge back at the detective.

Both men hit the wall this time, knocking James out cold from a blow to the back of the head. Lucifer took a blow to the mouth, blood immediately gushing from between his lips as he fell to the ground.

He was stunned, Nikki thought as she struggled with the knots. He was stunned but he was not out cold.

Hands at her arms shocked her. Her neck shot to the right.

Priscilla. She was free. Free and trying to undo the knots that held Nikki down. But there was too much wet blood dripping from the senator, slicking her hands and making them repeatedly fumble.

Lucifer moaned, quickly coming to.

Nikki's eyes widened. "Run," she whispered. "Go—now!"

The senator seemed not to hear her.

"Run!"

Priscilla's head came up. She didn't look very lucid. "I—I can't leave you."

"You're our only hope," Nikki frantically insisted, hysteria bubbling inside of her. "Go get help!"

The senator blinked. The iron-will determination she was known for finally took over. She quickly glanced to their momentarily felled captor, then back to Nikki. "I *will* be back." And then she was running, dashing down the watery stone corridor that would take her from this basement of horror.

Lucifer bellowed when he realized the senator had gotten free. He lunged up to his feet and stumbled after her.

Her heart racing, Nikki continued to struggle with the blood-slippery knots.

Chapter 29

Monday, July 28
4:07 A.M.

"Damn it," Kim muttered under her breath to Megan as they walked back and forth in the alley next to Jake's café in the Flats. This was the alley Nikki had originally been assaulted in. She knew—*knew*—that was significant. She didn't know how, only that it was.

"I wish Ben O'Rourke had been right about your dreams being voodoo, dear," Megan said as she frantically paced. The revolver was securely in her hand. "Because it would be nice if you could force a dream to come on right about now."

Kim stilled. Ben O'Rourke . . .

Ben O'Rourke.

Oh my God, she thought, memories flooding back. There had always been something about the detective that sent shivers down her spine. Something about him that told her he'd bring trouble into her life.

Was he to blame for this? Had she sat side by side in a car with the devil himself and not even realized it?

Ben O'Rourke had found one of the victim's bodies. Ben O'Rourke also possessed vivid, too-blue eyes . . . .

It didn't matter, Kim staunchly told herself as she resumed her pacing. All that mattered now was finding Nikki.

"What are you two doing here?" a male voice growled, about giving Kim a heart attack. Her pulse jumping, she stopped pacing and whirled around in her tracks.

"Oh, goodness," Megan squeaked. "I almost shot you, Detective. Don't frighten us like that."

Thomas frowned at the revolver in Megan's hand. "I'm pretending I don't see that, Mrs. Cox."

He turned his attention to Kim. His expression was stony, but she could see the naked vulnerability in it. He'd been searching hard for Nikki, she could tell. His breathing was ragged, perspiration covered his forehead, and his dark eyes were desperate.

"I've looked everywhere I can think to look," he rasped out. He drew in closer to Kim, resting his hands on her shoulders. "Please think. Your dreams—anything. Give me anything, here," he pleaded. "*Anything.*"

"Don't you think I'm trying?" she whispered, her gaze as tortured as his.

He briefly closed his eyes. "Yes," Thomas said quietly before releasing her shoulders and turning around to give her his back. "I don't know what to do."

Think! Kim told herself. *You can do this!*

"The scent of water is strong," she murmured. He slowly turned around to face her. "In my dreams," she clarified. "A dark, enclosed space. No windows. I smelled water and something rotting, garbage I think." Her face scrunched up a bit. "I didn't see it, but I smelled it."

Thomas stilled, trying to think.

"That's striking a chord in me," Megan murmured. "But why?"

He glanced up. "What do you mean?"

"I was raised in this city," Megan said thoughtfully. "And I've got more than a few years on you two." Her forehead wrinkled. "Now if only I could remember . . ."

"Please," Thomas choked out. "Let it come to you. Don't force it. No matter how much you want to, let it come out naturally or it'll get stuck."

Kim's teeth sank into her lower lip as she watched her stepmother's face.

"The sewers," Megan finally whispered, making chills run down Kim and Thomas's spines. Her eyes slowly rounded. "A little girl was killed down in the sewers about thirty years ago. There was an old abandoned boat shed with a passage that led to them. Kids used to dare each other to go down, all of us afraid, naturally." She swallowed. "They locked up that old shed ages ago, though. When that little girl was killed. They might have even torn it down. I don't recall."

"Where was it back then?" Thomas asked, his voice raw and gravelly.

Megan closed her eyes tightly, her face scrunching up as she tried to remember.

Kim's gaze slowly flicked up to the sky. Her eyes widened.

Déjà vu . . .

"The northwest docks," Kim murmured, recalling the vantage point of her most intense dreams, the direction from which the moonbeams had spilled down. Her heartbeat sped up as she turned her eyes to Thomas. "I'm positive. Go. *Now.*"

He did. Faster than Kim thought a man his size could move. She could only pray he reached Nikki in time.

"Call the police," Megan said, breaking Kim from her thoughts. "Tell them where he's gone so they can help."

Kim's eyes widened. "Thanks for remembering that," she said shakily, fumbling in her purse for the cell phone. "I'm so on edge I'm not thinking right."

"You did wonderful, honey." Megan's smile was proud. "Nikki will be all right now. We have to have faith."

Kim stared at her for a long, intense moment, her eyes searching Megan's. "You're the hero tonight. Not me."

Her face colored. "That's not true. I—"

"I love you, Mom," Kim said softly, making Megan's eyes widen. "I'm so incredibly proud to be your daughter."

Megan's eyelashes tried to bat away her tears, but they fell anyway. "I love you, too," she said on a shaky smile. "More than anyone or anything on earth."

Kim swiped at the tears falling down her face with the back of her hand. "We better do this later," she said with a wry smile. "I need to call the police."

After she'd made the call, Kim held out her hand and waited for Megan to thread her fingers through hers. They walked back to the BMW and got inside, deciding to wait the finale out at police headquarters.

"How sad for that little girl," Kim murmured as she started the BMW and put it in gear.

"Yes." Megan sighed. "I still vividly recall the day her body was found. Thirty years ago a murder that disgusting in scope was big news."

"I can imagine." She frowned, pausing a moment. "I'm curious . . ."

"What about, dear?"

"The little girl." Kim turned her gaze to the road as she slowly drove away. "Do you remember how she died?"

Megan nodded. "A tragic story, really. She was raped by her father down in the sewers. Her mother went crazy—not out of love for the little girl, but out of jealousy that her husband was interested in their daughter instead of her, if you can imagine."

"That's sick."

Megan sighed, agreeing. "Anyway, she killed her husband, then as a sort of symbolic punishment, she took their two children down into the sewers and tried to kill them both. Fortunately, her son escaped. But not until after the poor boy witnessed both his father and his sister's murders."

"How horrible."

"Yes, it was," Megan commiserated. "The little boy ended up being raised in foster care."

"Do you remember his name?"

"Michael," she said. "Michael Sorenson."

Kim's breathing stilled. Her eyes widened. "Oh my God."

*Nikki had prayed James would wake up before Lucifer re*turned, but that was not to be. Her only consolation was that he'd come back empty-handed, the senator nowhere in sight.

She hoped that meant Priscilla had gotten away, not been struck down and disposed of. Otherwise, she realized, her nerves so raw she couldn't stop trembling, she was as good as dead.

Something about him was different now. Lost, almost. His fake blue eyes didn't so much as blink as he walked toward her, nor pay the fallen detective any attention. Nikki would have thought disposing of James would have been his first priority, torturing her his second. But he was lost in his own twisted world.

"She escaped," he said in a monotone, his gaze faraway. "That wasn't supposed to happen."

Hope surged inside of her. *The senator had escaped.*

Nikki's eyes were wild, desperate. She didn't know if she was supposed to respond to him or not. She'd done a bit of research on serial killers since escaping Lucifer the first time and, while not exactly an expert on the subject, knew they tended to be very ritualistic in their thoughts and behaviors. Whatever intricate killing pattern he'd etched out in his brain had just been shredded to bits. That wouldn't keep him from killing her, though.

"What was supposed to happen, Michael?" she whispered.

Her breath caught in the back of her throat. Dr. Sorenson—her nemesis—she still couldn't believe he was Lucifer, that she'd known him all along. She had expected a bad man to look like a bad man, but Michael Sorenson, while always on the strange side, possessed a perfect face and an equally perfect physique.

He blinked. His gaze slowly found hers. "She was a liar. She was supposed to be punished like Lisa. She was supposed to be punished in front of you."

Oh dear lord he was crazy. What little hold he still had on reality was tentative at best. "Maybe you should go look for her again," Nikki said, hoping she sounded helpful. Anything to stall for more time. "Maybe she's still out there—"

"Shut up!" His nostrils flared. "You just want me to go away," he yelled. "I've loved you for years, and look how you betray me!"

Just as he'd "loved" every victim, she was certain. "No," Nikki said weakly, her heart pounding. "I want you to stay. I've never betrayed you."

Thomas please, she thought desperately. *Please hurry* . . . .

"You're a liar," Michael hissed, his jugular bulging. He came toward her slowly with the knife in his hand poised in such a way as to strike. His eyes flicked over her naked, splayed-out body. "You left me for *him*. For that . . . that *cop,*" he spat, the word distasteful on his lips.

Nikki furtively shook her head. "No, I didn't. I swear!"

She'd swear to anything to keep him calm, she hysterically thought. He was getting worked up, and history had taught her that when he was angry he liked to inflict pain. And death.

"Liar!"

"He made me go away with him," she lied, knowing Thomas wouldn't mind her saying what she had to. "Because he knew you'd get angry with me if he took me."

Thomas—hurry up and find me!

"I swear," she whispered, her eyes wide. "He made me go."

"Liar!"

"No!" She felt desperate as he stalked closer, the blood-stained knife gleaming. "Please calm down," she begged, her heart slamming in her chest.

"Liar!"

Nikki couldn't believe this was happening. Just couldn't believe it. Her teeth began chattering. She stared at him unblinking, her mind slowly beginning to disassociate from her body.

Michael stood before her. She was tied down, helpless. His teeth were gritting, his nostrils flaring. He held the knife in one hand and unzipped his trousers with the other one. "Master must punish you," he rasped out. "If you want me to love you again, then you must suffer in my name."

Her teeth were chattering, her mind was splintering. She heard his words, but they didn't register, made no sense, sounded far away. Nikki's mind was almost completely disassociated from her body now. She stared up at him, but didn't see him.

The knife sliced open a tiny cut above her heart. Not too deep, not too superficial. A second-rate surgeon's skill. She saw the cut, but didn't feel it. A hand roughly grabbed one of her breasts. She saw it, felt the pressure, but felt no pain.

This isn't happening, her disassociated mind continually reassured her. *It's just a dream* . . . .

"Suffer for me."

The voice was thick, aroused, and very far away. Nikki stared up at the mouth that uttered them, not comprehending what the words meant. She saw his penis. Erect. Ready. No comprehension of what that equated to. His hand wrapped around the base, guiding it toward her.

"Bastard!"

A big man slammed into Michael. Thomas? No—no, James. James! Nikki blinked, her mind trying to come back, but not totally cooperating. Everything felt fuzzy, like it was happening in a dream that made little sense.

Oh God, his hands were still chained. Her mind picked up on that.

The knife. It slashed down, tearing into James's already wounded shoulder. She heard a scream, saw the two men fall to the floor, then saw nothing else. She was tied down and they were out of her line of vision. She could hear them wrestling, could hear something that sounded like a bone cracking followed by another bellow of pain.

Help me! Nikki mentally screamed, her mind slowly snapping back. Sounds and smells were finally registering. *Thomas—help me!*

* * *

A naked woman burst out from what looked like the ground from his vantage point. Guttural sounds were coming from her throat as she climbed up onto solid ground and dragged herself up to her feet. She began to run again, stumbling in his direction. She fell once, but quickly pulled herself back up and continued to blindly stumble toward him.

It was the missing senator, Thomas realized, his heart racing as he ran toward her. She'd gotten away. Her torso was covered in blood, she needed help, but she was very much alive.

"Down there!" the senator moaned, her voice still raw and guttural. The closer he got the worse she looked. Luckily, he knew what she was talking about. Her words would have made little sense to the average passerby. "She doesn't have much time. Help her!"

His breathing was ragged, his adrenaline pumping. Thinking quickly, he pulled his T-shirt off, over his head, and, reaching her, covered her up in it. She was a tall woman, but rather slight, so she swam in it.

"Listen to me," Thomas said gently but forcefully. He grabbed her by the shoulders and shook her a bit, hoping he wasn't touching any wounds. Her eyes were wild and distant, a mixture of mental disassociation so common in victims, probably combined with the lightheadedness inherent with blood loss. "Do you hear me?"

Her teeth were chattering. "Yes," she finally whispered, her eyes unblinking.

"I have to go down there. Run to that building over there." He pointed out the closest one. "Do you see it?"

"Yes."

"Police are there. They will help you." Thomas had to get moving. He had to get to Nikki. "Go!" he ordered. "Run. *Now*. And tell them where I've gone!"

The senator blinked. "She saved my life," she murmured, making chills go up and down Thomas's spine.

There could be no mistaking which *she* Priscilla Harrington-Barnsworth was referring to. He could only pray Nikki hadn't given up her own life in the process.

"Go," Thomas said hoarsely as he ran toward the hole in the ground from which the senator had emerged. His heart was slamming in his chest. "Run!"

*Nikki's mind wasn't registering anything clearly—an innate bio-*logical protection that kept suffering at a minimum. But she was aware of her surroundings enough to know that she needed to get loose from the knots that held her immobile and helpless.

She could hear wrestling on the floor, could hear James and Michael repeatedly slamming into each other, but she had no idea which man would emerge the victor. She had to help James, she realized. She had to get free.

The positive aspect of mental freeze was that she was no longer shaking, no longer terrified. Nikki could methodically work at the knots that held her bound without trembling. And as luck would have it, without fumbling.

She tried to concentrate as she worked them, her mind slowly coming back as every knot fell loose. By the time her hands were free and she could work at the knots on her legs, her mind had snapped totally back. Unfortunately, so had her shaking hands and thumping heartbeat. Blood dripped from the one puncture wound Michael had dealt her, so she was careful to avoid the area so as not to slick her hands with wet blood.

James, she thought in horror as the first knot at her leg came undone, he was about to get stabbed. Oh, dear God—Michael was going to win.

Thomas followed the sound of two enraged men fighting. He was thankful for the loud bursts of noise because it helped him zero in on the exact location much more quickly. Water splashed around him, a few inches high at best, as he ran down the long underground corridor leading to a joint in the sewers, gun in hand and ready to fire.

When he rounded the corner he was stunned to find James and another man he didn't know wrestling, knocking each other back and forth into the concrete walls. Nikki—sweet lord, she was alive. Alive and freeing herself from Lucifer's bondage knots.

But which man is Lucifer?

Thomas's gaze flicked back and forth between the two men as he ran at top speed down the corridor. His heart was slamming in his chest. He didn't know which man to go after. If he made the wrong choice, the real Lucifer would be able to bring Thomas down while his attention was fixated on the innocent man.

James—

Please God, he thought, don't let Lucifer be James. He ran faster—faster than he'd thought possible.

Nikki was free a moment later. Thomas's muscles tensed and his eyes widened when it occurred to him that she was about to assault the real Lucifer. Oh no, he thought, horrified. He didn't want her that close. "Nikki!" he bellowed, running closer, almost reaching the corridor.

But he was too late. He heard a keening sound erupt from her throat as she flew into the air and jumped on the back of . . .

Not James. Thank you, God—*not James.*

Lucifer yelled, flinging Nikki off his back. She hit the concrete floor, her eyes wide with horror as she watched him raise the knife he held up into the air.

The rest happened as if in slow motion. Realizing he wouldn't reach them in time, and knowing he had only one chance to save her, Thomas came to an immediate halt, aimed the revolver's sights for the side of Lucifer's head, and fired. The shot whizzed out, the familiar scent and sound of gunpowder filling the corridor.

Lucifer's body lurched forward upon impact, the bullet through the head clean and precise. He fell to the ground a moment later, dead only seconds after he hit it.

It took Nikki a long moment to realize she was okay. By the time Thomas reached her side, his heart pounding in his ears, he could tell she was aware that it was over. In true Nikki form, she didn't cry, didn't lose her cool. She was trembling, her eyes were a bit wild, but she was okay.

He held his arms open. She gratefully, and shakily, went into them.

"Oh, thank God," Nikki whispered as he rocked her back and forth in his embrace. "Next time," she said in an attempt to lighten the mood, "don't wait for a dramatic ending."

Thomas gently squeezed her, not wanting to let go. "There won't be a next time." He tried to sound calm, together, but he realized his voice was shaking a bit. "Hell, woman, that's the last time I leave you alone without a babysitter."

She tried to laugh, but couldn't. "I love you," she whispered, gazing up into his dark, worried eyes. "Thank you."

He pulled her close, but not too tight, knowing she had sustained a wound above the heart. "I love you, too. And you're very, very welcome."

"I told you," an exhausted James said as he pulled himself up from the ground, "that I wasn't Lucifer."

Thomas put Nikki behind him, shielding her nudity from his partner. James looked pretty beat up. A sliced-up shoulder, a puffy black eye already turning purple. But he was alive.

"Be a gentleman," Thomas winked as he watched his best friend stumble toward him, "and give Nikki your shirt."

"Hell, I can't get it off," James muttered. He held up the cuffs. "Remember?"

"I remember," he whispered.

James sighed as he came to a standstill before him. "Her clothes should be over there." He jerked his head toward a black bag. "Bastard likes to keep them as souvenirs."

Thomas studied his face. "I've got a lot of questions, you know."

"I know." James nodded. He sighed again. "To make a long story short, I started to suspect the sewers during the days I was researching Lucifer when I was on the run. I didn't know if you'd believe me or not, so I took matters into my own hands."

"I'm glad you did, bro," Thomas murmured. "I was pretty tore up. Didn't know my ass from a hole in the ground. I don't know if I'd have believed you or not."

Nikki must have heard James's comment about where her clothes were, because a second later Thomas saw a shirt going over her head out of his peripheral vision. He turned his neck to gaze at her, watching as she made a wide path around Lucifer's body.

"Let's just get out of here," Nikki mumbled as she rejoined Thomas and James. "I want to go home."

"Hospital first."

She took Thomas's hand, then looked up to James. "Thank you. Priscilla and I would both be dead if you hadn't intervened when you did. Both times."

He nodded. "You're welcome," James said quietly.

Thomas stared across the corridor at Lucifer's felled body. James and Nikki turned their heads, following his line of vision.

"Please, Thomas," Nikki whispered, taking in his rigid profile. As if she could read his thoughts and the fact that he wanted to obliterate that corpse, even dead, she said, "It's over. You killed him. I want to go. Please. I can't stand being down here another second."

Thomas blinked. It *was* over. After all of these years, Amy's murderer was dead.

And Nikki, the woman he loved, was alive. It was time to let go.

Thomas nodded. "Let's get out of here," he said softly, his callused hand threading through Nikki's. James took to his other side, dragging himself along beside them. "Buddy, I'd like to give you a hug." Thomas's eyebrows rose. "But I'll take you out for a beer instead."

Chapter 30

Friday, August 22
10:59 P.M.

Between her demanding career and his, Nikki wasn't seeing as much of Thomas as she would have liked, but the time they did get to spend together, mostly at night and on the weekends, was always special. There were a lot of loose ends Thomas had to tie up from the Lucifer case, including the methodical search of Michael's home, which had turned out to be a regular house of horrors.

Dr. Michael Sorenson had tortured, raped, and murdered more women than the police had suspected. The combined estimate of Lucifer's assumed kills had been around ten. Nobody, not in their worst nightmare, was prepared to find evidence that the surgeon had raped, tortured, and murdered close to thirty women. But then, the CPD hadn't connected Michael's earlier, "unsophisticated" murders to the murders committed at the hands of Lucifer until the diary was unearthed. For the past several years, the victims had mostly been lured via the Internet. Before the Internet had been widely used, personal ads had been his modus operandi.

Finding Michael's painfully detailed journal enabled several Ohioan police departments to solve a multitude of their backlogged murder and/or missing-persons cases. Lisa Pinoza, it turned out, had played with Lucifer just as Priscilla had. Priscilla had pretended to be a willing submissive who wanted to meet a real offline Master. Lisa had pretended to be a single, high-powered career woman instead of a low-paid barmaid in a dead-end marriage. Lucifer had wanted to punish both of the women for their lies, symbolically leaving their hearts behind as proof they were not fit to belong to him forevermore.

God rest her soul, he succeeded in doing just that to Lisa Pinoza. Priscilla Harrington-Barnsworth, thankfully, had survived.

My heart all but stopped when I realized it was you—you, Nikki!—who answered my online ad. We were fated, my love. For months I've been plotting ways to bring you home to me, but the timing was always off.

Then the gods smiled upon me—and you came to me . . . .

Michael's diary had also detailed his lengthy obsession with Nikki. It had been difficult finding out just how frequently he'd masturbated to perverse fantasies of torturing and raping her, and how many close calls there had been on her life prior to when she'd placed the online ad at Dom4me.com. Reading the chilling passages had sent goosebumps down her spine, had made her feel like vomiting. Nikki could only be grateful fate had intervened on all his previous attempts at kidnapping her.

She still didn't quite "get" what it was Michael had seen in her to begin with, but she had her guesses. Mostly because his obsession with her, according to his diary, magnified a hundred times over upon her promotion at Cleveland General—the same promotion Michael had lost out on. It seemed surreal for Nikki to think something so simple as being beaten out at a promotion could cause her to become the focal point of a madman's fantasy life, but there it was. His several-months-long fixation on her had begun mere days after he'd murdered Linda Hughes.

For the first two or three days after Lucifer died, Nikki walked around in a daze half the time, her rational mind searching for a logical explanation for what could have possibly turned Michael Sorenson into the monster he had been. She realized there was little rationality to be had, yet for some reason her mind struggled to find at least something tangible it could grasp onto to explain it.

Kim and Megan had told her the story of Michael's sister and of how his mother had then tried to kill him when he'd been a boy. What Kim and Megan hadn't known, and what Thomas later uncovered, was that Michael had escaped his mother by killing her before she could kill him.

The only thing Nikki could figure was that each of Lucifer's victims, herself included, were a way for him to relive his mother's murder over and over, again and again, like a broken record that never stopped playing. A way for Michael to wield ultimate power over the woman who, in his mind, was all-powerful and godlike to him.

Nikki felt sad for the little boy Michael, who would grow up to never have a normal life, a normal thought, or a normal relationship. That he'd managed to make it through medical school and a surgeon's long residency was proof that he'd tried, at least to her way of thinking. In the end, of course, he had failed.

But as saddened as Nikki felt for the little boy Michael, she couldn't help but to breathe easier knowing that the adult Michael was now gone from the world, no longer able to inflict pain and suffering on others. Like a rabid dog foaming at the mouth, there was no cure for what Lucifer was.

A house divided against itself cannot stand:

Turning the detectives against each other was no small feat, my sweet submissive Nikki. But then I, your lord and Master, am no ordinary man.

Yesterday, James had been officially cleared from all charges. He was reprimanded for withholding evidence in the Lisa Pinoza murder case and as a consequence was forced to take an unpaid leave of absence from the CPD. A hearing was scheduled for the following month, at which time his future as a police officer would be determined.

Nikki decided to show up at that hearing whether or not she received an invitation. After all, were it not for James, she and Priscilla Harrington-Barnsworth would be dead.

I love you, Nikki. Tomorrow as I make love to Monica, it'll be your face I see as I thrust inside of her, your heart I long for throughout eternity . . . .

She's a sorry, pathetic substitute. But your Master has needs, and you are not here seeing to them as a loyal slave should. Still, this lets us prolong the inevitable just a little bit more, darling. The longer I wait, the more I crave you . . . .

Our unavoidable consummation will be beyond sublime.

In Nikki's soul, there would always be sorrow for Monica Baker-Evans. Monica had died because Lucifer couldn't have the victim he desired. Like a dead fish thrown Mafia-style at a marked man's door, she had been nothing more than a warning to Nikki of what was to come. Thankfully, it hadn't come.

You knew that woman, didn't you? That filthy bitch who thought she was saving you from me! She will *pay for her inter-*

ference. Do you hear me, Nikki? If it's the last thing I ever do I will find that woman's name and I will punish her like the whore she is for coming between you and I. She's tried to convince you I'm bad, hasn't she? All I want is for you to love me! I want you to belong to me forever, Nikki. Why can't you understand that!

Kim and Megan were doing great and were having a fabulous time forging the mother-daughter bond Roger Cox had thwarted all those years back. In the past eleven days alone, they'd already done each other's hair twice and given each other facials. Nikki would have laughed, but she found the situation rather adorable.

Kim was back to spending her weekdays at Eastern Academy. Classes would start back next week, so she was busy preparing for the students' arrival. She didn't like to talk about the Lucifer case, or about her old dreams, and Nikki couldn't exactly say she blamed her.

Nikki didn't like to talk about those subjects, either. Michael was dead, and it was time to move on.

The only thing about the Lucifer case Kim begrudgingly discussed at all was the enigma of Ben O'Rourke. Kim had been certain he was Lucifer until Megan had told her the horrible story about Michael Sorenson and his sister. From there it had been easy to put two and two together.

Still, there was something about Ben that Kim didn't trust. She admitted to Nikki that she'd had a few inexplicable dreams about the hard-nosed detective with the bad-boy reputation, dreams that led her to believe he would bring trouble into her life. Therefore, she avoided him like the plague.

Ben's "disappearance" the night of Lucifer's death had

turned out to be not much of a story. His mother had taken ill, he'd rushed over to help his brother get her to the emergency room, and in all the mania, his pager hadn't been turned on. Ben had been verbally reprimanded by the chief but, due to the nature of the emergency, thankfully not punished for taking off without permission. He was back to work now and was Thomas's acting partner until James was reinstated—if James was ever reinstated.

She wasn't supposed to signify much, just another lying bitch with an over-inflated sense of importance who needs to pay for her sins. Then I overheard you telling a nurse you're friendly with that you used to be jealous of the gangly senator once upon a time. I find such information . . . intriguing.

Will you feel jealousy when you watch your Master make love to her? I smile at the thought. My cock hardens at the thought! But no worries, darling. I won't keep her heart—only yours. For a brief moment I considered punishing you with the knowledge that her heart would belong to me forever—you did run from me after all!—but Priscilla is a lying slut who is unworthy of my eternal love. The thought of keeping her heart leaves me feeling decidedly unclean.

The senator managed to emerge from what could have been a potentially career-ending situation virtually unscathed. In fact, her online activities were completely shielded from the press. All of the publicity she garnered for being one of only two females who had ever escaped Lucifer alive (Nikki being the other one) was doing wonders for her campaign. Priscilla Harrington-Barnsworth would be reelected come November without a doubt, and probably by a landslide. Maybe Nikki would even vote for her.

Nikki smiled at her thoughts as she drove into the parking lot of her high-rise apartment complex. Nah. Probably not. But life, she concluded, does go on.

I have to have you, Nikki. I think about possessing you every minute of every hour of every day . . . .

Soon, you will be irrevocably mine. You escaped me once, but I'll return for you, my beloved. For the interim, I must say good-bye.

Good-bye, Michael.

In terms of her own life, everything was back to normal at the hospital. The entire staff had been shocked to say the least upon discovering that one of their own had been responsible for the grisliest crimes in Cleveland's history. The hospital had provided a trauma counselor for anyone who wanted to talk it out. Some had taken advantage of that service while others, like Nikki, had not.

Strange as it sounded, especially considering all that she'd gone through, Nikki didn't feel as though she was harboring any issues that needed airing. Those issues—fear of the unknown, fear in general—had died with Michael.

The only issue Nikki had to deal with these days was the surly, growling detective who'd moved into her apartment a week ago. She smiled as she climbed out of the Mercedes and headed toward the elevator that would take her to where Detective Grouch was waiting for her. She passed by his Cadillac on the way to the doors, the sight of it never failing to make her heart thump pleasurably . . . because it was proof that Thomas was hers.

It had taken him a while to let Amy rest in peace, and although Nikki knew he would never completely recover from her death, Thomas had, to a great extent, let go of his guilt in regards to it. A picture of his daughter hung in their living room—a photograph he could now smile at and remember the good times, rather than keeping it out of sight to avoid thinking about her.

Sinking her key into the lock, Nikki opened the front door. She could hear the television on, as well as the familiar sound of Thomas cursing under his breath as he attempted to not burn himself while cooking dinner. She grinned, loving that sound as much as she loved seeing his Cadillac parked in the garage when she came home from the hospital.

"I'm home," Nikki called out, throwing her keys onto a nearby table. "Hey, I think I smell spaghetti," she said as she rounded the corner and headed toward the kitchen.

Thomas frowned. "It was supposed to be meatball sandwiches," he growled. "They sucked, so I threw some spaghetti sauce on them. They ain't half bad now."

He was wearing a Harley-Davidson T-shirt, snug jeans, and a chef's apron—and looking as sexy as sin itself.

"Great." Amused, her eyebrows rose. "Can hardly wait to eat."

He bent his neck and gave her a quick kiss. "Don't be a smart ass."

She chuckled. "Sorry. So how was your day?"

"Oh—same old, same old. Glad it's the weekend. How was yours?"

"Not bad." Nikki watched him pour her a glass of wine, fascinated by the way his bicep bulged doing little more than moving his arm. "Any news on James?"

He nodded. "Looks like the senator plans to help him get reinstated," Thomas said as he handed her the glass of wine. "Said her rep would be showing up to his hearing."

"Thank God for that."

Thomas sighed. "Yeah. I just hope it's enough. He's been through a lot as it is."

They had dinner in the living room like they typically did, sort of watching television but mostly talking. She enjoyed these conversations as much as she relished what normally followed afterward.

Nikki's eyes studied Thomas. "You haven't tied me up lately," she announced, her tone teasing.

His eyebrows shot up. "It's been two days! You make it sound like I've been subjecting you to the missionary position for months on end."

She chuckled. "Sorry. Didn't mean to call your Masterly skills into question."

"It's not that." He ran a hand over his jaw. "It's just . . . hell," he muttered, glancing away. "I don't know."

Nikki looked at him quizzically. "Thomas?" She stilled as the possibility he might not be enjoying their sexual explorations as much as she did crossed her mind for the first time. "You don't like it?" she whispered.

He snorted at that. "Like it? I *love* it."

She released a breath she hadn't realized she'd been holding in. "Then . . .?"

Thomas sighed. Setting down his wineglass, he gave her face his full attention. "Nik, I've read all your books. I've read about how the bond between a Dominant and a submissive is supposed to be more intense than a normal couple's. I've read about how this happens because of the extreme trust the submissive places in the Dominant during sex and blah blah blah."

She frowned. "And?"

"And call me weird, but I don't want our 'intense bond' based on sex! I want to be loved for me, not because I can tie you up like nobody's business. Though I am damn good at that," he sniffed.

Nikki's eyes shimmered with amusement. Detective Grouch was damn good at something else, too—getting under her skin like nobody's business. "Yes, you are. And that has got to be the sweetest thing I've heard in my life."

His face colored. Her expression turned serious.

"Thomas," Nikki murmured, reaching over and placing her hand on his thigh. "The bond between us was intense way before we had sex. The books make for great reading, but sex alone could never have forged what we have together. That came from friendship, love, and mutual respect."

His face gentled as his hand slowly found hers. Their fingers laced together on his thigh.

The remainder of the dinnertime conversation was light. A joke Thomas had heard at work, Nikki's recounting of the yummy chocolate chip banana muffins she'd found at a new bakery en route to the hospital. Twenty minutes later, Thomas went into the kitchen to refill their wineglasses. But instead of bringing her another drink, he returned with something else in his hand that startled her.

Nikki's eyes widened. Her gaze flicked from the small velvet box in his hand up to his face. "What's this?" she whispered.

He frowned. "A new car," he grumbled. "I had it miniaturized just for you. Merry Christmas."

"It's not Christmas," she murmured.

Thomas sighed. "Okay, I'm sorry. Let me try to do this right." His eyebrows rose. "And no getting blubbery on me, now."

She rolled her eyes. "My heart, be still. You should write Hallmark cards in your spare time."

He grunted.

Nikki suspected she was about to get blubbery whether he wanted her to or not. When he came down on one knee, she was positive. "Oh, Thomas," she whispered. "I'm about to cry."

"As long as I don't, we're doing okay."

She chuckled, shaking her head slightly. “I don’t want to, either. I’m supposed to be the tough-as-nails surgeon.”

Thomas took out the ring and then looked deep into her eyes. She got a little teary, but not bad enough to qualify as blubbery.

“I’m going to marry you,” he rumbled out as he shoved the ring on her finger. “Thought you might want to know in case you need to buy a dress or something.”

Nikki blinked.

“I know most men ask, but I figure that’s kind of stupid because the chick could say no.”

Before she could contain it, she started to laugh. “You’re a nutcase!” Nikki said, swatting him on the shoulder.

He smiled. “But a nutcase who loves you,” Thomas murmured.

She smiled back. “I love you, too, Detective Cavanah.” She kissed him on the lips and slid her arms around his neck. “And I will definitely marry you.”

“Really?” Thomas drawled.

Nikki grinned. “Oh, yeah. This chick would never say no to you.”